NIGHT
CALLS

Rex. Anderson

By the same author
*Cover Her With Roses*

# NIGHT CALLS

## REX ANDERSON

St. Martin's Press
New York

*Design by Philip Denlinger*

Library of Congress Cataloging in Publication Data

Anderson, Rex.
  Night calls.

  I. Title.
PS3551.N379N5  1986     813'.54     85-25164
ISBN 0-312-57279-4

First Edition

10 9 8 7 6 5 4 3 2 1

For Holly, Roy, Luanne, Doyle, Marie, Jim, and Adryenne, who kept the faith, even though I didn't.

IT WAS after ten o'clock. Who'd be calling now?

"Hello," Chad said, ready for a wrong number.

A man calmly said, "I'm going to kill her."

"What?"

"You heard me," the man said. "I'm going to kill her."

Chad pulled the handset away from his ear and frowned at it. Putting it back into normal position, he said, "Who is this?" From old habit, he rubbed at his face, momentarily surprised at feeling naked skin there, instead of the brushiness of beard.

The man chuckled. "You don't know who I am."

"Screw off!" Chad said, and was about to slam the handset down into its cradle. But before he could do so, he heard what could only be a muffled cry of pain or fear. "What was that?"

"Her name's Marian," the man said.

"What the hell's going on?"

"I told you. I'm going to kill her."

Chad looked around his study. Bookshelves. A couple of framed posters. The glass wall of the atrium. The best lighting setup known to man. And above and to the right of the fireplace, alone on the fieldstone end wall, his new Roel Peña painting. "Who are you? Who are you calling?"

"You."

Chad looked at the clock on the credenza. 10:07 P.M. It was a steamy, springlike night outside. It was probably a normal night everywhere but in this room.

The man on the other end of the telephone line didn't

say anything. Instead, there was the sound of an open hand striking flesh, followed by a shrill squeal of sudden pain. Then the man said, "Hey, Marian, am I joking?"

Chad felt as if he were frozen.

He heard words now from the woman, not just voiceless cries. She sounded hysterical, terrified, hurt.

"He'll kill me!" she cried. "Help me! Marian Col——" There came hard, rattling sounds then and her voice was choked off. Chad was sure that the man must have dropped the telephone handset to the floor so he could have both hands free to force a gag back into place.

Now she was trying to yell out her address, Chad thought. He heard terrible, struggling grunts of pain and, maybe, the words, ". . . six . . . six!" and then, ". . . eight!" or perhaps, "Wait!" while the abandoned handset rocked toward a rattling stop on a hard floor.

Chad tried to think of anything. The minirecorder that he used to make dictation tapes for his secretary was in his attaché case behind the desk. It had come with wires with connections on their ends so that it could be used to record both ends of a telephone conversation.

Suddenly hopeful, keeping the handset pressed against his ear, he went around the desk, lifted the case onto its top, opened it. With the woman's struggling continuing in his ear, he fumbled with the recorder, trying to figure out whether he could make use of it. God knew where those wires were! Awkwardly, he held the recorder's perforated sound-in end partly across the earpiece of the handset while trying to continue to hear, himself.

The man spoke again. He was a little out of breath, but seemed amused, as if the struggle had been great fun. "She's a tiger, isn't she? Ate the gag right off her mouth. Tried to chew up my hand."

Chad said, "I don't know what you're doing. What the hell's going on?"

"Oh? Isn't this just some kind of silly joke? I thought I 3
was just calling you up, pulling your leg."

"What the hell do you want?"

"To talk to you. And I want you to hear me kill her."

"Why?" Chad said.

"I want some company," the man said, laughing. "I got lonely."

"Do I know you?"

"No."

"Then why the hell me?"

"I liked your number."

Chad heard bumping sounds then, and harsh raspings. "What's that?"

The man grunted with a sudden effort. There was a heavy crash and the woman cried out in agony.

"Trying to wiggle her chair away from me," the man said. "She's really something. Tough as a boot."

"You kicked her over," Chad said. With sourness rising up from his stomach, he pulled a yellow lined pad from the attaché case. Quickly, he scribbled down the numbers he thought he had heard the woman scream. And he wrote, "Marian Cole???"

The man said, "You're being pretty quiet."

"What the hell am I going to say? Who are you?"

"Just somebody that wants your company."

"This is a goddamned joke."

"Oh, yeah?" the man said. "Okay. There isn't any tied-up woman here, waiting for me to kill her." He struck her then, several times, hard, the sounds of the blows crackling from the telephone.

And then he said tonelessly, "You still think it's a joke? That sound funny to you?"

Chad's stomach hurt. "What do you want?"

"Just for you to listen. Just to start getting to know you."

"Getting to know me!"

"We'll have long talks and good times."

"You're goddamned crazy!" Chad said. "I don't know what you're—"

The man cut in with, "You'll be able to talk better the next time. Once you've thought this over."

"No next time, son of a bitch! There won't be any goddamned next time!"

The man laughed. "Listen," he said.

The woman's muffled cries went shrill and quavery. Then there was the thunderous explosion of a gunshot and she made no more sounds at all.

The line went dead.

FOR THE fiftieth time, Beth looked at the clock.

"Where is he?" she asked herself aloud. Wrapping her arms around herself, she paced out of the kitchen, through the dining room, into the family room, around the pool table, and then back into the kitchen.

She looked at the green telephone on the wall and shook her head.

For the fiftieth time, she sorted through the mail she'd brought in when she got home at six. A big, colorful, fold-out ad about books from the National Geographic Society. The Visa bill. A hokey, come-on,"You've won a prize!" letter from some so-called resort community at Lake Houston. The light bill. She made a face at the unopened Houston Lighting & Power envelope. God! The electric bill was always unbelievable.

She looked at the clock.

Where was Bill?

She paced to the family room again. Picking up the remote control from the pool table where she'd dropped it five minutes ago, she switched on the television and leaned back against the brass-bound edge of the table to watch the screen come to life.

A commercial. Why was it that whenever you turned the TV on, there was a commercial running?

She flipped away from it and got a Multiple Sclerosis spot. Flip. Muscular Dystrophy. It was late, so it was Public Service Time. Flip. Spina Bifida. "My God!" Beth said. Flip!

Suddenly, gunshots were blasting on the screen and two Oriental women were slammed backward into a cigarette rack. As they fell, the camera panned away, onto their killer, a slender youth with a nylon stocking pulled down over his face, and followed him as he ran out of the convenience store.

That stocky "Eyewitness News" anchorman zoomed onto the screen then. He said that this had been the reenactment of the robbery of a Seven-Eleven Store, during which the robber shot and killed the two clerks for no reason at all. He ended the spot by telling how you could call a catchy number—222-TIPS—for a one-thousand-dollar reward, if you knew anything about the killer. And they'd keep your identity a secret.

Beth watched the entire thing intently. She always watched the Crime Stoppers spots whenever she ran onto them. They had nothing to do with her, of course, but they were quick and sharp and different. They also weren't about some awful disease.

A rerun of an ancient segment of "Bonanza" began now. It was so ancient that Pernell Roberts was still one of the sons. The instant he appeared on the screen, Beth punched the "off" button.

She paced back into the kitchen.

It was 10:33.

She flipped through the mail.

She looked at the telephone and wrapped her arms around herself, shaking her head.

She looked around the kitchen. A chilled-water-dispensing, color-coordinated, self-defrosting, triple-doored, ice-making refrigerator. The toughest trash-masher made. The spiffiest, trickiest, solid-state dishwasher on the market. The biggest Cuisinart. A Waldorf-Astoria-class toaster. An over-and-under range with optional convection oven. A microwave oven that you could play tunes on. An industrial-strength can opener. Three stainless steel sinks. A faucet attachment that chuffed out steaming-hot water. A computerized clock that was just now achieving 10:34.

She shifted her weight forward, standing away from the Saltillo tile counter. She'd pace some more.

But she stopped as she heard the almost inaudible hum the garage-door opener sent into the house as it operated.

Moments later, Bill came through the utility room into the kitchen, and she met him by the trash-masher to kiss him.

He brushed past her, though, and went to the refrigerator, yanking off his tie with so much force that it zinged through his shirt collar.

She wrapped her arms around herself, stood back. "I was worried, Bill."

He pulled open a door of the refrigerator and got out a can of beer. "I was working late." He ripped the tab away, took a drink. "Why should that worry you?"

In a small voice, Beth said, "Well, it's so late."

"The Goldston contract. You knew about that. I still

ought to be down there working on it." He pulled open
the top of his shirt and rubbed his neck. "I'm starving."

Beth looked wildly around the spotless kitchen. "You
weren't here, and I just made a sandwich for myself. I
thought you'd send out for something. But I'll fix something. I'll fix you something."

Bill watched as she opened the freezer compartment
and looked inside. "I'm hungry as hell."

She closed the freezer, opened the big lower door.

She set a plastic milk jug out on the counter.

Bill said, "Just bacon and eggs. Think you can manage
that? Just bacon and eggs'll do fine."

Beth took a deep breath and stared blindly into the
open refrigerator. Weakly, she said, "We're out of eggs."

"We're what?"

A little louder, she said, "I forgot. I ran out of eggs. I
forgot them when I went by the store."

Bill wheeled around and started going through the stack
of mail. Over his shoulder, he said, "What's wrong with
you? How the hell can somebody run out of eggs?" Taking
a drink of beer, he set the can clatteringly down on the
countertop.

"I forgot."

He slapped the National Geographic ad down onto the
counter and picked up the Visa bill. "Well, something,
then. You had a sandwich. I'll take a sandwich."

He flipped the Visa bill aside, picked up the Houston
Lighting & Power envelope.

Beth set out mayonnaise and bread. She tried to think
what else she could use to make a sandwich.

The beer can clattered loudly against the tile. Bill said,
"How come you didn't open up the light bill?"

They had always joked about the outrageously high bill.
Beth forced a chuckle and a Mr. Magoo voice and said,
"Not me, fella. I wasn't about to look at that thing."

She heard paper ripping.

She tried to think what to put into the sandwich. There'd been one chicken breast left, and she'd used that in her own.

She could hear Bill's breathing now, rasping and harsh.

She knocked over a jelly jar and it rolled and rattled echoingly until it bumped to a stop against the side of the refrigerator compartment.

Behind her, liquid sloshed and the can bottom clanked against tile. Paper rattled. She managed to get the jar turned upright.

"Goddamn it!" Bill shouted.

Beth whispered to the refrigerator, "What's wrong?"

"Two hundred and fifty-four dollars!" he said. "And it's not even hardly spring yet. And you've got the air conditioning on right now. Two hundred and fifty-four dollars! No goddamned wonder. You could hang meat in this place."

Beth stared into the refrigerator.

"Look at me! Why the hell won't you look at me? You think I'm talking to myself?"

She turned and Bill waved the crumpled electric bill in her face. "Look at this! And there's lights on all over this goddamned house! You've got the air on full blast right now!"

She waited.

The bill dropped out of Bill's hand. He grasped her upper arm, closing his fingers down hard, pulling her toward him.

She gasped, strained up onto tiptoes, trying to relieve the pain.

"Can't you talk?" Bill snarled, his face flushed and damp-looking.

He shook her, the fingers of his left hand cutting into her arm like clamps. "Answer me when I talk to you!"

She couldn't. The odor of beer and stale after-shave clouded metallically, chokingly, around her.

Bellowing with rage, Bill slammed his right hand, fisted, into the side of her face.

FOUR RINGS. Five. Six. Chad was about to hang up, but the telephone was answered as the seventh ring started.

"Hello?" Diane said, her voice slow, drowsy.

Chad knew that voice well. He stared at the yellow lined pad and stabbed short, hard marks onto the paper. "It's Chad."

She trilled a sleepy little laugh. "Oh. Well, hi."

His face flushed hotly. "Sorry to bother you."

She giggled. "No bother."

Chad remembered that giggle. He remembered when he had thought that giggle was about the greatest sound in the world. That hadn't been very long ago. The pencil lead snapped and the broken end gouged deeply into the pad. Dropping the pencil, sitting up straight, he said, "You didn't call me a little while ago, did you? Trying to joke around?"

Diane laughed. "Call you? Huh-uh." A little aside, but without bothering to cover the mouthpiece of her telephone, she said, "Did I call him a while ago?" and made that giggle again. Near her, a man laughed.

Feeling like an idiot, Chad hung up.

He tugged at his chin, found nothing but a day's worth of stubble, and jerked his hand away.

The notes on the yellow pad. Looking at them made the woman's cries play back through his mind.

Shaking his head, he opened the bottom desk drawer and got out the White Pages, flipped open the cover, and dialed the number of the Houston Police Department.

A woman answered with a slurred, "Houston P'lice."

"Yeah," Chad said, feeling suddenly tongue-tied, feeling idiotic all over again. "Well, I need to talk to somebody."

"Go ahead. What is it?"

Feeling more and more the fool, Chad said, "I got a call a while ago. A man talked to me and then shot a woman."

"Shot a woman! What location?"

"It was on the phone."

"On the telephone?"

"Yeah."

"Call the phone company in the morning—they take reports on threatening calls," the woman said, and hung up.

Chad punched out the numbers again and a man answered. This time it was, "Houston Po-lice."

"Don't hang up on me," Chad said.

"Why, I wouldn't do that. What do you need?"

"A man called me a while ago. While I was on the phone, he shot a woman."

"Where'd this happen?"

"I don't know. It was—"

"Well, who was it calling you?"

"It was an anonymous call. I don't know. He just—"

"'Anonymous call.' Eight-thirty in the morning, you call the phone company and report that."

"Wait a minute," Chad said, and realized he was talking into a dead line.

This time, he pounded out the number. When another woman answered, he said, "I want to talk to a policeman.

I heard a shooting, and I want to talk to somebody about
it."

"Heard a shooting? What do you mean?"

"I heard a woman get shot during a phone call, and don't you hang up on me. Put a policeman on the line with me."

It took a while, but finally, there was clicking on the line and a voice said, "This is Officer Reason. So you got a threatening phone call." It was a woman's voice, and good-sounding, except that her tone showed that she was used to getting the late-night weirdos shoved off on her.

"Not a threatening phone call," Chad said. By now, he had the story just about all together. "What happened was that a man called. I don't know who he was and I don't think he knew me. He said he was going to kill the woman that was with him. She was screaming. I heard her. Finally, there was a gunshot, and the woman was silent and the man hung up."

"Have you been drinking?"

"No."

"Who are you?"

"Chad Palmer."

"Jack Palmer?"

"Chad. C-H-A-D."

"Ah. What's your address?"

"Thirty-one ninety Bissonnet."

"What's that?"

"A town house."

"Phone number?"

"Five-five-five–three-one-five-five."

"Is that listed, or unlisted?"

"Listed."

"Married?"

"No."

"You live there alone, Mr. Palmer?"

"Yes."

"How long?"

"About two and a half years."

"Are you calling me from there?"

"Yes.'

"Date of birth?"

"Fourteen August 1953."

"Occupation?"

"I own a lighting company."

"Lighting?"

"Chandeliers. Track lights. Ceiling fans. The store's on Buffalo Speedway. Let There Be Light, Inc."

"Oh, sure," Officer Reason said. "I've seen it."

"I'm not in the habit of making screwy phone calls to the police, Miss Reason."

"*Officer* Reason. I didn't say you were, Mr. Palmer."

"I recorded part of the conversation."

"Recorded? How?"

"A recorder I use for work. I don't know how well it came out, but I tried to record it."

"What do you mean? Haven't you played it back?"

"No. Not yet."

"Do it now. Turn the volume up and let me hear what you've got."

Working with the recorder, rewinding it too far, fast-forwarding past a dun letter he was composing, Chad finally got the tape to where it had been when he started holding the recorder against the telephone earpiece.

The sound quality wasn't very good, but with the volume all the way up, the man's voice and the woman's cries came through with chilling clarity. Chad played it through twice, the recording picking up from when the man said, "She's a tiger," to the ending when the gunshot sounded and was followed by the buzzing of the dead line.

After the second time, Reason said, "I've never heard
anything like that."

Chad had to laugh. "I haven't, either."

"Is this funny, or something?"

"Hell, no. I wasn't laughing for fun. I was laughing because there doesn't seem to be much else to do."

"All right, Mr. Palmer. Sorry."

"Okay. Before I got the recorder going, the woman said her name, or part of her name. And what might be part of her address."

"What did she say?"

As he was about to answer, Chad heard the Call Waiting beep and, on the other end, Reason heard its static.

Quickly, she said, "Are you expecting a call?"

"No."

"Get it. If it's him, keep him talking as long as you can."

Chad depressed the switchhook, took a deep breath, and said, "Hello."

It was the man. He chuckled and said, "I'll bet you were talking to the cops. I could hear you switchhook me on."

"Yeah, well," Chad said. "I'm just trying to figure out what this is all about." Starting the recorder, he fitted it against the earpiece of the telephone once again.

The man said, "Tell 'em I said 'hi.' And what this is all about is me thanking you for a pleasant evening. That's all."

"That woman—"

"She helped, too."

"What's your name?" Chad asked.

The man laughed. "I don't know you that well yet. Not yet, Chad."

Hearing the man say his name sent gooseflesh racing up Chad's back. "At least, you can tell me why the hell you're doing this."

"Later. You'll understand later. But right now, I'm

pretty tired. It's been a long day. I just called to say, 'Thanks,' and 'Good night.'"

"You're just going to leave me hanging."

The man chuckled. "We'll talk about it later, Chad. Okay? Right now, good night, good buddy. Talk to you soon."

The line went dead.

Chad depressed the switchhook, released it, bringing Officer Reason back onto the line.

"You didn't keep him talking very long," she said.

"As long as I could."

"It was him, for sure?"

"Yes."

She did noisy things with her telephone and a third line was added. She said, "Mr. Burton? You there?"

"Yeah."

"Did you get anything?"

He was annoyed. "Well, hell, no, I didn't get anything. You gotta get those people to keep talking long enough for me to get into the computers. I can't do anything, if they're going to hang right up."

"Okay," Reason said. "Sorry. Thanks, Mr. Burton."

Back on a clear line with Chad, she said, "Stand by there, Mr. Palmer. We'll be at your place in about fifteen minutes."

BILL WAS on his side, his back to Beth, each of his indrawn breaths causing that almost inaudible clicking sound at the back of his throat that meant he was deeply asleep.

Slowly, carefully, a fraction of an inch at a time, Beth
snaked sideways on the bed, moving away from him. Each
time it was the turn of her upper body to move and she
had to use her elbows, tensing her right arm caused it
to ache and shot hot spears of pain into her breast. Her
face throbbed. Her left cheekbone felt swollen and fever-
ish.

When at last she felt the edge of the mattress under her
back, she brought her left leg down so that her foot was
on the floor, and turned her body. When the weight of
her right breast shifted, the pain of it was suddenly so
sharp that it seemed to be grating inside her bones.

Biting her lip to keep from crying out, using both hands
to support her aching breast, she finally stood up. With
careful, silent footsteps, she went around to Bill's side of
the bed.

In the weak glow of moonlight through the curtains, he
looked pale and innocently boyish. Even with the thick,
prickly feeling in her face and the hot ache gnawing at her
breast, Beth found herself almost drowning in protectiveness.

Without thinking, she reached out to pull the sheet up
over him and gasped aloud with the pain that stabbed into
her breast.

Bill stirred. His eyelids flickered.

Beth stared down at him, let the sheet edge drop.
"God! I can't even do this right!" she shouted inside her
head. But he didn't wake fully. He shifted just a little and
then sank into deep sleep again.

Holding her aching breast, Beth fled from the room,
hurried down the hallway to the other bathroom.

In bright light, she saw that there was a red blotch
down the left side of her face, and puffy swelling all
around the eye. There was a smaller blotch of scarlet on
the side of her breast. God, it hurt!

She ran cold water onto a washcloth and pressed the cloth against her breast, catching her breath at the shock. And then the shock was finished and the coldness felt more wonderful than she could believe.

But her eye . . .

Without thinking about it, she pulled the washcloth away from her breast and pressed it to her face, trying to tell herself that the cold would keep it from going bruised and purplish.

That was the important thing—to keep from having another black eye. Another accident? She felt sick at the thought of having to make jokes about another silly accident, passing herself off as the all-time world-class klutz. But what else could she do?

Why did she do such stupid things? Eggs! What idiot ever runs out of eggs? And that electric bill. Why couldn't she learn to be careful of things like that?

Her breast throbbed horribly, but she just let it throb, and sopped the cloth in cold water again and pressed it to her eye. "Don't let it go black! Don't let it go black!" she begged again and again, inside her head.

WHEN CHAD opened the door to Officer Reason, he was struck momentarily speechless by the look of her.

She was tall and slender. She wore a plain beige linen suit and serviceable, low-heeled shoes. Her hair was very blonde and wound tightly around her head so that it looked like a shiny golden helmet. Her eyes were flashingly green.

"Mr. Palmer?" she said in a moment. "Is something wrong?"

"Uh, no," he stammered. "No. You're Officer Reason?"

She smiled and nodded and Chad stepped back, hoping he wouldn't trip over something.

"You said, 'We,'" he said, as he showed her into the study.

She looked around the room. "I always say, 'We,' when I'm going to a man's home at night on police business." Spotting the recorder on the desk, she went to it, picked it up. "I'd like to listen to this, Mr. Palmer."

He watched her settle into one of the two stuffed chairs across from the sofa and work the controls of the recorder until the sounds of the conversation came out into the room. She listened intently, her face showing nothing.

After Chad had heard as much as he could take, he said, "At the end of this, there's that second call."

Reason's voice was rich and pleasant against the tinny sounds of the woman's screaming. "You got that? Good." Smiling briefly up at him, she shifted her hand slightly and now he was able to see that she wore no rings.

Leaving her with the recorder, he went to the kitchen for coffee. When he returned with the pot and mugs on a tray, the second conversation was just ending.

Reason took her coffee black. "Before you got the recorder going, the numbers you heard. Six-six-eight?"

"I think so. Six-six, I'm sure about. But the other could have been 'eight' or 'wait.' I was pretty shaky about things just then."

Reason tilted her head toward the fat Houston Residential Directory open on the desk. "Were you looking? Did you find anything?"

"Page after page of Coles, Colemans, Kohls, Colberts, Coleridges. A couple of Marians. But not with a six-six-eight address. Not even six-six."

Frowning, sipping occasionally at her coffee, Reason played the tape through again. After it ended, she said, "What else did he say? Before you got the recorder working?"

Chad sat on the corner of the desk and pulled the yellow pad around. "I made some notes. While I was waiting for somebody at the Police Department to stop jacking me around. He said I didn't know him. He said several times he was going to kill her. And he did."

"You're absolutely sure you don't know him."

"I don't think so."

"The voice doesn't seem familiar at all?"

"No."

"He called you Chad."

"Yeah. In that second call. The first time, I thought he'd just dialed a number at random and got me. But he must have picked my number and my name out of the phone book."

"Do you have friends who play jokes like this?"

"No. I don't think so," Chad said. Thinking about Diane, he rubbed his jaw.

"Why are you doing that?" Reason asked.

Embarrassed, he pulled his hand away. "I always had a beard until just a couple of days ago. I shaved it off Saturday morning. But I still reach for it and wonder why it isn't there."

Reason looked at him intently, as if trying to picture him with the beard.

He felt the stammers coming back. Quickly, he said, "Do you think it was a joke?"

Reason stood up and turned away to look at the painting on the fieldstone wall. "Somebody can tape women's screams off about ten TV shows in an evening. And then talk along with them."

"Do you think that's what happened?"

Standing with her back to him and her head at an angle **19**
as she studied the painting, she said, "It sounds real."
Then she turned toward him, smiling. "I like your house.
I love that painting."

Chad grinned, for the first time in hours, it seemed. "I
just got it. I figured out where to put it and had it hanging
about five minutes and was standing right here, looking at
it, tickled to death, when the phone rang. As late as it
was, I figured it'd be a wrong number, but I was hoping
it'd be somebody I knew and I'd get to say, 'Hey, I was
just standing here, admiring my brand-new, very own,
genuine, original, real Roel Peña painting.'"

"But it wasn't somebody you know," Reason said. She
bent, picked up the recorder from the coffee table, and
held her finger poised over the "eject" button. "May I
take this tape?"

"Sure," Chad said. "There's a dun letter on the first
part of it that I was dictating. It sounds pretty violent, too,
but don't take it too seriously. It's to somebody that's jacking us around about paying for three twenty-five-hundred-
dollar chandeliers."

Reason raised an eyebrow in wry sympathy, snapped
out the cassette, dropped it into her purse, and adjusted
the strap over her shoulder.

"Has this happened before?" Chad asked. "This guy
calling somebody? Killing somebody?"

Reason smiled. Her teeth were just irregular enough to
be perfect. "You mean, is this the latest in a bizarre and
brutal series? No. There hasn't been anything like this."
She set a business card on the corner of the desk.

Chad looked at it. Her name was Sharon. "What happens now?" he asked.

She moved toward the study doorway. "I don't know,
Mr. Palmer."

Walking with her along the hallway, he caught the faint

scent of her perfume. It was light and sunshiny. Somehow, it filled him with loneliness.

"It's up to him," she was saying when they reached the front door. "Will we find that woman? Will he call you again?"

Chad stood in the doorway and watched her go down the walk to her Mustang and get in it and drive away. The air was cool, but damp and thick, and smelled vaguely of mildew.

A siren wailed in the distance, probably on Kirby Drive. It was late enough that the traffic cops would be starting after their nightly quota of drunk drivers. That siren was lost in the distance. Another one started. It was nearby and very loud.

Chad closed the door, locked the sound and the night outside.

BILL HAD not moved when Beth crept back into bed. She was dressed now, in a nightgown with a brassiere under it. She hated sleeping in a brassiere, but the support of it dulled the pain in her breast.

Her eye was another thing, though. It didn't hurt. There was only a hot, tight feeling to the skin there. But she knew that, in spite of the cold cloth and all her wishing, it would be full purplish-black by morning.

"Damn! Oh, damn!" she thought.

For a moment, she pictured herself bolting up out of bed, snatching up her purse, running through the house.

To the garage. Into her car. And away. Into her car and away. And . . .

Away where? Without Bill? It was unthinkable! What would she do without Bill?

Suddenly, she was crying and couldn't stop. The paroxysms of breath, no matter how much she tried to control them so she wouldn't wake Bill, clawed at the hurt place in her breast.

The crying did wake him.

He turned toward her and, for a moment, was up on his elbow, looking down at her, seeming to loom monstrously over her in the darkness. Then he was holding her and whispering, "Why are you crying, Beth? What's wrong? Don't cry, baby. Please don't cry."

She couldn't stop.

He moved his hands over her, petting her as a mother pets a fretful baby. He touched her breast and she choked off a scream.

He felt her hand come up reflexively to push his hand away and shield the hurt place, heard her choked sob of pain. His voice went gentle, plaintive, and he moved as if to shield her from any threat, whispering, "Oh, baby, baby. I'm sorry." His lips brushed the hand she held over her breast. "Don't cry, baby."

She turned into the protectiveness of his hard, warm, prickly chest and cried.

"It'll be okay, baby," he said. "Don't cry. Please don't cry. I'm sorry, Beth. But you just get me so mad. You know what a temper I've got, baby. Why do you do it?"

She couldn't stop crying.

Bill's voice was going hoarse and broken now. "I'm sorry, baby. I'll make it up to you. You know I will. You know how it makes me feel when you get me so mad. I feel like dirt, I'm so sorry. I don't ever want to hurt you.

But you just push me into it. I love you, Beth. I couldn't love anybody else."

CHAD HADN'T slept very well. The Snooz-Alarm got some heavy usage before he finally got up.

In the bathroom mirror, he saw that his upper lip still looked about four inches wide and his cheeks and chin seemed obscenely naked and pale. It had been just three days now since, suddenly, without really thinking about it, he had let the morning trim job get completely out of control and ended up with a naked face for the first time since junior year at Rice. Maybe in another six or eight months, he'd get used to the way it looked.

Pulling on a bathrobe, he went downstairs, started the cranky coffee maker, and went out front to see if he could find his morning paper. He was pleasantly surprised to see the rolled-up *Post* on the step right at his feet. Amazing!

Stepping over it, he reached out and flipped up the top of the mailbox and pulled out the mail. Nothing much.

Traffic thundered toward downtown along Bissonnet thirty feet away, but the air was crisp and clear, almost fresh. A breeze from the north, Chad realized, was bringing dry inland air to the city, for a change. He thought that he really should run this morning and take advantage of the rare, unhumid day. But he didn't. He wasn't a dedicated runner, just a guilt-driven one, and the guilt wasn't very strong this morning.

Picking up the paper, he went inside.

It was 8:08. He frowned at the belching, wheezing coffee maker, wondering if it were worth stinking up the house with hot vinegar to clean out the thing's pipes. But he didn't feel guilty enough to do that, either. He sat down at the table, thinking he'd just browse through the paper and take it easy and not go into the store until 9:30 or so. Hell, he was the owner, wasn't he?

Then he remembered that the Spring Sale ads had gone into the *Chronicle* yesterday afternoon and would be in the *Post* this morning. Well, the coffee maker should be able to dribble out an entire cup of coffee while he shaved and showered and dressed. He'd better get moving and get to the store as soon as he could.

Standing in front of the bathroom mirror, foam smeared over his face, he had just decided to start the beard growing back when he remembered the man who had called him last night.

Everything else was shoved out of his mind. When he paid attention to his reflection in the mirror again, he saw that he'd already shaved his upper lip and right jaw. Starting up the beard again would have to wait another day.

BETH'S EYE and her cheek were a mess. The eye was just a glassy slit and the cheek was purplish-sickish-looking.

"I called in sick," she said to Bill.

He was almost through with his coffee, ready to rush off to work. "It'll be okay, honey. You work too hard, anyway.

As hard as you work for that woman, you ought to be able to take a little time off now and then."

"Will you be late tonight?" she asked, already hating the loneliness of the day ahead.

"The Goldston contract."

Suddenly, she noticed that she had left the light in the utility room burning. With her breath catching in her throat, she hurried over and switched it off.

As she turned back into the kitchen, she saw that Bill had gotten up from the table and was coming back from the hallway.

She picked up her coffee cup, leaned back against the counter.

At the table, Bill lifted his cup and finished his coffee.

The air conditioning hummed into electricity-sucking life then. That's why he got up! To lower the thermostat!

"Hot as hell in here," he said, picking up his attaché case.

Beth stared into her coffee cup. Cold air washed over her.

"You just relax," Bill said, pecking a kiss on her uninjured cheek. "I'm the one's got to hurry off. You're getting to take it easy."

His footsteps faded off through the utility room. The garage door opened and closed. Frigid air clouded around Beth.

She threw the coffee cup and it smashed against the dishwasher, the violent motion surging pain through her breast. Good!

In the hallway, she twisted the dial of the thermostat all the way down to forty-five degrees. There was another one at the foot of the stairway and one in the hallway upstairs. Savagely, she turned both of them as far down as they would go.

"What am I doing?" she said aloud, as she crossed the

bedroom through a gale of chilled air. "I don't know!" she shouted as she fell into bed and jerked the covers up around her head.

)UARE foot of the ceiling of Let There Be
showroom was choked with examples of
ld be constructed around one or more light

nged from light fixtures to chandeliers.
of glass—smoked, bronzed, etched,
tained, pearled—and of brass, alumi-
late, wood, porcelain, plastic, shell,
plate, cast iron. There were mar-
thousands of fine leaded crystal
avy, ornate chains. And there
h were nothing but shaded
ns ranged from the gaudily
ce, to sublime creations of
way toward transforming

and, from many of the
with bargain prices.
had to wolf lunch in
setting a good ex-
after one o'clock,
nload the only
e of the pre-

chandelier

al
gs
les-
the
mer.
, and
e tele-

and I'll
eemed to
owing the

." Without
button and
futile anger.
the bleached
ring her, Chad
shing a smile at
ency."
h her secretarial

you have?" the skinny, bleached, prospective buyer asked. In only two years, she had body-surfed her way from the steno pool to the marriage bed of the major owner of one of the very major oil companies. She was now in the process of seeing that her new husband built her a "Home" that would be "A Real Showplace" in River Oaks.

"Absolutely," Chad said, happily crumpling the red sale tag in his pocket. He'd seen her coming, and pulled off the tag. She'd demand a discount, but would be insulted by a markdown.

Suddenly, the speaker system overrode the Muzak with the voice of Gina, his secretary, saying, "Chad, line two."

He grimaced and turned toward the counter to sign her to take the number. Then he grimaced again. This were so busy that she was working the floor like a sa clerk. She had hurriedly answered the telephone, pu line on hold, paged him, and gone back to her custo

"I'll be right back," he assured the bleached lad went over behind the counter and snatched up th phone. "This is Chad Palmer. . . ."

"Hi, Chad."

He rushed on with, "Let me get your number . . ." But suddenly, all the lights in the store s swirl around him. "Who is this?" he asked, kn answer.

"It's me."

"Let me go to my office. I can't talk her waiting for an answer, he punched the "hold jammed the handset onto the telephone in

Forty feet away, on the showroom floor lady began impatiently tapping a foot. Igno went to Gina and touched her shoulder, fla her customer. "I need you, Gina. Emerg

Propelling her along with him, throu

and bookkeeping alcove, into his office, he made the "be
quiet" sign with a finger across his lips and punched in the
flashing button on his desk telephone and lifted the handset. "Still there?"

"Sure, buddy. What's going on?"

Digging into his inside jacket pocket, Chad found Officer Reason's card. He dropped it on a scratch pad and
started writing while saying into the telephone, "What do
you want?"

On the pad, he wrote, "Call her! Tell her *he's* on the
phone with me *now!*" and shoved the pad across the desk.

As the mystified Gina hurried out with it, the man said,
"I thought we'd just have a nice chat."

Fumbling the recorder out of his attaché case, Chad
said, "So, you know who I am, for sure." This morning,
first thing, he had located the telephone hookup wires in
the bottom drawer of his office desk. But now, as he
pulled them out of their plastic envelope, they sprang out
in a bewildering jumble.

"Sure, I know who you are, Chad," the man said. "I
made a point of that."

What wire went where?

He took a deep breath. Making a fierce, internal effort
to relax, he swiveled his chair around so he could look
through the window in the front wall of his office.

Gina stared fixedly at his note while she spoke rapidly
into her telephone. Out on the showroom floor, his best
clerk, Alice—God love her!—had abandoned a lesser customer and was reverently listening to the bleached lady
tell her how expensive and imposing her new "River Oaks
Home" was going to be.

"Why me?" Chad said into the telephone while his suddenly calm fingers attached the recorder's wires in their
proper places.

"Why not?" the man asked.

"Did that actually happen last night?"

"What do you think?"

"I don't know what to think," Chad said. Motion made him look toward the window to see Gina pressing his note against the glass. Written across it in big letters was "SHE'S NOT IN—WHAT NOW?"

He shrugged and shook his head.

"It was real," the man said.

Chad turned his chair away from the window. "Why did you kill her?"

"For fun."

"My God! Why'd you call me?"

"It made it more fun."

"But why the hell me? Why not somebody else?"

Sounding utterly sincere and open, the man said, "You seem like somebody I can be buddies with."

"I have good times with my buddies. Football games. Golf. Jogging. Drinking beer. I don't have any buddies that call me up and kill people."

"Give it a try."

"Listen," Chad said, trying to fight down his anger. "Do you know me?"

The man laughed. "You sound like that credit card commercial."

"This isn't funny. Are you somebody I know?"

More laughter. "Have the cops told you how to talk to me?"

"No."

"But you've talked to the cops."

"Damned right, I have."

"Didn't they tell you all kinds of neat, little psychological things to say to me?"

"No."

"Not yet, huh?"

"Yeah. Not yet."

"You'll try all those tricky things they tell you, huh?"
"Yes."

"Why?" the man asked.

"To try to stop you somehow."

"Why should you want to stop me?"

"That's dumb. Because you killed somebody. I guess you did, anyway."

That amused the man. "You're something else, Chad. Still that 'I guess' stuff, huh?"

"Where is she, then?"

The man chuckled happily. "Have they got your phone lines all fixed up with tracing stuff yet? And bugging stuff?"

"No."

"Are you telling me the truth?"

"For Christ's sake, I don't care enough about you to lie to you," Chad said, his anger close to getting out of control.

The man laughed.

There was light tapping at Chad's office door. Without turning, he waved the tapper away.

"They will," the man said. "They'll have half the wires in town fixed up to track me down."

The office door opened and Chad turned his chair around, ready to vent his anger on the intruder. But it was Officer Reason.

Into the telephone, he said, "Yeah. They probably will."

Reason mouthed, "Is that him?"

Chad nodded as the man said, "You can tell them it's a waste of time and money. But they'll do it anyway."

Reason sat down in the visitor's chair on the other side of Chad's desk. Today, she was wearing a navy blue suit, and her hair was like a golden helmet again. Touching the

wires running from the recorder to the telephone handset, she gave Chad thumbs-up.

"Why's it a waste?" he asked the man on the telephone.

"It just is."

"Listen, what am I supposed to call you?"

"Do you like talking to me, Chad?"

"No."

"Why don't you just hang up, then?"

"I want to try to catch you. And stop you. And see you
get what's coming to you."

The man seemed pleased. "I like you," he said solemnly.

Biting back his anger, Chad said, "Did you know that
woman?"

"You mean, before I killed her?"

"Yes."

"No. I didn't know her. I never saw her before last
night."

"Why her, then?"

The man said, "I guess I'd better let you go now. I enjoyed talking to you, but . . ."

"Wait a minute," Chad said. "Why now? What's your
hurry?"

"You've got your big sale going on. I don't want to take
you away from business. So, go back to work. Bye, buddy.
Talk to you later."

The line went dead.

Feeling drained and used, Chad hung up the telephone. Out on the showroom floor, he could see the
bleached lady striking Jet Set poses. She wasn't very good
at it and kept having to adjust the sling of her hip, the
angle of her elbow, the jut of her chin, to get each pose
just right, like the women in the photographs in *Town
and Country*.

He remembered how naturally and perfectly Officer

Reason had stood to look at the painting in his study last night.

He pulled the wires loose and slid the recorder across the desk to her.

Now, she looked very businesslike. She stood, dropped the recorder into her purse. "I'd like for you to come with us, please," she said. "I'll listen to this in the car."

COCOONED IN the electric blanket while the air conditioner labored on, Beth slept away most of the morning as if she were drugged. By midday, though, she was sated with real sleep and began to drift and doze. In the drifting times, she constructed a scenario in which she and Bill lovingly faced and solved their problems.

She was drifting now, and shifted luxuriantly in the warmth of the covers, turning so that part of her swollen cheek was exposed to the chill of the room. The cold felt wonderful. Smiling, floating, she built her scenario again.

She and Bill were in the locker room, deep under the stadium, while the very walls vibrated with the cries of the thousands of spectators in the tiered seats above them watching the Cotton Bowl Game.

She said, "Something's gone wrong, darling. It's been wrong, but it's getting worse and worse. I won't be so stupid, I promise. I'll be more careful when things are bad for you. But you've got to try to get away from taking your temper out on me. I love you so much, but I'm getting so afraid, and we have to do something."

As the crowd cheered wildly, Bill said, "I'll be careful, Beth. I will. We can't let these things come between us."

She began to doze and the scenario floatingly turned into a lilting dream of her favorite memory. The place was the same, but Bill was younger. Up above, the crowd still roared at the progress of the game, but Bill was down here in the locker room. He still wore his uniform with RHODES and the huge proud number 20 on the jersey, but one shoe was off and that leg was up on a bench, ice packs heaped around the swollen knee. He was crying bitterly.

Stealthily, Beth slipped into the locker room. She wore her cheerleader's uniform and, ridiculously, there was an orange pom-pom tucked under her arm.

She wept, also. She and Bill had been dating for two years now, and engaged since last summer. For all that time and before it, Bill had been fighting to protect his fragile knees, to keep them safe and whole enough to get him into the pros and fame and riches.

And this was his last college game. Quarterbacks weren't getting Heisman Trophies in those days, but he'd been nominated twice, and pro scouts were in the Cotton Bowl today. All he had to do was still be standing up at the end of the game.

But he wasn't. Not five minutes ago, he had taken an evasive step, twisted, slipped, and the sound of cartilage breaking in his knee had seemed like thunder.

The other cheerleaders would be mad as hell at Beth for slipping off. If someone walked in on her in the locker room, there'd be a huge uproar. But that didn't matter. Bill needed her.

Overhead, the crowd roared as Beth held Bill and they wept together.

"That's it," Bill said in misery. "I'm finished now."

Beth could already see the headlines in the sports pages: BILL RHODES—GREAT HANDS—CHEESE KNEES.

"Twenty more minutes," he was saying. "All I needed was twenty more minutes. But this finishes me, baby. Nobody'll sign me now. Nobody! What am I going to do?"

And now, Beth's half-asleep dream-memory moved into the really wonderful part. "What are you going to do?" she said, holding Bill even more tightly, letting that silly pom-pom fall rustling to the floor, wiping her wet face against her sweater sleeve. "What *we're* going to do now is graduate, Bill Rhodes. And study for your CPA. And get married in August just like we planned. That's what we're going to do. And live happily ever after, football or no football."

"This washes me out of the pros."

"We don't need the pros. We've got each other. I love you, Bill Rhodes, whether you can play football, or walk, or anything. We don't need anything but each other."

And then they held each other and cried some more, while the crowd overhead went crazy, as if it were cheering them, and not the touchdown pass that Bill's replacement had just thrown.

Half asleep, Beth smiled at the memory.

And then she jumped and cried out at the sound of the doorbell!

Who the hell? Who had the right to startle her out of that nice dream? Well, they'd give up. They'd give up.

She stretched a little, turned her face, luxuriated in the warmth on her body and the soothing coolness on her face.

"Bill, we have to talk," she'd say to him. "We have to do something about our problems. I'll try to—"

The doorbell again!

They hadn't given up all that easily. Well, they would!

Angry now, Beth stared at the ceiling.

More ringing!

Stop it! Let me alone!

But the ringing didn't stop. It became continual.

Angrily, Beth unwrapped herself from the blanket, grabbed her robe, and wound it around herself against the icy air of the room. At the window, she pulled the drapery a little aside and looked down.

A powder-blue Seville sat in the driveway, a magnetic Century 21 sign stuck on the driver's door. Alma!

There was no letup in the ringing. Alma wasn't the type to give up on anything she started. Besides, from the front step, she could look over through the window in the garage door and see Beth's car inside. She knew Beth was home and wouldn't let up on the doorbell until she answered the door.

Not angry now, just wishing this were over, Beth went out of the bedroom. Pausing only to reset the thermostats, she went down to the front door. The tile floor of the entryway was like ice!

Her heart racing, she looked through the peephole.

Alma Henderson was a short, compactly built woman, fifty-five years old, with medium-length, wavy hair that was a mixture of black and steel-gray. When she was barely twenty, she had gone to work as receptionist in a small real estate office. Ten years later, with everything against her, she had opened her own and had made it a success through sheer toughness and hard work. Beth loved working for her; Alma was one of the few women she really respected or liked.

But at this moment, her face was set in a frown and she looked as if she were getting close to kicking the door in.

Taking a deep breath, Beth opened the door about two inches. Trying to sound groggy, she said, "Oh. Alma. I was asleep."

Alma peered through the opening. "I came by to see how you're feeling."

Beth's feet were freezing. Bringing the good side of her face to the gap, she said, "Lots better now than when I called in." In a moment, she added, "I only have to run to the bathroom about every ten minutes now," aware as she said it how lame it sounded.

Alma wasn't amused. "Aren't you going to let me in?"

"I need to go again right now," Beth said. "Thanks for . . ."

Her voice trailed off as Alma pushed the door far enough open to step inside. "You can at least offer me a cup of coffee."

Moving back, grateful for the warmth of the carpeting, Beth tried to keep her face turned to hide the bruise. But Alma was too quick for her. "What's wrong with your face?"

"I stumbled. That's all. Getting out of the car last night. I wasn't thinking and . . ."

Not waiting to hear her out, Alma headed for the kitchen. "It's cold as hell in here. Is there any coffee made?"

When Beth reached the kitchen, Alma had already dumped out the morning's filter and grounds and was rinsing the pot. Her purse hung by its strap from the back of one of the chairs at the table. There would be a gun in it—Alma carried a gun with her, always. A surprising number of women these days were doing that.

Seeing the dried splatters of coffee on the floor and the scattered fragments of the cup, Beth forgot about the gun. She knelt and began to pick up broken china, talking at the same time, as if that would divert Alma's attention. "I guess I left the thermostat on low this morning when I went back up to bed."

"You're barefooted," Alma said, as a piece of broken cup crunched under her shoe. "Sit down. I'll sweep that up."

Beth sat down at the table and tucked her icy feet up under her.

"I thought you had to go to the bathroom," Alma said, using a thumbnail tip to separate one filter from the rest.

"No. It's okay."

Pulling off the top of the coffee canister, Alma spooned coffee into the filter. Another fragment of china crunched against the floor.

"I dropped my coffee cup this morning," Beth said.

Alma slid the filter holder in place. "Right smack against the front of the dishwasher, looks like." Now, she poured water into the top of the coffee maker. "The Jacksons called about the Barnes place."

Beth looked up with interest, but her face fell as Alma continued with, "You weren't there, so I had to turn them over to Roseanne. She'll blow it. You know she chokes on anything with more than a bath and a half."

"Oh no," Beth said. "And I worked so hard on them."

Alma sat down opposite Beth. "You had to take three days off last month." She moved the sugar bowl to the exact center of the table. "How's Bill?"

"Working so hard," Beth said. "It's tax season. He's working late every night."

Alma was staring at the bruise on Beth's face. "Uh-huh."

Quickly, Beth said, "Things are just so hard on him right now."

The coffee maker burbled softly, sending rich odor into the air.

Alma kept looking at the bruise until Beth turned away and stared at the microwave.

Alma stood up, opened the cabinet, and brought out coffee mugs. "Can you drink some? Or is your stomach still bothering you too much?"

Miserably, Beth said, "I can drink some."

Alma gingerly pulled the pot aside and intercepted the stream of coffee with a mug. "The Morgans called and wanted you to take them over to that place on North Boulevard again this morning. I took 'em myself. Didn't want to take a chance on somebody else making a botch of the deal." One mug was full. She switched it for the empty one, deftly avoiding spilling even a drop onto the hot plate below. "Ran up and down stairs for an hour and a half, flushing johns for them."

Beth giggled.

Alma replaced the pot, returned to the table, and set down the two mugs. "I think they'll go with it. But that cuts your commission in half because you weren't there."

Beth nodded and sipped gingerly at the coffee.

Alma waited until Beth had replaced her mug on the tabletop before she spoke again. "I've got the personal things out of your desk in the car. I'll mail your final check."

Beth was stunned. "My final check! Alma—"

Without raising her voice, Alma cut her off. "You don't think I buy these nitzy little accidents you have all the time, do you? And how many times a year can somebody have the flu?"

"Please, Alma. You can't—"

With more force, Alma said, "The hell I can't. I'm not going to put up with it any longer. You get going pretty good, and then he beats hell out of you, and I get some half-assed excuse, and you're out for a week. Maybe you like it. But I don't."

Beth's heart was pounding. Tears stung at her eyes. "Like it!" she cried. "Like it? How can you say that?"

"You keep sticking around for more, don't you?"

Beth was speechless. Her eyes hurt. Her feet were

freezing! She wrapped trembling hands around the coffee mug and stared into it.

"How come it's like a meat locker in here?" Alma asked. "What's the story on that?"

Dully, Beth said, "I got mad. It was the electric bill that got him mad—last night. And this morning, he said, 'It's hot as hell in here,' and just turned it down." Lifting away one hand, she made an angry twisting gesture in the air. "Like that."

"And you got mad and slung your coffee cup, and really turned the air conditioning on. After he was gone."

Beth nodded.

"Well, that's something, at least."

"Bill and I have to talk," Beth said into her coffee mug. "I've been thinking out what to say. We have to talk about this."

Sipping from her mug, Alma raised an eyebrow in approval. "Did you get it all thought out?"

Beth nodded.

"Well, tell me about it. Let's see how it sounds."

Beth floundered. ". . . that we have to work it out. We have to stop having fights. I'll try to stop making him mad. And he needs to try not to . . . well . . . get so angry at me."

Alma's eyebrow went up again, but not in approval. "Why beat around the bush?"

Beth looked at her blankly.

"Just say it right out. He beats you. Abuses you. You're a battered wife."

"Alma!"

Standing, pouring more coffee into her mug, Alma said, "What's the matter? That really bothers you, doesn't it? Just say it like it is. He's a wife-beater."

Beth shook her head. "He loses his temper."

Alma rolled her eyes as she sat down again. "What are

you telling me? That Yuppies aren't wife-beaters? Maybe
you think they're all mechanics or bus drivers. Just because Bill Rhodes makes good enough money to buy off
knocking you around with a color-coordinated trash com-
pactor, you think it's different?"

Beth thought she was going to cry.

"Try saying this to him. Say, 'Bill, I love you, but if you
ever lay a hand on me again, we're through.'"

Spewing coffee, the mug spurted out of Beth's hands.
Alma caught it just before it rattled off the tabletop. "Why
can't you try saying that?"

Beth shook her head. Coffee was starting to run off onto
the floor and she looked wildly at the paper towels.

"Just sit still," Alma said. "Why can't you just say, 'Bill,
don't you ever hit me again'?"

Beth was crying now, staring desperately at the coffee
as it overflowed the tabletop rim and spattered onto the
floor.

"Because he'd knock hell out of you for saying it, that's
why," Alma said.

In a moment, she pulled Kleenex from her purse and
handed it across to Beth, then stood and pulled away a
stream of paper toweling to mop at the tabletop.

Beth said, "Why are you doing this to me?"

"Trying to get through to you how much trouble you're
in."

"Not with Bill. I'm not in trouble with Bill. I love him."

Alma pointed at Beth's face. "Right there, I can see
where his knuckle hit. About another half inch higher,
and you wouldn't have an eye left."

"I have to talk to him. We have to talk this out."

"So you talk. What'll happen?"

Beth shook her head in agony.

"You know what'll happen. Nothing's going to change
until you both get help. My God, Beth, where have you

been? It's all over the news all the time now. What are you going to do, just wait around until one night you find yourself pouring gasoline on his bed?"

Aghast, Beth cried, "Stop it, Alma!"

"Stop, hell!"

"What can I do?" Beth asked, crying again.

"He's got to have help to deal with his sickness. And so do you."

"Help? What help?"

"Don't play dumb with me. You know what I mean. Therapy. Professional therapy."

Beth's eyes went wide. "He'd never do that!"

"Fine. The hell with him, then. Get help for yourself."

"He'd never let me. He wouldn't. Never! I'd have to leave him."

"If that's the only thing that'd get the point across to him, it's well worth it."

Beth couldn't breathe. "I couldn't. I couldn't leave Bill."

"Suit yourself. But it's getting worse, and you know it. And getting more often. I can show you your time sheets and tell you that. You'll be leaving him next time. Or the next time after that—getting carried off to the hospital."

Whispering, Beth said, "Where would I go?"

"My son's town house just sits there empty."

"He'd kill me!" Beth cried.

Silently, eloquently, Alma lifted her hands.

OFFICER REASON and Chad rode in the back seat of the police car while a uniformed policeman drove. Using the headset attachment of Chad's recorder, Reason listened to the recording of the latest call.

Chad rode in silence. The morning's sunshine hadn't held, giving way in midday to a thin, high overcast that was steadily going grayer and gloomier.

The policeman drove them south on Buffalo Speedway and turned west on meandering North Braeswood Boulevard, taking them into a section of the city where someone years ago had been so enamored of the Scottish word "braes" that it had been repeated endlessly in street names. Street signs flashed Braesforest, Braesrun, Braespark, Braes-this, Braes-that. Finally, the driver took them onto a meandering street called Braesriver and they traveled through quiet, tree-shrouded blocks of well-kept, sprawling, one-story houses that had been built in the 1950s, when electricity for air conditioning was cheap.

Chad's stomach grew hollow and cold as he watched the street numbers of the houses they were passing.

6233. The 6300 and 6400 and 6500 blocks. Ahead, in the middle of the next block, several police cars were parked in front of a house in whose drive stood a white Cadillac hearse. The house was the standard one-story ranch style, built of a combination of Mexican brick and white clapboard. Elaborate trellises over part of the front porch and around the front windows were tangled with rose vines just beginning to get into full leaf for spring. In the front yard stood a wrought-iron sign whose black-painted ivy vines and leaves wound intricately around the white-enameled number, 6608, and the name, Koehler.

The drive wasn't wide enough for both the hearse and a car, so Reason's driver bumped over the curbing and drove half on the drive, half on the spongy lawn, and stopped only when the front bumper of the police car was nearly nudging the knees of a pudgy policewoman who sat on the front step.

She waved casually at Reason's driver and glanced at her shield, motioning permission to enter the house.

The living room was immaculate. A glass-fronted cabinet held Boehm porcelain roses of different colors. Over the dusty-pink velvet sofa hung an oil painting of a bouquet of roses of the same color.

"Her name was Marian Koehler," Reason said. "She owned a fabric shop in Westbury Square. Lived here alone. She didn't show up to open the shop this morning."

Two more paintings of roses hung in the dining room. This room was as perfect as the living room except for the vase of pale yellow roses sitting in the center of the glossily polished table. The roses were past full bloom and the water in the vase had begun to look thick and greasy. They should have been thrown out last night.

"One of her employees tried to call her this morning," Reason said. "Didn't get an answer. Then, when she didn't show up by lunchtime, she came to the house. She had a key."

They passed next through a small sitting room which, unlike the other rooms, looked as if it had been used for day-to-day living. A lipstick-stained cup with coffee dried brown in its bottom sat on the coffee table. The rag rug on the hardwood floor was faded and old, as was the afghan crumpled at one end of the worn sofa. Across the room, a seven- or eight-year-old walnut console television set

hulked under bent rabbit ears that were festooned with
wings of wrinkled aluminum foil. The only perfect thing
here was another painting of roses. These were red.

"She was fifty-two," Reason said. "She went to a movie
last night with the woman that came looking for her today."

A man in a blue blazer stood in the bedroom doorway,
giving instructions to a uniformed cop. The cop hurried
off and the man grinned at Officer Reason.

"Hey, Sherry! Hi," he boomed. He was about thirty-
five, with short reddish hair and a wide, boyish face.
Looking at Chad, the grin disappeared. "This the phone
friend?"

"I'm the man he called from here," Chad said.

Reason didn't seem to notice the instant animosity between the two men. "Chad Palmer. This is Lieutenant
Burke."

Chad nodded and waited to see if Burke would offer to
shake hands. He didn't.

Reason frowned past Burke's shoulder. "Why's the
body still here?"

Burke laughed. "Danny ran out of film. Sharp, huh? He
ran down to the station to get some more." Chuckling, he
looked back into the bedroom. "She's not in any hurry."
He nodded toward the front of the house. "The TV people
still out there?"

"We didn't see any," Reason said.

"Shit!" Burke said, and then shrugged it off.

Reason said, "Tell us about it, Ross."

Burke looked unhappily at Chad and then stepped aside
to allow him and Reason to enter the bedroom. "You start
getting sick or anything, Palmer, just run on back outside.
We're not finished here yet."

The room smelled of rose-scented powder and heavy,

flowery perfume. There was also the thick odor of meat which has been left too long in the refrigerator.

The floor was fine old hardwood with small throw rugs here and there, all of them patterned with roses. When Marian Koehler was shot, her chair had toppled over backward and she had died on a little yellow rose rug.

Burke pointed toward a panel of the bedroom curtains, bunched and tied in a loose knot to keep it out of the way. "He got in there. Forced the lock. Easy."

Between the bedroom doorway and the closet, a woman's purse lay open on the floor with lipstick, pens, an Excedrin tin, folds of pink Kleenex spilling out of it. The day's mail had been dropped near it. The closet door was partly open and a pale pink jacket matching the skirt worn by Marian Koehler's corpse lay crumpled on the floor where she had dropped it in terror just as she started to slip it onto a satin-padded hanger.

Burke said, "He got in that window and waited on her. In the dark, looks like. Looks like she walked in and flipped the light on and reached in the closet and got the hanger before she looked around and saw him."

Moving to the foot of the bed, Burke touched the shiny brown toe of his shoe to the pink Princess telephone that sat on the floor. "He sat right here, on the foot of her bed, and shot the shit with you, Palmer. While she was sitting there, tied to that chair, watching him. Looks like—just like it sounds on that tape of yours—when he was ready, he just sat right here and raised up his shotgun and let her have it—POW!—right up her nose."

Chad saw the dark, dried pool of blood on the yellow rose rug and backed up, turned away, to look anywhere else, except at the body.

Reason said, "Are you finding anything, Ross?"

Burke made a disgusted sound. "Naw. I think he must

of had on rubber gloves. We vacuumed all around on the
bed. Might get some hair or something."

Reason motioned toward the body whose waxy-white legs stuck awkwardly over the wooden seat of the toppled-over chair. "Anything sexual?"

Burke shook his head. "Doesn't look like it. Before or after. The Pathology spooks'll have to find out for sure, but I don't think so. I think he just got off to killing her."

He turned suddenly, his movement swirling the old-meat smell around Chad. "What's your connection with her, Palmer?"

Trying not to breathe, Chad said, "Connection? None!"

"She stiff you for a bug-light, or something?"

"No."

Bending slightly, Burke pinched the toe of one of Marian Koehler's shiny black shoes. "This how you handle your bad debts?"

"No!"

Burke shrugged and moved away from the corpse toward Reason, seeming to forget all about Chad. "I wish those TV people hadn't left so quick." Grinning, he looked back at the corpse. "Too bad, Marian. I thought we were gonna get you on the 'Lip-Smackin' News,' but you can't win 'em all."

He wheeled suddenly on Chad, grinning no longer. "How much it cost to get that guy to blow her up for you?"

Startled, Chad turned. "I never even heard of her!"

"That's enough, Ross," Reason said.

Shrugging again, Burke gave it up and stepped toward Reason, leaving Chad staring at the mirror that tilted slightly down toward the dressing table.

His eyes changed focus, and he was looking directly into the reflection of Marian Koehler's ruined face.

Chuckling, Burke said, "Hey, Sherry. I guess you better take your pal outside now."

AS FAST as Beth filled a bag or suitcase or set out a bundle of clothing, Alma would carry it down to stow in Beth's car or hers. As she returned from one such trip, the telephone was ringing and she found Beth staring at the set on the bedside table.

"You're going to have to answer it," Alma said.

Taking a deep breath, Beth lifted the receiver and said, "Hello."

Bill sounded boisterously happy. "Hey, honey, I didn't think you were going to answer."

"I was asleep."

He chuckled. "Get that rest, baby. But wake up for a minute. Have I got a news flash for you!"

His happiness was contagious. She looked guiltily at Alma who was gathering up an armload of clothing. "What, Bill?"

"Five glorious days for two in glorious Puerto Vallarta. A month from day after tomorrow."

Alma disappeared through the bedroom doorway. "Puerto Vallarta?" Beth said, her body feeling suddenly like water.

"Yeah, honey. Wait'll you see this place we're going to stay at. No hotels for Beth and Bill. I got us the penthouse of this big villa that's got waterfalls all down the front of it. Wait'll you see the pictures! Private pool, whirlpool, ser-

vants, everything. We'll live like a king. How's that
sound, hon?"

Beth pulled aside the curtains and looked out at the
gloomy sky. "Wonderful."

"Now, you go on back to sleep," Bill said. "I'll have the
tickets and everything when I get home. It'll get you all
excited. Now, I got to get busy and make us some money.
Bye, baby."

"Good-bye," Beth said.

When Alma returned, she said, "He's taking me to
Puerto Vallarta next month."

"Puerto Vallarta. That's really something."

"We have a villa. He says I won't believe how beautiful
it is."

Alma nodded as if she were impressed. "A villa. In a
month, you say?"

"Yes."

"A month. What are you going to wear? A veil? That'll
be about time for him to beat you black and blue again."

"Alma . . ."

"Or maybe he'll be real careful and not bust you in the
face until after you get back. Maybe he'll just slug you in
the belly. Or break an arm. You can tell everybody you're
klutzy and you tripped getting on the plane."

"Please, Alma. I don't know what to do."

"Terrific! He beats you to a pulp, and buys you off with
a trip to Mexico." She swung her arm to take in the whole
house. "He's filled up your kitchen with gadgets, and now
it's travel."

"It's not that way," Beth said.

"Not that way, hell! Not what way? Puerto Vallarta for a
black eye is what way it is. Listen, why don't you go for a
broken nose next time? That ought to get you Jamaica, at
least."

"You're pushing me around, too," Beth said. "Just like Bill does."

"Oh hell yes, I am!" Alma said angrily. "When was the last time I busted you in the face?"

"WHAT'S THIS?" Chad asked, as Reason took papers out of her attaché case and set them on the kitchen table. On the counter, the coffee maker wheezed and choked.

"Formal authorization for us to put a tap on your home telephone," Reason said. "And on the lines at your store."

Chad looked at the smudgy photocopies. "You think he's going to do this some more, don't you?"

"He said he would." Tapping a fingertip on the forms, she said, "The forms state that only the case in point—Marian Koehler's murder case—will be of interest to us." She smiled up at him. "But just between us, don't be dealing any dope, or anything."

In mock disappointment, Chad said, "Oh hell!" And then, "Other than that, how does it work?"

"We've got taps in place on other lines. Legal ones, of course. We'll just run your lines through the phone room with the ones already tapped. Yours will be flagged for tracing, too. Not just recording. So any time there's an incoming call, there's an alarm, and there'll be live surveillance just long enough to be sure whether it's him or not. If it is him, they'll hot-line the phone company for a trace."

Chad grinned. "With all the calls we get at the store, it's going to get kind of busy."

"When they need to, they pull in help from other departments."

"From Vice, I hope. That ought to be right up their alley, messing around in people's private lives one way or other."

Reason laughed. "Not from Vice. That's a money-maker."

"Oh, sure," Chad said. "Shortchange Burglary and Homicide. But don't fool around with the important stuff."

The coffee maker had finally trickled out enough coffee for two cups. Chad rose, poured them, and sat down again.

"You could clean out that thing," Reason said. "Just run some vinegar through it—white, I think. It dissolves the lime and mineral deposits."

"It stinks up the whole place," Chad said, looking at the wiretap consent forms. "I won't feel right about this unless I can tell my employees."

Reason sipped carefully at her coffee. "Tell them. It shouldn't make any difference. If word gets out, it won't hurt. He told you he knew we'd be doing this. I don't think I'd tell them exactly why, though."

"If he calls, how long will it take them to trace it?"

"If he's calling from this exchange, thirty seconds. If he's calling from another one, maybe a minute. No longer. Everything in Houston's electronic."

"Thirty seconds!" Chad said, smiling. He started signing. Halfway through the stack, he said, "That lieutenant—Burke—wasn't exactly overjoyed with me."

Reason sipped coffee, didn't answer.

Chad signed the last form. "Are you involved with him, or something?"

Her eyes flashing green, Reason said, "I was. For a

short time. It wasn't anything important. If that's any of your business."

"He wears a ring. He's married."

"May I have those forms now, please?"

Chad straightened the papers into a neat sheaf. "Do I have to keep on calling you Officer Reason?"

Sitting back, sliding the papers into the attaché case, she said, "Are you working up to some kind of pass, Mr. Palmer?"

He grinned and leaned back in his chair. Marian Koehler's bedroom seemed a million miles away now, not just seven or eight miles and an hour ago. "Sure I am. You're a beautiful woman." Leaning forward again, resting his elbows on the tabletop, he said, "Or do I have to ask Lieutenant Burke's permission?"

"Go to hell," she said, without much force.

Chad chuckled. "Fine. But it's 'Go to hell, Mr. Palmer,' then."

She smiled. "You're a nice man. But not while this is going on."

Chad looked at her attaché case. "All I've got to do is keep him talking for thirty seconds, or maybe a minute, and the bastard won't be going on any more."

"That's the plan."

Chad said, "Did you always want to grow up and be a policeman?"

"God, no! I'm a geologist. But there's not much demand for geologists right now."

"I thought there always was."

She laughed. "Not in Houston. Not with the shape the oil business is in these days." She stood up. "But if you think I'm wrong, I'll be happy to pass your name along to some of my classmates the next time I'm in McDonald's buying a hamburger from them."

Chad stood, too. Through the window over the sink, he

saw that it had begun to drizzle. It was going to be a normal, gloomy springtime Houston evening.

A moment later, as he opened the front door, he said, "One thing I want to ask you. Do you believe what Burke does? That I had something to do with it?"

"I don't think so."

"You don't think so," Chad said.

Reason put out her hand, felt the misting rain. And then she was running lightly down the walkway toward her car.

"I HOPE you or Beth—one—thought about money," Linda Janssen said. She was the first visitor to the town house that Alma's transferred son and his family had left sitting empty three months ago. She arrived bearing a big white paper bag and a potted rubber plant.

Taking the plant, setting it on the table in front of the draperies, Alma said, "Of course, we thought about money. We did the drive-through teller on the way over."

Linda, forty-four, thin and attractive, was Alma's roommate. She wore an old Houston Gamblers sweatshirt, faded blue jeans, and a pair of super-clean but pitifully worn Adidas sneakers. Sitting down on the sofa, she ripped the paper bag down the side, flipped off the top of the cardboard bucket, and pinched off a piece of fried chicken crust. "I hope she cleaned the son of a bitch out," she said, popping it into her mouth.

"Fifty percent. To the nearest penny. You know Beth."

Alma picked her purse off an empty shelf in the built-in bookcase and sat down at the other end of the sofa.

Linda sampled the chicken again. "That old boy used about four herbs and spices too many, if you ask me." She opened the paper carton of french fries.

Looking over, she saw Alma lighting a cigarette with a cheap plastic lighter.

Linda stared. "When the hell did you start that again?"

"It was a rough day. I picked them up when I was getting Beth's groceries."

Shaking her head disapprovingly, Linda pulled the pack from Alma's purse and took one for herself. "Not a bad idea. Quitting's such great fun." Tentatively, she drew in smoke, exhaled. "I give her twenty-four hours."

"Knock it off," Alma said.

Chuckling, Linda looked around the living room. Vanilla candles burned on saucers here and there, doing a good job of dispelling the musty, shut-up odor. The bookshelves were empty. The walls were blank except for an old mirror. The only things on tables were the rubber plant, the fried chicken bucket, and a dead telephone. "Mommy Alma's Rescue Mission," she said.

Alma said, "She'll make it. She's scared, finally. And mad, too."

"Mad. At Bill, or at you?"

Alma laughed.

Beth came into the room, looking shiny and pink, except for the deepening purple of the black eye. She had taken a shower and felt immeasurably better.

Linda greeted her, gesturing grandly. "I'm here for the housewarming! Food, gift, guest. What more can you ask?"

Beth was surprised at how welcome the food looked. She hadn't bothered to eat today, she realized.

"We need some napkins and plates," Linda said. "And something to put out these nasty cigarettes in."

Beth brought paper towels, plates, and a jug of wine
from the kitchen.

When there wasn't much left but a mess, Linda leaned back, smoking. "Well, Beth, what do you think? Is this just a trial run, or are you really going through with it?"

"What do you mean?"

"I left my son of a bitch five times."

"You!" Beth said.

Linda chuckled. "You thought it was irreconcilable differences, huh? Not quite."

"I knew about Alma, of course. But not you."

"Well, here I am. Poster Child of the Battered Wives Society." Grimacing, she stubbed out her cigarette. "What did you do? Call him, or leave a note, or what?"

"A note."

Linda nodded and started dumping chicken bones and greasy wads of paper toweling into the cardboard bucket. "It's going to be real tough, but you've got to stand your ground."

"I just have to think," Beth said. "Tomorrow, I'll talk to Bill and we'll make some plans about getting some help. To work this out."

"On the phone," Alma prompted.

"Yes," Beth said. "Until he cools down and thinks about what's been happening to us."

"What about the telephone here?" Linda asked.

Alma looked at the dead set. "They'll hook it up tomorrow. I called Liz at the phone company. The bill'll come to our house." She grinned evilly. "Guess what name it's in." Breaking into laughter, she answered herself. "Rhoda Williams."

Beth and Linda looked at her blankly.

Laughing even harder, she said, "Rhoda Williams! Bill—William Rhodes!"

Now they caught it. All three laughed.

"It's funny right now, Beth, but you'd better get serious about it," Alma said. "Don't you give out that number to anybody. When you call your mother tomorrow, you give her the office number, and our home number, in case of emergency. And don't give out this address, either."

"All right," Beth said. "But this is going a little far."

Linda said, "Dream on, Snow White. You be careful when you go someplace, too. Bill's going to be looking for that red car of yours. Just keep an eye out for him."

Beth looked unbelieving.

Linda raised an eyebrow at Alma, asked Beth, "Who's your car registered to?"

"Registered to?"

"Where's the title? Did you bring it?"

"Well, yes. It's in my purse."

"Whose name's on it?"

"Name? Mine, I suppose. Why?"

"My car was in my husband's name. The third time I tried to leave him, he reported it stolen." She took another cigarette, rummaged for the lighter. "I spent the night in jail for stealing my own car, and I still went crawling back to him again. Poster Child of the Wimp Society, too."

Beth shook her head. "Bill's not like that."

Linda shrugged.

"We've just let things get out of hand," Beth said. "That's all. I'll talk to him tomorrow, and we'll work it out."

Linda stuffed the rest of the mess into the bucket, stood up, headed toward the kitchen. "She's not ready," she said over her shoulder.

"This is all silly. Bill loves me," Beth said.

"Sure he does," Linda said as she returned. "What do you think he'd do to you, if he walked in that door right now?"

ALMA HAD offered to spend the night, but Beth wouldn't hear of it. She'd have felt silly, needing a baby-sitter but, more important, she wanted to be alone. She needed to think.

This was just an unpleasantness that would have to be endured, this being off in a strange place, alone, not sure that Bill was all right. He'd be angry at first, when he came home and found her gone. But then he'd get worried, just as she was. At this minute, she was certain that he was at home, reading her note again and again, saddened over the fact that they'd let things get so out of hand that she'd had to escape.

Her mental picture of his anguish was comforting for a moment. But then there crept in the painful thought that Bill, at this instant, was in pain, and she had caused it.

She fled from the thought, went walking through the town house, busying herself with looking everywhere and at everything, checking to see how many closets there were, inspecting the bathrooms, trying the windows to make sure they were locked.

This was a nice place, although small compared with her house. Two bedrooms, two baths, and a sundeck upstairs. Downstairs, the living room, dining room, kitchen, and a bedroom with a glass wall and sliding door that opened onto a small enclosed patio.

The upstairs bedrooms were larger, but the patio had made her decide to use the one downstairs. She could open the sliding door and have fresh air. It would be perfectly safe because the patio was enclosed. Right now, it was empty, but it would be pleasant with a few big potted plants. As if she were going to be here that long.

The furniture wasn't exactly wonderful, of course— Alma's son had taken the best of it along. But he had left an antique mirror in the living room that Beth loved.

She checked the locks, being particularly careful to see that the door between the kitchen and garage was locked. Bill was always on her because, at home, she was always forgetting to lock that one.

She took another shower then and got in bed, settling down to watch television, holding a heating pad alternately to her face and her breast.

She felt safe and warm and drowsy. Almost immediately, she dozed off. Waking a little later, because the heating pad had gotten too warm, she found Pernell Roberts' face smiling at her from the television screen as a late-night rerun of "Trapper John, M.D." began.

Muzzy with sleep, she stared at him, thinking for a crazy moment that she was actually looking at Bill.

A commercial began. Wonderful-looking boys and girls danced wildly on a beach guzzling orange soda.

Beth plunged into bottomless depression.

She stared at the telephone on the bedside table, picked up its handset, verified that it was dead.

She hated this!

Longingly, she pictured herself running to her car, racing home.

But no! This was just an unpleasantness that would have to be endured so that things between her and Bill could be set right again. Just a temporary unpleasantness.

BETH'S TELEPHONE was turned on just after two o'clock. She was ready—more than ready.

It would go like this: Bill would answer, the strain of the night's worry showing in his voice. She would say, "Darling, it's me. I'm all right." "Oh God, Beth!" he would say. "I've been scared to death!"

Quickly, her heart racing, smiling, she punched out the numbers for the private line that didn't even appear on his secretary's telephone.

He answered, "Rhodes."

The sound of his voice rocked her wonderfully. Breathlessly, she said, "Darling, it's me. I'm—"

Cutting her off savagely, Bill shouted, "Goddamn it! Where are you?"

"Bill, please. I'm—"

"Don't you 'Bill, please' me, goddamn you!" he roared. "I'll teach you to run out and hide on me! Where in hell are you? You better be home! I'll show you—"

Trembling, shuddering, she pulled the handset away from her ear, rattlingly replaced it in its cradle.

"YES," CHAD said, answering his desk telephone.

"Line one."

"Yeah. Thanks, Gina." The flashing button. "Chad Palmer."

"Mr. Palmer, Officer Reason here."

He smiled. "How are you?"

"Fine. We just got your wiretaps up, and I wanted to check them out with you. What line did I ring on?"

"One."

"Good. The surveillance people ought to be listening to us right now, if everything's hooked up right. Give us a signal, Lenny, if you hear us okay."

Static.

"Okay, Mr. Palmer. This one checks out. Let's hang up and I'll call you right back on the next line."

"Okay," Chad said.

When the second button began to flash a moment later, he answered, "Good afternoon, Let There Be Light."

"That sounds awfully Old Testament, Mr. Palmer."

"Yeah, well."

"Now, Lenny, let there be static."

There was.

"So far, so good, Mr. Palmer. Number three next." This time, Chad answered with just "Hello."

Mr. Palmer?"

"Yeah. You want to score some coke, huh?"

The static came this time without being requested, so loud that Chad had to jerk the handset away from his ear.

"Jeez!" he said, when he tried listening again. "Your old buddy, Lenny, doesn't have much sense of humor, does he?"

Reason laughed. "She. Okay, let's try the next one now."

A few minutes later, after the last line had been checked, she said, "Fine, Mr. Palmer. That takes care of the store. When you get home, call my office number and ask for Sergeant Andrews. He'll call you back and check your home line the same way."

"Sergeant Andrews," Chad repeated. "Okay. But when will I talk to you again?"

"When the man who killed Marian Koehler calls you the next time."

IN THE three days since her temporary move to the town house, Beth's nerves had become frayed. Her emotions whipsawed. She laughed at the most stupid things. She cried for no reason at all. She had never, in her whole life, cried as much as in just the last three days.

But earlier this morning, after another telephone call to Bill, she had decided that she had had enough—more than enough—of this wimp-stuff!

"Beth, baby," Bill had said. "Thank God, you called!"

She felt faint, she was so overwhelmed with the fact that he wasn't angry and yelling.

"Enough's enough," he said. "Every time the phone rings, I just go crazy because it's not you."

"Thank God!" Beth breathed into the telephone. She was trembling with happiness. If it were possible, she'd jump right down the wires to him.

"I'm going to come get you right now, baby," he said. "I can't stand it another minute."

He sounded so nice!

"No. Meet me at the doctor's office," she said joyously. "That's what I've been trying to talk to you about. The doctor's office at ten."

"Doctor's office? What doctor?"

"I'm talking to a therapist today. About us. And now, you can, too."

There was a long silence and then he said pleadingly, "We don't need any therapist, baby. We just need each other. That's all. And that nice trip to Puerto Vallarta's coming up."

"Please, darling. He'll help us so much."

Another, longer silence. Finally, Bill said, "Where are you, Beth? I'm going to come and get you right now. We don't need any of this therapy-stuff."

Beth was the one pleading now. "Bill, we do need it."

His voice went cold. "I've had a bellyful of this. I'm going to come and get you and take you home where you belong."

"Just an hour, Bill. We just sit and talk to him for an hour."

"I'm not talking to anybody about things between you and me. And you're not, either. Now, goddamn it, where are you?"

She couldn't think what to say.

"Where are you? I said."

"No," she choked out. "Not like this."

He bellowed, "You tell me where! I'm going to take you home and put some sense into you!"

"No!" she cried into the telephone and then caught her breath at how strongly she had said it and how much she meant it.

"Don't you say No to me, goddamn you!"

She was angry! My God, she was angry! "I meant it! If you're going to be like this, good-bye!"

She hung up. She hung up on him!

"That's it!" she had said aloud to the lonely rubber plant
in the living room of her borrowed town house, as she
shoved the telephone away.

"Mrs. Rhodes?"

She looked up to see the gray-haired woman at the reception desk smiling at her.

"Go on in now," the woman said. "Through that door."

Beth stood, adjusted her dark glasses, picked up her purse,
smiled at the woman, and started toward the doorway.

In her mind, she ran through what she would say, what
she had worked out after deciding that she'd had enough
of being a wimp and would get her life moving again.
She'd say, "Hello, Dr. Wray. I'm an abused wife, and I've
had enough of it. What do I do?" And then they'd go to
work straightening out her life and her marriage. "My
husband couldn't come along, Doctor. What do I do to
bring him around?"

She pushed the door open, meaning to continue, to get
in one more flashing-quick rehearsal. But suddenly, it all
fell to pieces. "Oh my God!" she found herself thinking.
"What am I doing here?"

A voice said, "Mrs. Rhodes, please come in."

She teetered at the edge of panic, wanting only to slam
the door shut and run away. But she forced herself to
close it quietly instead and step on into the office.

There wasn't any couch. There were shelves stuffed
with important-looking books. Big windows looked out on
the massive downtown buildings.

Numbly, she approached the desk.

A man had half risen to greet her. He was short and pudgy
and wore a three-piece suit, the vest of which looked tight
and ready to pop open. "I'm Dr. Wray," he said.

Their hands touched for a moment over the desk. His
fingers were burningly hot. No. Hers were cold!

"Please be seated," he said.

Beth looked for the chair, touched it, fitted herself down into it. What was she doing here? Who was he? A stranger!

He settled into the leather chair behind the desk, smiling to try to ease her nervousness. It didn't work.

She tried to see him differently. He was an old, close friend of Alma's. He'd been struggling into practice and had helped Alma when she had that awful time with that awful husband of hers. He was very good. He made wonderful things of stained glass, Alma said.

But he was still a stranger.

Suddenly, Beth began to feel as if she needed to go to the bathroom. But how could she? She had gone at five minutes until the hour, just so this wouldn't happen.

Dr. Wray was looking down at papers on an open file folder on his desk. "Beth Rhodes," he was saying. "Twenty-nine. Married to William R. Rhodes for seven years." He tried a warm, pleasant smile again. "Alma Henderson asked me to see you as soon as possible." He tried a gentle joke. "This is as soon as possible."

Beth managed a nod. Her eyes were stinging. Thank God for the glasses!

"Why are you here, Mrs. Rhodes?"

Her throat was powder-dry. Somehow, she said, "Didn't Alma tell you?"

He spread out his hands, palms up. "She asked me, as an old, dear friend, to work a dear, young friend into my schedule as soon as possible."

"That was all?"

"You'll have to tell me yourself why you're here."

The Wimp Society, sure enough! Why the hell had Linda said that? What a dumb thing to say! Wimps were men, not women. It had been a stupid thing to say.

Dr. Wray leaned back and smiled. "That's something, anyway."

Beth was startled. "What?"

"I caught a little flash of anger. That's better than nothing at all."

She turned away, found herself looking out of the window. That building was Commerce One. Bill's offices were there, not ten blocks away.

"Would you remove your dark glasses, Mrs. Rhodes?"

"My glasses?"

"Yes, please."

Her fingers felt like sausages as she fumbled off the glasses, folded them, tucked them away into her purse. The light hurt her eyes.

Dr. Wray studied her. "I understand your feelings. Talking about private things with a stranger can be very difficult."

"With anybody," Beth said. She wanted to keep her black eye turned away from him, but that meant that she had to look directly at that building, practically right into Bill's office window.

"Your eye. That happened when? Two or three days ago?"

"Three days ago."

"Have things like that happened before?"

Reluctantly, she nodded.

"When was the very first time?"

Beth looked wildly around the room. "The first time?" she asked weakly.

"Yes, Mrs. Rhodes. When was the first time your husband beat you?"

Her bladder again. It was going to explode! "He loses his temper."

"All right. When was the first time your husband lost his temper and beat you?"

She tried to be angry, but all she could be was afraid. "Christmas," she whispered. "Christmas night."

"What Christmas?"

"After we were married."

"The first Christmas after you were married?"

Beth nodded.

Paper rustled as Dr. Wray turned over the Personal History Form she had filled out when she arrived at the office. "Ten August," he read. And now, he was counting along his knuckles. "To twenty-five December. Four and a half months. And when was the next time?"

"The next time," Beth said hopelessly. "Oh, the next time. It was a long time."

"How long?"

"Just before my birthday."

Dr. Wray looked at the form again, counted along knuckles again, asked, "When was the last time before three days ago?"

"A month ago. About a month."

"And before that?"

"About a month," Beth whispered.

"The man beats you, Mrs. Rhodes. He has, it seems, for almost as long as you've been married."

"He has a terrible temper."

"Yes. You mentioned his temper before. Does he beat up the people he works with? Does he beat up your neighbors?"

"No. Of course not."

"Of course not. His bad temper he reserves for you, then."

Beth stared at her hands knotted on the sides of her purse.

"Isn't that what you're telling me, Mrs. Rhodes?"

"I don't know," she said, whispering it.

"I have a bad temper, also," Dr. Wray said.

Beth flashed a look at his face, looked back at her hands.

"At any moment, your monosyllabic answers might anger me to the point that I'd reach across my desk and strike you in the face."

Beth looked at him now, astonished to find him smiling. "You wouldn't do that."

He chuckled. "Of course, I wouldn't. But what if I did? What would you do?"

She floundered for a moment. "Well, I'd run out of here. And I wouldn't come back. I'd report you to somebody."

"You might even be inclined to hit me back."

"I might."

"I'm a virtual stranger. We have no ties. Why is that different from when your husband strikes you?"

"I don't know."

"Why are you so afraid of me?"

"I don't know," she said, and breathed deeply. "I wasn't afraid. Before I got here. I was looking forward to seeing you—to getting started."

"I'm no one to fear, Mrs. Rhodes. You'll get angry with me from time to time. Sometimes, no doubt, you'll hate me. But don't be afraid of me." He shifted in his chair, dangerously stressing his vest.

Beth stared, sure that it was going to give way, but miraculously, it didn't. For the first time, she smiled.

"Have you left him?" Dr. Wray asked.

"I'm living in a different place. Since day before yesterday." She changed position also, leaned over, and put her purse on the floor, astonished at how stiff her fingers had gotten.

"The man beats you at increasingly frequent intervals and it takes you seven years to leave him."

"I love him."

"Tell me about him. Describe him."

"He's a year older than I am. He's athletic—he was an All American football player and then he hurt his knee.

He has dark hair. He looks like Pernell Roberts, when he was on that Western."

"'Bonanza.' What kind of work does he do?"

"He's a CPA. He has his own firm. He's very successful."

"Does he love you?"

"Of course."

"Of course, he loves you. And he gives you that black eye. And other injuries."

Beth twisted her hands together, wished she hadn't put down her purse.

Dr. Wray said, "He's physically abused you for seven years. Why have you remained with him?"

"I love him."

"Other than love, why?"

"He needs me."

"He needs you. He can't take his bad temper out on bowling or softball or mowing the lawn. He needs you for that."

Beth was silent.

"Actually, it isn't that he needs you, Mrs. Rhodes."

She looked blankly at him.

"It's that you need him."

She looked down at her hands.

"You need his abuse, Mrs. Rhodes."

"You're supposed to help me," she said. "But you're hurting me."

Very gently, Dr. Wray said, "Have you ever said that to your husband?"

Tears stung at her eyes. "No."

"Why haven't you?"

She couldn't answer.

"Because you're afraid of him?"

"I don't know."

"Does he talk about his childhood?"

Surprised at the change in subject, she looked up. "His childhood. Yes. Some."

"Did he enjoy it?"

"He didn't have a very happy childhood. Things were hard for his family."

"How does he feel about his father?"

"He died when Bill was in high school. He worshiped him."

"His mother?"

"He's very careful of his mother. He'll do anything she wants him to. And he's always afraid I'll do something she won't like."

"Have you ever?"

Beth smiled warmly. "No. She's wonderful."

"Do you and your husband have any problems other than this?"

"No."

"No sexual problems? Or money problems?"

"Neither one. None at all."

"That's good," Dr. Wray said. "You're very fortunate."

"We have a wonderful marriage," Beth said. "Except for that."

"'That,'" Dr. Wray repeated. "Let's put 'that' into perspective then, shall we? Statistically, the chances are very great that either you or your husband will be dead by the other's hand within another seven years, if some fundamental change isn't made in your relationship."

Beth stared at him.

"Well, I have scared you, after all. But now, you're scared of something real. Keep that fear in mind. It will make what we have ahead of us seem less difficult and much more worthwhile."

"HELLO. THIS is Chad Palmer."

Reason tensed. Into her telephone, she said, "Is something happening?"

"No. That's why I called you. To ask the same thing."

Wearily, she leaned back in her chair. "No. Nothing."

"It's been two weeks."

"I know. We'll leave the taps up for another week. If he hasn't called by then, well . . ."

"If he hasn't called by then," Chad said, "will you have dinner with me?"

"I work nights, Mr. Palmer."

"All right. Breakfast."

She laughed lightly, happily. "I'll think about it."

"Nobody's listening. I'm calling from a pay phone."

She laughed again. "In that case, I'll think about it very seriously."

AFTER THAT first visit to Dr. Wray, Beth cried for two days.

But the next session was easier.

After the third one, she wrote a five-page letter to Bill, cried herself to sleep, and got up early the next morning and drove to the nearest post office substation to mail it.

Finally, after what seemed an endless two weeks, her black eye had faded enough that she was able to go back to work.

Her desk was overflowing with new properties—Alma had refused to let her do any work at all at home, saying, "No way. I want you rarin' to come back, not half bored." Gleefully, she dug into the mass.

Halfway through her second cup of coffee, she found herself intrigued with the photograph of a colonial-style house on Memorial—"'Home' on Memorial," she corrected herself mentally. When you sell real estate, they're "homes," not just houses, at least during working hours.

It wasn't the home that intrigued her. It was the majestic-looking animal standing beside the woman in the foreground of the photograph. It was a Doberman pinscher. He was beautiful. He seemed absolutely certain of himself and of his world.

"But they're so dangerous," she told herself.

A shadow fell across her desk, and she looked up, a little startled, and saw Bill standing there.

He was dressed for the office, in the gray flannel suit Beth liked most.

"I didn't see you," Beth said, heart flurrying.

His face looked hurt. "Beth, honey, where've you been? I've looked everywhere for you. I call here, and nobody'll tell me anything. I've been driving by this place two and three times a day, looking for your car. You don't even call me any more."

Beth tried to neaten the stack of papers. "You won't discuss anything. You just get angry."

His face full of misery, he said, "I miss you, baby. I'm no good without you. And our trip's coming up."

Beth shook her head.

"Why are you being like this to me?" Bill asked piteously.

"I try to talk to you about it. And you just yell."

"I was scared for you, baby. I just lost hold of myself when you called, I was so scared."

"My letter. I said it all. And you still wouldn't talk to me."

More pain. "That letter! My God, Beth. Who put you up to the things in that letter?"

The photograph was atilt against her stapler. With steely gaze, the Doberman assessed her courage, or lack of it.

"No one put me up to it."

"I want you home with me. Where you belong."

She stared right back at the Doberman, shook her head strongly, looked up at Bill. "No. Not like this."

Bill's eyes flickered up and behind her. She heard Alma say, "Everything okay out here?"

Bill looked up at the ceiling. "Yes, it's okay. I'm just talking to my wife. It's nothing to you."

Alma said, "Beth, is everything all right?"

Turning, Beth saw her leaning against the side of her office doorway ten feet away. "It's all right."

Bill bent forward, spoke in a hoarse whisper. "I want you home with me."

"I told you about that in my letter. Have you started seeing a doctor yet?"

"I don't need any damned doctor. I need my wife."

His anguish was gone. All there was in his face was anger seething, near explosion.

"It's no good, then," Beth said, saying it strongly, even though her breathing was ragged. "I'm not going to take it any more. That's all there is to it."

With his chin, Bill pointed angrily over Beth's shoulder. "Is she behind all this?"

"Nobody's behind it. Please just go, Bill. I'm not going to try to talk to you when you're mad."

He reached forward and grabbed her upper arm.

"Let go of me!"

"I want you out of this goddamned place. So we can talk. You come on out of here."

She shook her head. "You're hurting me."

Alma's voice was cold and hard. "You let go of her, Bill Rhodes."

He glared up at her, didn't loosen his grip. "You want her. Is that it? You think you've got her, don't you, you old bitch? But I got news for you." He jerked roughly at Beth's arm. "Goddamn it, I'm taking you out of here!"

She tried to pull away. "No!"

Bill grunted deep in his throat, raised his other hand to bring it crashing into her face.

"Don't you do that!" Alma snarled.

Hand upraised, Bill froze. He stared at Alma, his eyes widening.

"Let go of her," she said.

Slowly, his fingers loosened, and Beth pulled away. Her arm felt numb. Pushing back from her desk, she looked around.

Alma held a pistol, motioned with it toward the entrance. "Get out of here. Now!"

Bill frowned at her, his jaw working, his hands clenching and unclenching.

"I said, 'Get out of here, son of a bitch!'"

"She's my wife! You got no right!"

"Get!" Alma said, spitting the word, lifting the gun muzzle to bear directly on his face.

He folded. He wheeled around, bumped against the half-partition between the office and reception areas, left it shuddering behind him as he stamped to the plate glass front door and pushed it open so violently that it belled hollowly.

Alma came to Beth's desk. "Are you okay?"

"Yes," she said. "Yes!"

"IT'S YOU!" Chad said, his system going into full alert.

"Sure. You sound like you gave up on me."

"It's been over two weeks. I almost did." He checked the time. Somewhere, in some kind of equipment-jammed "phone room," a cop should be hot-lining the telephone company to get a trace going. And then the cop should be calling Officer Reason to tell her the killer was on the phone with Chad Palmer again.

The man chuckled. "I wouldn't forget my old buddy, Chad."

"Where are you?"

"In a house. Waiting."

Gooseflesh climbed up Chad's neck. "What?"

"Waiting. In the dark."

"What do you mean?" Chad asked, not needing an answer.

"She does needlepoint. You ought to see this place. Needlepoint stuff everywhere."

Chad tried to picture that phone room. What if they were all asleep in there? What if they'd gone down to the break room to drink coffee and tell war stories?

"You there?"

"Yes. Sure, I'm here."

"What time is it? I can't believe it. There's even a needlepoint cover on the commode, but there's not a clock in the place with a lighted dial."

"Eight-twenty," Chad said.

"When I was looking around, I saw her calendar in the kitchen. She's got this meeting tonight. I just wonder how long we have to wait."

Chad's heart went cold. "We? Why are you saying 'we'?"

The man laughed, ignored the question. "How'd your big Spring Sale go?"

"Why the hell would you say 'we'?"

"You've got a chandelier on display I really like. Brigatti's the brand name, I think. But none of them were on sale."

Chad shook his head in frustration. "No. We don't put those on sale."

"There were seven or eight that looked like they were all made by the same company. This one, in particular, I really wanted. No froufrou stuff, just a terrific light. But boy, are they expensive."

"So you've been in the store."

"Sure."

"Was I there?"

The man chuckled. "Yes."

Chad said, "You're in some woman's house right now."

"Yeah."

"Why?"

"You know why."

"Don't do that. Get out of there and leave her alone."

"She's mine, Chad. The Needlepoint Lady. She's mine."

Chad saw that two minutes had passed since he answered the telephone. They should be completing the trace at any second now, if they hadn't already. At any second, police cars would be racing toward a darkened house.

"Why do you kill?" he asked.

"Because I like to."

"Like to! How can somebody like that?"

"It makes me feel like I've made things be okay. Kind of like you feel when you start feeling good again after you've been sick. Alive and well."

Chad tried not to think about what he was hearing. Leaning back in his chair, he pictured police pouring into the darkened bedroom where this man talked so cheerfully about being alive and well, tearing the telephone out of his startled hands, slamming him against the wall.

"Why so quiet?" the man asked.

"Just realizing how fucking-awful this is."

"Awful? Why?"

"I'm here, on my phone, talking to somebody that's waiting for a woman he doesn't even know to come home so he can terrorize and kill her."

"What's awful about that? I don't see anything awful about it."

Chad rocked forward, pulled the handset away from his head, trying to crush it in his hands, wanting to smash it against the fieldstone wall. Instead, he put it back to his ear. "I saw Marian Koehler. After you killed her."

"Hey! Really? They really let you in her house? I can't believe that, Chad. That's terrific."

"Damn you!"

The man laughed. "Gets to your tender sensibilities, huh?"

Chad look at the ceiling. He wanted to break things, wanted to rage and shout. But he breathed deeply and carefully. "Why don't you tell me who you are?"

"That'd be dumb, wouldn't it?"

Chad needed to move around. He stood up, paced to

the sliding door of the atrium. "You seem to know all about me, so why shouldn't I know about you?"

"That's different."

Chad paced back to the desk. He looked at the clock for what seemed to be the thousandth time. What the hell was wrong? He pictured beer-gutted cops, lolling around in that equipment-choked phone room, smoking confiscated grass and giggling while the alarm on Chad Palmer's telephone tap went unnoticed. He remembered how Lieutenant Burke had joked about the police photographer's running out of film. Maybe this week that efficient photographer was running the phone room.

"How old are you?" he asked, to be saying something, realizing as he said it that he'd been hearing an odd noise for some time. A faint tapping?

"About your age," the man answered. "Around thirty."

Tapping? "Where are you from?"

"Middle America," was the answer, but Chad barely heard it.

Hurrying out of the study, he headed for the front door, toward that discreet tapping. "Did you grow up there?" he said into the telephone, knowing that the long cord would just reach.

He keyed the bolt lock open and twisted the knob. Reason pushed the door open and came inside, turning to close the door quietly behind her.

"Yes," the man answered.

Chad asked, "When did you come to Houston?"

Reason had been off-duty. She was wearing sneakers and blue jeans and a man's cream-colored oxford cloth shirt. Her hair was loose, falling wavy and golden around her face.

"Six or seven years ago," came from the telephone.

Reason pointed toward the study, passed Chad and went in. She pulled a small spiral notebook from her purse, but dropped it back inside when she saw the yellow pad ready on the desk.

"Do you like it here?" Chad said into the telephone as he watched Reason write a note.

"Yeah. I love it here," the man said. "I've really found myself here."

The note said, "They can't trace the call!!!"

Chad pulled the pencil out of Reason's hand, slashed a huge "WHY??" onto the paper.

Reason put out her hands in a gesture of futility.

Chad sank into the chair behind the desk, angrily shifted the telephone handset from right ear to left, jerked at the trailed-out cord so that it looped messily into the corner behind him. To the killer, he said, "So you found yourself. How'd you do that?"

Reason waved a hand, pantomimed, "Be right back," and left the study.

The man said, "I didn't know who I was. I wasn't anybody. But here in Houston, I've got some identity. I know who I am and what it's all about. I'm somebody."

Through the doorway, Chad saw Reason kneeling down, plugging the yellow telephone from his kitchen into the dining room outlet. As she came into the study with the telephone, he let himself boil over. "You're somebody, all right! Some goddamned sneak-murderer."

Reason pantomimed, "Drop the phone."

Chad leaned forward, lifted his handset and let it fall on the hard top of the desk. As it did, Reason lifted the handset of the yellow telephone.

Retrieving his handset, Chad said, "Sorry about that."

"So, as I was saying when you so clumsily interrupted me, you don't approve of me, do you?"

Chad picked up the pencil, ripped away the top sheet of paper. "No, you son of a bitch! I don't."

Furiously, he wrote, "He's in a woman's house! Waiting for her! They've got to do something!"

The man said, "You're not being much of a buddy."

"Get out of there. Why can't you just please get out of there, and leave her alone? What's she ever done to you?"

Reason read his note, picked up the pencil, wrote, "Do what?"

Chad fell back into his chair and listened to the man. His voice now was lower and paced so that he sounded thoughtful and sad. "You still won't give me a chance, will you?"

"I'll give you anything you want," Chad said. "Money. I'll get money for you. Anything. Just tell me."

The man just laughed.

"Damn you!" Chad said. "What the hell kind of chance do you give them? Sneak in like a thief and wait and scare hell out of them and torment them and kill them, like you were some goddamned animal!"

His stomach churned. Reason touched his hand and he jerked away in reflex, and then looked up, realizing it was she. She touched him again, just for a moment, trying to lend him strength.

The man hadn't answered. Chad made his voice go calm. "Tell me where you are. Let me come and get you. I'll come and get you and we'll go somewhere and talk this out. Just you and me. Please."

"Fool!"

Chad closed his eyes, swallowed down bile. "Let me do that. I'll get you out of there. We'll talk it over like buddies should."

The man laughed. "You don't expect me to—" There was a sharp intake of breath. And then, hoarsely, he whispered, "I hear her coming in. She's here! She's finally coming in to me."

BETH SPENT the evening in utter self-indulgence.

For as long as she could remember, she had gathered and tossed into a drawer all the beauty-product and personal-care samples she had been offered, promising herself that she would try them someday when she had the time. When she was packing to leave Bill, she had dumped out that drawer into a suitcase, feeling silly about taking such unessentials, but determined, nevertheless, to haul them along, just because they were hers and hers alone.

And now, she certainly had the time to experiment with them.

She lolled in a bubble bath, shaved her legs and underarms with microscopic care. She shampooed her hair, applied a rinse guaranteed not to change, but to brighten irresistibly, and followed that with a conditioner that nobody had bought even though the commercials had insisted every woman would be forever sexless and lonely without it.

That completed Body, Legs, and Hair. The project now was Face.

Trying not to breathe too much of its vicious stink, but determined to use it, nevertheless, she slathered the vile green plasticky mess of something called Masque Magique over her face. When it had solidified, she peeled it away, aghast at the debris it had squeezed and sucked from her skin. Shuddering, she rolled the gloppy mess into a ball and flushed it away down the commode.

The clear, healthily-glowing look of her face in the mirror made the unpleasantness of the procedure worthwhile. The only flaw was that the discoloration of the
black eye lingered on like a pale green shadow across her
cheekbone.

She set to work with foundations and masking sticks.
Some of her combinations only accentuated the bruise,
but finally a concoction improbably named Cherry So-
prano turned out to be perfectly concealing.

Humming, soaringly happy, she painted, brushed,
smoothed, patted, blended, until she was finished with
her face. Then she brushed her hair, shaped, pinned,
touseled, until it, too, was perfect.

"My God!" she breathed, staring at her reflection in
awe, hardly daring to believe she was looking at herself.
She didn't look made up or artificial; she looked glowingly,
cleanly, healthily good. She looked as good as all the girls
at the prom thought everybody thought the other girls
looked.

"Prom! What prom?" she suddenly said aloud to her
reflection. In seconds, her pleasure turned to desperation.

She fled to the bedroom, sat huddled on the edge of the
bed, and jabbed out her home number on the telephone
dial.

It rang and rang and rang.

"Where are you, Bill?" she cried.

She dialed his office number, aching to hear his voice.

But there was no answer there, either.

She told herself that she had made a mistake in dialing,
tried both numbers again.

Still no answer.

She smashed the handset into the cradle.

The bathroom smelled like a whore's underwear.
"Damn!" she shouted at her reflection.

Picking up a lipstick, she wrote, "FUCK YOU, BILL RHODES!" on the mirror.

Letting her robe slip off to the floor, she started to write the same message on her naked belly. But the bruises on her arm, caused by Bill's angry grip just three days ago, caught her attention.

"No! I won't think about that!" she said, and with the lipstick, hid the bruises with smeary red flower petals.

Inspired now, and giggling, she stuck an iridescent-green bottle cap in her navel and used an eyebrow pencil to draw an eye around it.

Laughing, she painted her left nipple with blue eye shadow, the right one with green, and drew curly-lashed eyes around them. She lipsticked her nose red, stuck a finger in mascara, and painted a huge black mouth around her lips, and a sloppily star-shaped beauty mark on her cheekbone.

She laughed, waved, winked, whistled at her reflection, did bumps and grinds. For a while, it was all great fun.

But not for long.

Dipping a finger in silver eye shadow, she smeared great teardrops on her face and beneath the painted eyes on her breasts and belly.

When she began to weep real tears, she stumbled into the shower, turned the water scaldingly hot, scrubbed all of the colors off her body, and watched them swirl scummily down the drain.

CHAD HAD bitten raw his lips and the inside of his mouth. His shirt was clammy with perspiration. He had stopped long ago looking at the clock; it seemed that this had gone on forever.

"It's time," the man said.

The woman moaned. She had screamed herself hoarse. Lately, she had been able only to moan.

"No!" Chad shouted.

He was answered by the thunder of a shotgun blast. A moment later, the telephone was hung up and there was only the whine of the dial tone.

He hung up his own telephone, finding that his fingers were cramped and aching.

Reason smashed down the handset of the extension, lifted it immediately, and dialed with savage jabs. "What in hell is wrong with you people?" she said, in a rough, angry voice.

Chad stared off, away, at nothing. All he could think of was that it was finally over.

"So Burke is there. Fine!" Reason said. "Put him on here, son of a bitch!"

The woman's screaming started up in Chad's head again.

Forcing himself to stand, he went out of the study, away from everything, into the dining room across the hallway, pulled open the door of the liquor cabinet. Wrenching the cap off a bottle of bourbon, he sloshed an inch and a half into a glass.

The woman had screamed forever!

He drank down the bourbon, gasping aloud as it seared his throat and seemed to set hooks into the raw places in his mouth.

Reason's angry voice carried from the study. "He was on the phone for one hour and fifty-seven minutes, Ross! What the hell went wrong?"

Chad set out another glass, poured more bourbon, went back to the study.

Reason sat at the desk now, frowning at its top as she listened on the telephone.

Chad set one of the glasses in front of her.

She wrapped her fingers around it as if she were trying to crush it. "Damn it, Ross! I knew they were having problems at first. They told me that when they beeped me. But they had another hour and fifty minutes! For God's sake, this is 1985! They trace calls with computers now!"

She picked up the glass, drank an inch of the bourbon, and shudderingly set it down. "Ross, they . . ." Breaking off angrily, she listened some more.

Chad took another drink. He wanted to rush out, get to some place where there were noise and music and people he'd never seen before.

Reason was saying, "All right, Ross. Okay." Her voice was lower now, her hand open and flat, palm-down on the desktop. She looked defeated. "I see. Fine, Ross. Goodbye." She hung up, looked at the floor.

In Chad's brain, the woman's muffled screaming started up again. "What went wrong?" he asked, to kill the sound.

"He's calling you in some way that makes it almost impossible to trace."

"How?" Chad said, looking at the telephone as if it were a chunk of bleeding meat.

"Routing his calls through a PBX, and through one of those non-Bell long-distance companies somehow."

Feeling lost, Chad shook his head. "Long-distance?"

"Somehow, he's piggybacking his calls. They go out of town and back in again. Screws up their damned computers."

Chad drank the rest of his bourbon, looked hopelessly at the empty glass. "It's going to happen some more. And you don't know how to find him."

Reason stood up, came very close to him, her hair falling wavy and golden-fine around her face. "We'll figure out something. There's got to be a way."

Chad felt the warmth of her, caught the scent of that light perfume, and stepped back. "I don't know what to do. This is the first safe place I've ever had. In my life. But now, this son of a bitch can call me up whenever he wants to, and show me I never knew a damned thing about being safe."

He turned away from her, looked at the painting, and then turned away from it also, suddenly afraid that the way he felt now might ruin more of the things he cared about.

"When you find this one," he said, "whatever you do, don't take me there."

THE RECEPTIONIST was in the back of the office, trying to remember how to operate the Mr. Coffee, so Beth answered the telephone herself. "Good morning, Century 21—Henderson Associates."

"Beth! Hello, hon."

She looked out toward the street, remembering the gunky mess in her bathroom this morning. And the gunky mess she had made of herself last night. When Bill was nowhere to be found.

"Hello," she said.

"How are you, baby?"

"I'm fine, Bill. How are you?" The rushing traffic on Kirby Drive smeared across her vision.

Bill lowered his voice. "Missing you all the time. You just don't know how I miss you, baby. I can't stand that house without you."

That voice had never before failed to affect Beth, and now was no different. Her entire body went damp and achy. A flush of red started up her throat, onto her face. "Don't, Bill. Please."

"I had this dream about you last night."

She breathed in sharply and clenched her hand so that the nails dug into her palm.

"It was so real. But I woke up, and you weren't there. Please come back home. I can't stand this any longer."

From somewhere, she dredged up the strength to say, "You know what you have to do."

"Do?"

"When you start therapy, then I'll see you. Not before."

"I have started," Bill said.

"You . . . what?"

"I started therapy."

A pulse of wonderful warmth started in Beth's breast, washed all through her. "You've started! That's wonderful. Why didn't you tell me?"

He laughed. "You didn't give me a chance, baby. Listen, now can I see you so we can talk?"

"When did you start?" Beth asked.

He laughed ruefully. "You don't know how I felt after I

finally settled down the other day. After I pulled off that stunt in your office, I felt like a fool, baby. And I went right out and got me a therapist. Just like you want."

"I'm so happy," Beth said.

"And you apologize to Alma for me, will you? You tell her I said I was real sorry."

"Of course."

"So, when are we going to get together?" He paused, and then hopefully provided the answer. "How about right now?"

Beth wanted to jump up and rush out to her car. But she laughed and said, "Oh, I couldn't. I've got two showings this morning I can't change."

He was disappointed. "Well, how about lunch?"

"Lunch! Yes. At twelve?" Then she added, "But I can't take a very long one, darling. I've got an appointment at one-thirty."

"How many showings you doing in a day, anyway?"

"Oh no. One-thirty's with my doctor. You know how important that is."

"Sure," Bill said. "Absolutely. I can't wait till my next one."

CHAD GOT up late, feeling dirty and depressed. So he ran, running farther than he had in years, just slogging along through the muggy, overcast morning.

The exercise helped.

Back in front of his town house, perspiration running off his body, he picked up his *Houston Post* and, shrugging, picked up the neighbors', also, from where they had been dropped almost together, barely clearing the curbing. The neighbors' paper, he carried up their walk and tossed through the bars of the locked gate, into their enclosed front courtyard.

He had cut across the lawn to his own front door and was fishing the mail out of his mailbox when he heard a car pull up and park. Turning, he grinned happily to see Sharon Reason getting out of her car. Mopping at his face with his sopping T-shirt, he waited at the door for her.

She was dressed as she had been last night, when word of the man's call to Chad had found her at bowling. The only difference in how she looked now was the fatigue in her face, and her hair, which was now tied up in a ponytail.

"I thought you'd be at the store," she said, passing him to go inside. "I went by there first."

"I ran," Chad said. "Maybe I'll go to the store later on." He followed her down the hallway, toward the kitchen. "You've been up all night, haven't you?"

"Yes. Good, you've made coffee, Chad."

He was startled that she had used his first name. "Sure. Started it going before I left."

Wearily, she went to the coffee maker. "We have to talk. There are a million things we have to do."

Chad looked down at himself. "Have some coffee. I'll be down in a couple of minutes."

He rushed through the shower, put on jeans and a T-shirt, and came back downstairs to find Reason with a glass of water, washing down a pill she took from a folded-over Kleenex.

"Is that speed?" he asked.

She tucked the tissue into her shirt pocket. "There's no other way. I can't say, 'Screw off,' to the office and go jogging."

"Fine," Chad said. He poured coffee for himself and sat down at the table across from her. "Have you found her?"

"No. Who knows when? It was just luck that that woman friend of Marian Koehler's took it on herself to go check so soon. Just luck she had a key. Lots of women don't have friends they trust with a key. I don't." She smoothed her hair back, tucked away a couple of strands that had escaped the rubber band. "Did you have a rough night?"

"It wasn't terrific. I was glad to see daylight. But running helped."

"Do you think he's one of your customers?"

"He could be."

"He said he'd been in the store. He talked about some kind of chandelier."

"Anybody can come in the place and look around."

"I wish you'd gotten into that more. I wish we knew if he'd ever bought something there."

Chad got up, brought the coffee pot to the table, and added coffee to their cups. "Sorry I didn't say all the right things. I haven't had too much experience talking to maniacs."

With an edge of irritation in her voice, Reason said, "Stop it, Chad."

With a little irritation of his own, he said, "Are we Chad and Sharon now? Or is it Chad, but definitely still Officer Reason?"

"I'm sorry."

Sitting down, he said, "You're on speed, and I didn't get a hell of a lot of sleep. I'm sorry, too. What's all this we have to do?"

"Your customer files. We need them. And it's Sharon. All right?"

He smiled. "All right. Why the customer files?"

"We're going to call all the men and run voice-print comparisons."

"How? There must be thousands. Some guy drops in to buy a couple of light bulbs because he's in the neighborhood. I'm not exactly General Electric, but I get a lot of traffic."

"You don't even have the name of somebody that just buys some light bulbs, do you?"

"If it's check or credit card or charge, we do."

"We'll call all we can get. Half of what I was doing all night was trying to get a computer set up to run voice-print comparisons with what we recorded last night."

Chad frowned questioningly.

"We call and say, 'Hello, is this Joe Jones?' What's somebody going to answer? Not too many different things. First, of course, there's 'Hello,' when they answer. Then there's 'Yes,' or 'No,' or 'Yeah,' or 'Who's calling?' or 'I never heard of him,' or a few other things. We've pulled stuff like that out of what he said last night. When somebody answers, there'll be the computer on the line, too, whipping up a print of what they say. We compare that with prints of the same word or phrase he said last night, and when the two match, we've got him."

Chad was frowning more now. "What are you going to say when you call? 'This is the cops calling you to hassle you about your relationship with Let There Be Light, Inc.'?"

"Of course not. You won't be connected with it. We're going to tell them it's a phone campaign to get them to use their seat belts."

Chad nodded with relief. "Okay. That could work. If he's a customer."

"It's something to work on, at least. Another thing, why don't you put those chandeliers he likes on sale? Ross Burke thinks that might be a good idea."

"You're kidding. That's not sale stuff."

"It's a shot, isn't it? Would it break you, or something? Would you rather cut your profit a little, or keep on being a phone buddy with this maniac?"

Chad put up his hand in surrender. "Okay. Put like that, I'll red-tag 'em."

"You need to call somebody at the store and tell them we can pick up the customer files."

"Right."

"You also need to tell your people that, if anybody—any man, anyway—shows any special interest in those chandeliers, to try to find out who he is. Without being obvious."

"Okay. What else?"

"Listen to the tape of last night's call a couple of times. See if you can pick out anything you might not have noticed when you were in the middle of it."

"It ran through my head all night long while I was trying to sleep," Chad said. "I don't guess it'll hurt me to listen to it a few more times."

"A couple of other things. I want a key to your front door. So that, when he calls next time, I can get in without any trouble."

Chad nodded.

"And we want to run another phone line in here. With another set. So that, when he's on your line, I'll still have some way to call out."

"Okay. Sure."

"Also, before the next time, we're going to get a psychologist with you to help you with what you say to him."

"Next time," Chad said, watching his hand form a fist. "Something I've been wanting to ask you—does your Lieutenant Burke still think I'm involved? More important, do you?"

"No," Reason said. "God, no. Nobody thinks that. Burke was just taking a shot in the dark."

"No, you don't think so? Or, no, for sure?"

"I never really thought that," Reason said. "But you get wary." She rubbed at her eyes. "Last night. When you said this was the first safe place you'd ever had. What did you mean?"

"I was feeling sorry for myself."

She waited.

"Shooting off my mouth."

She persisted. "What did it mean?"

He shook his head, but finally said, "It was so hard getting this. I didn't even feel safe when I was a little kid. And I got thinking about that last night."

"Children are safe," she said, but looked unsure.

"We were always getting kicked out of some place we were living in. My dad was a musician—a pretty bad one. Sometimes we had to live in the car and somebody was always about to repossess that. And he and my mother believed in sharing all that with us—my sister and me. I started worrying so much I couldn't sleep before I could even spell the word.

"Then finally, four years ago, I was working at the store and it went on the market. I lied a lot and bought it on bluff and spit. Lived in the warehouse for almost eight months because I didn't have money for an apartment. Or a car.

"But then things started working out pretty well. There got to be always enough money to make the payroll. I didn't have to shuffle the bills around any more. And I bought this place. Got used to being safe. And being able to buy things I wanted. Like that painting in the study. I got real used to not worrying.

"And then, POW! that son of a bitch started calling me. And I was sitting there last night, and I was, all of a sudden, just that little scabby-kneed kid again, sweating blood because the rent wasn't paid, and it was cold and rainy outside, and I was scared."

THE MORNING'S long run had been good therapy for Chad. But after Officer Reason—Sharon, now—left, the little itches of insecurity prompted by talking about his childhood began to expand into ugly worries. He told himself that he was being stupid, but that didn't help.

Finally, he changed into the pin-striped suit in which he always felt the most serious and successful and drove to the store. He knew differently, but deep down he was sure that, when he got there, he'd find the doors padlocked and his bankers and major suppliers waiting to tell him he was finished, while gangsters in Houston Lighting & Power uniforms cut off the electricity.

Everything looked normal, though, as he parked his car and went around to the showroom entrance where the lights of a hundred crystal chandeliers twinkled out at Buffalo Speedway through the long plate glass wall.

But as soon as he walked inside, he saw Gina agitatedly waving a piece of paper at him, and his heart froze with the certainty that it was a summons, or worse.

But it wasn't. It was a deposit slip. And Gina's agitation was actually glee. "The check came in this morning's mail!" she crowed.

$7,959.38 showed on the deposit slip. The long-delayed payment for those three $2,500 chandeliers.

Even so, Chad was determined not to cheat disaster. "It'll bounce," he said.

"Stop it!" Gina said. "I ran it right over to his bank and got a certified check for it. That's what I deposited." Stalking away from him, into her alcove, she switched on her typewriter and made it chatter disgust at him until he crept past into his office.

Settling down at his desk, he went through the routine he'd followed at least once a week since buying this place.

He double-checked everything. All the insurance policies were up-to-date and paid. Friday's payroll was covered. The bank notes were current. Year-to-date sales were up 16.2 percent, even in the wake of the recession that was trying to linger on in Houston. The bills were paid, and there was still money in the bank. The IRS wasn't auditing. If Gina were embezzling, she was doing it both gently and skillfully.

Refusing to believe it, he checked all the figures yet another time, and set the results into a formula for figuring Net Worth. The bottom line was so satisfying and so real that even today's insecurities had to go to rest.

It had been not so very long ago when going through this routine had sent him running sweating and panic-stricken out onto the showroom floor, practically pleading with any available customer to buy something—anything.

But not today. Sitting back, smiling at the black-and-white proof of his solvency, he picked up the telephone to call his sister. A happy, joking long-distance call at the sinfully high daytime rates was one of their time-honored ways of putting the ghosts of their childhood worries in proper perspective.

Midway through dialing, though, he stopped. No. Good old Dr. Laura Palmer-Reed would have the whole story of the Rose Lady and the Needlepoint Lady out of him in minutes, and he didn't need to be dumping that on her.

He replaced the receiver and stepped out into Gina's office. "Call the florist, would you? Have them send a dozen yellow roses to my sister."

"It's not her birthday."

Chad shrugged. "Send three dozen."

Gina punched a button on her telephone number file. "What about a card? Or is this going to be a mystery, like everything else?"

"No mystery. Just 'Love, Chad.'"

Back in his office, he found the program for the Roel Peña Showing at the Fremont Gallery, took one more quick look at the papers on his desk, told himself that this was an investment, called, and bought Number 14 on the list.

Settling down to work then, he pored over an inventory printout, checking off the items to be put on sale along with the Brigattis. When he was finished, he went into Gina's office and sat on the corner of her desk.

"What now?" she asked, pointing at the sheaf of papers in his hand.

"Why do you say it like that?"

She rolled her eyes. "The telephone lines are bugged. The police came in and carried out half our files. What now?"

WHEN SHE reached the restaurant, Beth ducked into the powder room for one last check on her new makeup, and to spend a few moments telling her reflection to calm down. "Don't be so excited," she said silently. "So Bill has started therapy. That's just the beginning." Sternly, she forced her breathing to go slow and even.

Bill had arrived before her. When she saw him rising from the table, wearing the blue blazer and camel slacks she'd given him last Christmas, her mirror work was forgotten. He must have gotten a haircut just this morning, and the cut seemed to accentuate the little bits of gray at his temples.

With a start, Beth realized that it wasn't just the haircut. There really was more gray there now than there had been the last time she had really looked at him—something she hadn't done that awful morning at the office. Wrenchingly, the gray reminded her of the break in their lives.

Bill was wasting no time, however, on memories. Warmly, he kissed her cheek. Solicitously, he held her chair while she sat down, and then hurried over to sit down himself, pausing only to pull the bottle of champagne from its bucket-stand beside the table. "This is a celebration," he said, filling glasses.

He lifted his in a toast and Beth followed suit. "To my beautiful baby," he said. "God, how I've missed you. You look like a million bucks."

Beth drank. She wanted to jump out of her skin and dance.

Reaching inside his jacket, Bill handed an envelope across to her.

"What's this?"

"Open it."

She did. Airline tickets and a brochure featuring that villa in Puerto Vallarta. White marble and palm trees and blue private pool, Mexican tiles, red and yellow hibiscus.

"Thursday week," Bill said.

"It's beautiful. It looks just as wonderful as you said."

Bill raised his glass again. "Let's drink to it. To beau- tiful Puerto Vallarta."

Beth smiled, but shook her head. "First, we should drink to something really important. To getting help, Bill, so we can straighten out our lives. I am so happy about that!"

"Sure," Bill said. "Here's to help."

They clicked glasses. Bill drank. But Beth used her glass to hide a sudden frown, barely wet her lips.

"Now, to the trip," Bill said. "I can't wait! It's going to be just like our honeymoon all over again, baby."

Once more, Beth went through the motions of drinking a toast. Her heart was beating too fast. Surely, she was wrong!

She looked around the restaurant, as if the very richness of it would reassure her. But in the shadows near the ceiling, an ugly, leprous water stain showed in the elegant flocked wall covering. She turned away, toward the happy laughter at the table nearest theirs, and found the man to be sixtyish, at least, and sweatily short-breathed, predatory, not happy; the "woman" was just a child, looking as if, at any moment, she'd have to skip off to make it in time for her afternoon shift at McDonald's.

Looking back at Bill, Beth said, "Don't go so fast. I've got to talk this trip over with Dr. Wray. It could undo everything, if we moved too fast."

Bill said nothing, just looked hurt.

"What does your therapist think about it?"

Bill smiled now. "He thinks it's the best thing we could do. Get away together. Just the two of us. Where some outsider can't interfere with us. He said if I hadn't already told him about it, he was going to suggest something just like it. He says for us to relax and take a nice trip away from everybody."

Beth's heart was quite steady now. "Well, then, Dr. Wray will probably say the same thing. How often do you go to your therapist?"

"Monday, Wednesday, Friday. At four." He raised his hand, signaled. "I guess they better start bringing us some food now. I don't want you to be late."

Beth asked, "What's your doctor's name?"

"I don't want to talk about that guy," Bill said. "I want to talk about us." He probed at the brochure with a fingertip. "Look here, hon. This purple flower? Bougainvillea."

Smiling, Beth said, "You can tell me his name."

Bill sat back, worked up his boyish, innocent look. "You sound almost like you're checking up on me."

Calmly, Beth said, "You're lying. You haven't started therapy at all."

Bill was rocked. He looked desperately around, said, "Oh, come on, baby. How can you—"

She cut him off. "Stop it. And stop calling me 'baby.' I've always hated it."

Earnestly, Bill said, "I only told you what you were so bound and determined to hear. We don't need that phony stuff. We can work things out ourselves. If I can just get you away from that interfering old bitch for a while."

Beth picked up her purse, pushed back her chair. "I'm sorry, but you know how it's got to be."

Bill touched the brochure, shoved it across the table. "Just look at this place. We can work things out, if you just give me the chance. Alone. In a nice place like this."

Beth shook her head. "Puerto Vallarta. If I fell for this, next time I'd find myself going for a broken nose so you'd take me to Jamaica. The hell with that! I'm going to get well. With you, or without you."

Bill's face hardened. "Don't you just try and walk away from me."

"Well, this is wonderful! When you get mad, I'm supposed to start thinking, 'Oh, I deserve for him to knock me around!' But I don't any more. You just watch yourself, boy. You so much as touch me again, I'll have you in jail in five minutes. You're not ever going to beat me again. And you can get started on not wanting to. Or you can just stay the hell out of my life."

She stood up, and she left.

RED SALE tags fluttered from a third of the chandeliers hanging in the showroom, including the cluster of Brigattis. Chip postured artistically at the plate glass window as he painted "48 HOUR SALE" in huge red figures and letters.

Chad was on his way out when his telephone buzzed. Instead of answering it, he took another step, opened the door, and looked questioningly at Gina.

"A man asking for you," she said.

Chad grimaced.

"I'll tell him you left."

Shaking his head, Chad went back into his office, punched the flashing button, and said, "Hello."

"Hi, Chad."

His belly went cold. "What do you want?"

"Well, gee, buddy. You don't sound very happy to hear my voice."

"I'm not." He reached up for his mustache, to tug at it nervously, but jerked his hand away when he felt only bare skin. Angrily, he reminded himself that his beard and mustache had been gone for weeks.

The man said, "I thought you'd be all exhilarated and energetic after you did all that running this morning."

"How'd you know about that?"

"I make it my business to know about you. You're my buddy. We're in this together. I want to look out for you."

"We're not in anything together. Except you decided to start calling me, inflicting your goddamned craziness on me."

"Who's the blonde chick?"

Chad dropped into the desk chair. "What?"

"Tight jeans. Blonde hair. Great tits. Came to your place this morning when you got through running. Got you strutting around, scratching your chest, showing off."

"A friend."

"Nice friend."

"I wish you'd come to see me in person, instead of just spying on me," Chad said.

"Oh, yeah?"

"I don't know if I ever really wanted to beat the shit out of somebody before. But I do now."

The man seemed pleased with Chad's anger. "Hey! A macho attack. You sound like that blonde chick's with you right now."

"Give me a chance at you, son of a bitch! Just show your fucking face to me, don't spy on me!" Realizing the futility of his anger, he pulled away the handset, let the man's voice sink unheard into the desktop.

Finally, though, he had to lift it back to his ear. The man was saying, ". . . where are you? Chad? Chad! Answer me."

"Yeah."

"Where'd you go? What happened?"

"Leave me the hell alone."

"I like you, Chad. I need your company."

"Let me go," he said, flattening his hand on the desk-top, pressing down hard to arrest the shaking.

"Have they found the Needlepoint Lady yet?"

"This is all of this!" Chad said. "You've got to let me alone."

The man laughed. "Okay, buddy. Don't want to wear out my welcome, do I? I got to go, anyway. Bye."

Open dial tone whined in Chad's ear. He had to use both hands to guide the handset back onto its cradle.

"I USED up absolutely everything I had," Beth said. "By the time I got out of that restaurant to my car, I'd have turned around and crawled back to Bill on my hands and knees, if he'd come out after me."

"I think you did remarkably well," Dr. Wray said. "It was your first real crisis on your own. I'm proud of you."

"Will he keep on like this? Why can't he see that he needs help?"

"You talk as if it's easy. But you didn't exactly come rushing for help at the first sign of a problem, did you? It took you seven years. And then you had to be pushed."

"Pushed," Beth said, and waved it away. "Last night, I tried to call him. To beg him to come and get me."

Dr. Wray looked at her impassively.

"He didn't answer. Not at home, or at the office."

"When crises arise, you know you can call me. At any time."

"It wasn't a crisis! I just couldn't stand it any more."

"Luck plays a part in our lives, also. Last night was your night for luck in that Bill was out somewhere." He steepled his fingers. "But you can't rely on it. You came through today with an admirable show of strength. Now, just gather that strength and be ready for the next time."

"Oh, God!" she said, leaning back, feeling as if her legs had turned to water. "The next time. And the next. Oh, dear God!" She shook her head. "When I drove away from the restaurant, I was thinking how it could all be so easy. And I was wanting it to be."

"Easy? In what way?"

"What always used to bother me was having to lie about why I couldn't come to work for a few days. And then still having a bruise or the end of a black eye when I did go back. And knowing, eventually, that nobody believed me.

"But I could just quit working. I could just be a housewife. Then there wouldn't be anybody I'd have to lie to. Whatever happened, I could just stay in the house and get over it without people knowing about it.

"I don't really have to go through all this—all these awful feelings—and probably lose Bill, too. I could just quit working and stay home."

Dr. Wray studied her across his desk. "Of course, you could. That certainly is one solution."

She stared at him.

"That would be very nice for you. Doing nothing much but watching 'All My Children' and memorizing recipes. Making the occasional quick trip out to the emergency room."

"You make me so mad sometimes!"

Dr. Wray looked at her blandly, his stubby fingers checking the buttons of his vest, one by one, to see if they still held against the pressure of his belly.

"I noticed something today," Beth said. "When Bill gets

that mad look, he's really ugly. Really, really ugly. I just never saw that until today. And it made me mad as hell!"

She sat up straight, lifted her fist, shook it, brandished it at the big building that loomed in the window. "Bill Rhodes, you piss me off!" she said.

Dropping the fist, she shifted around to look away from the window completely. "I don't know how you stand this, Dr. Wray."

He lifted his eyebrows.

She explained. "Listening to this day after day. I couldn't do what you do at all." She cast about for an example. "If this were a book, I'd hate it."

He showed interest now.

"Well, if this were a book, I'd have some awful things to say about it."

Dr. Wray leaned forward. "Awful things to say about the book? Or about the people in it?"

"About the people."

"What things? I'm interested. Criticize this book for me."

"All right. The woman. I don't like her at all. I don't have any sympathy for her. She's a wimp. One minute, she's strong; the next, she's nothing. She goes back and forth so fast, she confuses me. And the man. He's so awful, I don't know how she could ever have fallen in love with him." She sat back, sneaked a look at her watch, and winced inwardly to see that the session was barely half over. "This is silly," she said.

"No, I think it's fascinating. Please go on. Not about why she fell in love with him, but why he's so awful."

She looked at the ceiling. "He's repulsive. The only time he's charming is when he's trying to trick her into coming home. He's just not believable in a book."

"Why not?" Dr. Wray asked.

"He's such a complete monster. If you're going to make

the book any good at all, you'd have to make him different. More complex, maybe. Anguished. He could be ill—maybe almost mentally ill—but not such a repulsive monster."

When she didn't continue, Dr. Wray said, "Go on."

"No," Beth said. "I don't think I like this. You've let me get myself into some kind of corner, and it bothers me."

"You're not in a corner. You know that."

"It feels like one."

"The only corner you've gotten yourself in is because you're pretending this book is a Silhouette Novel, and not the one you're involved in."

"That's silly."

"You're criticizing as if you were someone who doesn't know there are such things as abused wives, or abusive husbands."

Beth fidgeted. "I certainly do know. . . ."

Dr. Wray raised a hand, shushed her. "In the context in which we're dealing with these characters of yours . . . no . . . that's enough fiction. In the context of you and your husband, you are confused, afraid, wildly emotional. Your husband, in this context, is repulsive, charmless, diseased, every inch the monster. He's been interrupted in his established cycle of anger, release, contrition, new anger, et cetera. His every reaction to you, until he gets you into his possession once again and achieves temporary release from the violence which drives him, or until he undergoes effective therapy, will be nothing other than, in your own words, charmless and monstrous, or in mine, violent.

"He is not anguished. He anguishes over having lost possession of the thing with which he periodically achieves a temporary rest from his personal demons—you."

Beth was looking at him stonily.

Dr. Wray smiled gently at her. "Not half as pleasant as a nice romance novel, is it?"

She didn't answer.

"You're sitting there thinking how wrong I am, that I've completely misread everything, that someone like you couldn't have possibly fallen in love with someone so terrible."

"I don't know what to think."

"You'll remember that I steered you away from telling why your book character fell in love with him."

"I suppose you did," she said coldly.

"You think I'm being absurd, so I shall be. No romance novels. No realistic ones. Let's try a fairy tale now. You're Cinderella, looking for your Prince Charming, casting your glass slippers here and there, hoping the right fellow will pick one up and find you. Several do. Gently, they fit the slipper to your foot and are devastated when you turn your back and walk away without interest. But comes another Prince. With another of your slippers. You see the anger in him as he tries to fit it on your foot. If it won't fit, you think he'll smash it and probably smash you, also. And now, you're interested. You fall into his arms. He's exactly what you were looking for."

"That's awful. That's disgusting," Beth said, but without much force.

Gently, Dr. Wray said, "No. It's only human. It's awful and disgusting only if we refuse to recognize it, and fail to try to make it better and happier."

CHAD FOLLOWED the thick gray telephone cable through the kitchen, up the hallway, and into the study. It was held out of the way by masking tape that stuck it to the baseboards, he noted gratefully. At least, they hadn't drilled holes all over the place.

In the study, there was enough of the cable so that the new telephone set—an automatic dialer—could be carried to the far corner of the big room or out into the atrium, to be as far away from the regular telephone on the desk as possible.

Now, it sat on the coffee table in front of Officer Reason, who smiled up at him, as she hung up from a call.

He set the brown-paper-wrapped painting he carried against the side of the fireplace and turned toward her, frowning at the exhaustion on her face.

"Can I get you some coffee?" he asked.

She shook her head. "No more. I'm finally going home to bed. God! Sleep."

"Did you hear it a while ago, when he called me at the store?"

She looked down at the carpeting. "I heard about it."

"From Burke?"

She shook her head again, harder. "No. From one of the surveillance people."

"He saw you this morning. Coming in here."

"They told me."

"Where do you live?"

"Just off Hillcroft."

"An apartment?" Chad asked.

"Yes. Why all this?"

"Do you live alone?"

"Yes, I do. Why?"

"You'll have somebody go home with you, won't you?"

"Oh, for God's sake, Chad!"

"You get a cop to see you home—even Burke—or I'll do it, myself. We don't know how crazy that bastard is. I didn't like the way he sounded about you on the phone."

She stood up from the sofa, walked over to the glass wall of the atrium, and craned her neck to look up at the sky.

"It's crappy outside," Chad said. "You could cut the air with a knife." He pulled off his jacket, opened his vest, gratefully loosened the tie. "Call somebody to follow you home. Get him to check inside your place."

"That's silly," Reason said, turning her head slowly, rubbing the back of her neck.

"No, it's not."

She gestured toward the wrapped painting. "What's that?"

"Don't change the subject."

"Okay. I'll get somebody." Wearily, she moved over to the desk and sat back against it. "Is that another painting?"

Grinning, he knelt, peeled away the paper, and crossed the room to stand beside her, to look at it from a little distance. "When I went to the opening, I couldn't decide which of them I had to have. I had to flip a coin. Anyway, they're an investment."

Reason turned toward him. "Pretty good for that scared little kid, huh?"

"Not too bad."

Looking at the painting again, her voice going low, she asked, "Did they hurt you? Your parents? Is it all right to ask that?"

"They weren't like that," he said. "They were terrible parents, but they never hurt us. They were sweet and silly and about ten years old emotionally. But they'd have died before they'd hurt us—physically, anyway."

"I've wondered about that all day," Reason said, rubbing her eyes. "Since you told me about them this morning. That's the completely horrible thing about this job—the abused children." Tilting her head stiffly, she rubbed at her neck.

Chad touched her arm, turned her so that her back was toward him, and massaged her shoulders. "You're tied in knots."

"God, that's wonderful!" she said, allowing herself to relax back against him for a moment. Then she brought up her hands, touched his fleetingly, and moved away from him.

Looking at the new painting again, she said, "It's happier than the other one."

"Did anything happen today?" Chad asked. "They haven't found her yet, have they?"

"No. Nothing happened."

"Needlepoint. I keep thinking about that. My grandmother did needlepoint. My sister and I used to get to stay with her sometimes, and she made chocolate-chip cookies and sewed needlepoint Snoopys and Pogos for us. And now, this woman's dead, and no one knows where she is."

Reason turned reluctantly from the painting. "Nothing's turned up in the voiceprints."

Chad grimaced. "Have they figured out how to trace his calls yet?"

She lifted her hands in futility, spoke sarcastically. "Oh, sure, they have."

Chad waited.

"They've figured out how to trace him, all right. The only problem is it'd take something like three hours, maybe four or five."

"What the hell are you talking about?"

Reason explained. "He's using their computers against them. Switchboards at big companies are computers. He calls into one of them and gets it to call another switchboard at another company and gets it to hook him into one of those long-distance companies—MCI, Sprint—and gets in its computer and uses it to call a switchboard in Dallas. Then he uses that to call back to Houston, to some other switchboard here, and makes it call you.

"He piggybacks the calls all over the place. All it takes

is a bunch of code numbers and he sits there and punches them into a phone and sends his call all over, to hell and back, and finally to you. To trace it, they'd have to locate and get into every one of those computers."

Chad rubbed his beardless face. "Then tracing's no answer."

"No."

"What is?"

Reason frowned at her watch. "I wish I knew. Right now, I just know I've got to get home and get some sleep."

"Call somebody," Chad said.

She nodded tiredly, moved toward the automatic dialer on the coffee table.

And then Chad's telephone rang.

Reason faced around as if her body had been charged with electricity. Grinding his teeth together, Chad stared down at the set.

It rang again.

Hurrying to the desk, Reason put her hand on the extension and looked at Chad, waiting.

As the third ring began, he answered and Reason lifted the handset of the extension.

"Chad, this is Gina."

Relief flooded through him. Smiling toward Reason, he said, "It's Gina. At the store."

"A man just came in and bought two of the Brigattis," she said. "His wife had been wanting them a long time, waiting for them to go on sale, he said."

Chad asked, "Who is he?"

"He paid cash."

Chad groaned.

"Mike got the tag number off his car, though," Gina said. "It's eight-six-seven–Z-X-W."

Chad repeated the number. "Terrific! Thanks. And thank Mike for me. I'll talk to you later."

Reason was already bent over the automatic dialer. "I'm Badge Number seven-one-seven-one-four," she was saying. "I need a vehicle ID—eight-six-seven–Z-X-W. And I'll wait."

"It couldn't be, could it?" Chad said.

Reason gritted her teeth. "Oh, who knows?" she said, half-wildly. Into the telephone, she said, "Yes. Give me the name and address."

And suddenly, she was laughing.

"What the hell?" Chad said.

She was laughing out of control. Fumbling the handset back into place, the laughter became sobbing and tears began to roll down her cheeks.

Chad put his hands on her shoulders. "What is it?" When she didn't, or couldn't, answer, he shook her.

She fought away from him, rubbed harshly at her eyes. Finally, she was able to push words through the hiccups and sobbing giggles. "He bought them!" she said. "Ross Burke bought them!"

CHAD NEVER ran two days in a row. It was something he talked himself into a couple of times a week for exercise or, much less frequently, for mental therapy.

Yesterday, he had run an unusually long distance because he was angry and depressed; this morning, he came outside dressed for running because that was the best excuse he could devise for spending time in front of his

house while he tried to figure out how the man kept
watch on him.

He was pleasantly surprised to find that the weather
had changed completely overnight. It was his private
opinion that springtime in Houston was just a long, dreary
foretaste of the eventual triumph of mildew and cock-
roaches. Sometimes, though, there was inserted a day like
this one of azure skies and crystal air.

Opening his mailbox, he found it empty. The mail was
late today. This block was at the beginning of the route,
and he was spoiled into expecting the mail to be delivered
at the crack of dawn.

His newspaper was there, though, out on the strip of
grass between the curbing and sidewalk. Obviously, the
wonderful day hadn't inspired the hulking high school boy
who delivered the *Houston Post* to extend himself. The
neighbors' paper was there, also.

Picking up both of them, Chad went far enough up the
neighbors' walk to lob their paper between the bars of the
gate.

Looking into the courtyard, he saw that the paper he'd
tossed in yesterday was still there. So, the Mullins were
off again. It would be in the news in a week or so about
some famous heart patient somewhere in the world who'd
been attended by Houston's renowned heart surgeon.

Dr. T. R. Mullins—Chad didn't even know his neighbors well enough to know what the initials stood for—
would be one of the surgical team that did the real work,
but only the Renowned One would get the press. That
didn't seem to bother the aloof Dr. Mullins or his wife too
much, though. They kept very much to themselves in
their double-wide town house, with their His and Hers
Mercedes.

Chad grinned, a little envious at this moment. Dr.
Mullins might not be having too great a time, sweating

over some aging personage's rotted-out heart for the glorification of his famous boss, but the dumpy Mrs. Mullins would be having whatever she considered a ball while she waited for him in Cannes or Majorca, or some other glamorous spot.

Oh, well. Reminding himself that he wasn't standing out here in this wonderful sunshine to envy the neighbors, Chad dropped his own newspaper beside his front door and started warming up as if he were going to run, looking casually all around as he did so.

His town house was on the corner, at the end of a three-block row of town houses on the north side of Bissonnet. With their garages built in back, for the most part, their fronts, of various styles and widely differing types of brick, were reserved for shrubbery-flanked entryways or—like the Mullins'—small gated courtyards behind narrow, manicured lawns.

Across Bissonnet was the little independent city of West University Place. Facing Chad's row of town houses, virtually mirroring it, were more town houses. But behind them was the true West University, a quiet little island of narrow, tree-shrouded streets lined with Ray Bradbury 1930s houses. It was Chad's favorite place to run, away from the rush and steel and glass of surrounding Houston.

There was motion in the shadowy inset entryway of one of the West University town houses, Chad realized. It had been there for some time.

Stretching, bending, he kept watch on the entryway. The person there was dressed in blue or gray. A tiny spot of light flashed. Could it be reflected from binoculars?

Now, however, the person stepped out of the shadows and Chad grinned at his paranoia. It was a woman in a blue dress, standing away from the entryway to admire the cleaning job she'd done on the small glass panes flanking her front door. In her hand was a bottle of glass

cleaner which once again caught light and flashed it down
the street at him.

He stopped his warm-up. Someone could be watching from the windows of any of the houses across the street. Or from the parked cars, or those passing along Bissonnet. Across the street that ran along the side of his place, there was a strip shopping center. There were delivery trucks parked there, and shoppers' vehicles, and there were expanses of shop windows.

Grimacing, Chad accepted the uselessness of what he had tried to do. Five hundred anonymous callers could be zoomed-in on him at this moment, counting the hairs on his legs, and he'd never know it.

He pulled off his T-shirt and used it, wadded, to wipe perspiration from his face and chest. Maybe he did need to run a little today for therapy, after all. Maybe he needed a run today just as much as he had needed it yesterday.

Balling the T-shirt, sticking it between the burglar bars over his front window, he moved slowly down the sidewalk, walking up onto his toes to stretch his calf muscles.

Pausing on the island in the center of Bissonnet to let a group of cars pass, he glanced around toward the front of the Mullins' place, thinking how lucky they were to be off somewhere. He could stand a little time just now in Cannes or Majorca himself. Cannes or Majorca, hell! Right now, a little time hiding out in the middle of the goddamned Gobi Desert sounded terrific!

The last car passed and he started running into the placid West University streets. Almost immediately, he fell into that odd, insulated world of the jogger.

Pleasant scenes flickered in his mind. A golden, safe Gobi, dotted with tall palm trees encircling clear, cool pools of water, the nearest telephone a million miles away. Sharon Reason, her hair floating free in warm sunlight.

The times when they had touched. Those few moments when he had worked his hands at her shoulders, pressing knots of tension out of them.

Finally, with a twisting disorientation of time and place, he found himself back in front of his home, rubbing at his perspiration-soaked body with the T-shirt, the running finished.

Footsteps sounded behind him. Turning, he saw a young woman, dressed in a drab, bluish mail carrier's uniform, standing spraddle-legged a couple of feet along the walk leading to his doorway, a fat leather bag weighing down her left side. She was looking around in bewilderment.

"Thirty-one ninety?" she asked desperately.

"Here it is," Chad said, moving aside so that she could see his mailbox and street number.

She sighed, swiped at her sweaty face, and plodded up the walk, digging into the bag. "How can somebody run around in this hot weather, Mister? Air like peanut butter! I'm having trouble just walking."

Chad laughed. Air of crystal, yes, but laden with humidity, as usual. "Detroit, I'll bet."

She flashed him a smile. "Yeh."

"You'll get used to it."

She handed over his mail. "No, I won't! Yesterday, I was freezing my tail off inside the station, boxing mail. Today, out here in the hot, filling in on a route—day-off relief. Now, how'm I supposed to get used to the air conditioning you people got, *or* the heat?"

Chad chuckled.

Smiling, she shrugged and hitched up the bag. "Oh well, I got to admit it beats sitting around home waiting for the Japs to buy the Mercury plant and open it back up." Waving, she spotted the Mullins' mailbox and set off toward it.

Smiling, Chad waved good-bye to her. But the smile faded as he looked around, seeing once again all of the windows, all of the places his caller might have used— might be using at this moment—for a vantage point.

He wondered wryly if, next time, the man would mention his chat with the relief mail carrier.

LIKE DAMP charcoal, mildew outlined the tiles around the base of the shower enclosure.

Grunting disgustedly, Bill twisted the water off, stepped dripping out onto the rucked-up bath mat, and grabbed the towel. Rubbing at his face with it, he swore at its sour smell.

Throwing it angrily onto a pile of dirty towels in the corner, he yanked open the linen cabinet, stepping backward reflexively as a cockroach dropped from the inside of the door and scuttled off behind the commode.

"Goddamn it!" he yelled.

There was only one clean towel left. He pulled it out and dried himself, looking angrily around the bathroom.

There was a dark circle in the bowl of the commode. The lavatory was a mess of soap scum and razor stubble.

The bedroom was in no better shape. Stalking around it naked, he picked up shirts, socks, underwear, crumpled slacks, until he estimated that he had jammed about a week's worth into two pillow slips to drop off at the cleaners'.

But that hadn't even made a dent in the soiled clothing

that had accumulated over the last three weeks. And the goddamned place smelled like dirty feet!

He sat down on the foot of the bed, shook his head, tried to think what he was going to do. Cupping a hand over his knee, hiding the pale surgery scars, he said, "Damn it, Beth!"

DR. J. L. PULVER was a red-haired, painfully thin man who looked anywhere from thirty to fifty years old. He took his coffee with both cream and sugar and smoked menthol cigarettes. He was wearing a brown tweed jacket, camel slacks, an off-white oxford-cloth shirt, and a brown corded-silk tie. All of his clothing was of excellent quality, but on him, it looked ill-fitting and rumpled.

On the coffee table in Chad's study sat the beat-up-looking tape recorder Pulver had awkwardly shifted from right to left hand when Officer Reason introduced him to Chad.

Settling down into a chair opposite the sofa, Chad said, "Officer Reason tells me you're an adviser to the SWAT people."

"Right."

This morning, Reason was wearing a pale beige suit, paler even than her hair. "Dr. Pulver has also started working with the Crime Stoppers people," she said. "I didn't know about that until on the way over here."

Pulver nodded modestly, tapped ashes off his cigarette.

Chad indicated the recorder. "You've listened to the conversations."

"What's he up to? What going through his mind?"

Pulver chuckled, turned toward Reason. "I'm the psychologist. Would you please tell him that? I'm supposed to ask the questions."

Chad laughed. "Fine. You're the psychologist. What's going through this guy's mind?"

Pulver studied his cigarette. "What do you think is going through his mind, Mr. Palmer?"

Chad lifted his hands in surrender. "Maybe that he wants help. Not like therapy. But an accomplice, maybe."

"Do you feel like an accomplice?"

"No!"

Pulver hunched forward. "Will he be able to make you an accomplice?"

"No," Chad said, with much less force, and added, "I don't know."

Painstakingly, Pulver stubbed out his cigarette in the ashtray. "What is your strongest feeling when he's talking with you, when he's with one of his victims?"

Chad fidgeted, looked around the room. "Talking about this isn't as easy as I thought," he said finally.

Sitting forward, Reason started to rise. "Perhaps I should leave you two to talk alone."

Pulver shook his head. "No, no, no. You're needed." Turning sternly to Chad, he said, "There's no place here for therapy-jitters, Mr. Palmer. I assure you that your discomfort does not compare with that of his victims."

"Wanting him to finish it," Chad blurted out. "That's my strongest feeling."

"Finish it?"

"Wanting it over with. Wanting it finished."

"What is 'it,' Mr. Palmer?"

Chad rubbed at his face. "I wanted him to go ahead and kill her."

"The first victim? Or the second? Or both?"

"The second one, yes. I don't know about the first one. It went so fast, and I wasn't sure it was really happening."

Pulver waved away the initial cloud of smoke from a new cigarette. "What do you think of him?"

"That he kind of likes it when I'm tough on him. But he wants to feel that we're close, somehow. He keeps calling me 'buddy.'" Pausing, he pointed at the recorder. "You know that."

Pulver drank coffee, said nothing.

Finally, Chad continued, feeling as if he needed to choose his words with care. "I've had this crazy thought that he's maybe not doing violence against these women so much as against me." He looked at Pulver, at Reason. "I don't know. I guess that's silly. When I say it out loud, it sounds dumb as hell."

Pulver chuckled. "Remarkable."

Chad's face went hot with embarrassment. "Well, you asked."

There was silence while Pulver seemed to lose interest in Chad completely and seemed, instead, to be studying the automatic dialer at the other end of the coffee table.

Taking a drink of coffee, Chad looked toward Reason, but she was sipping coffee also, her gaze on the ficus tree whose leaves shivered in the slight breeze in the atrium.

Pulver said, "Would you happen to have a telephone answering machine, Mr. Palmer?" He turned to Reason. "Or I suppose the Police Department could furnish one."

Chad was puzzled. "An answering machine?"

"Yes," Pulver answered, looking as if he were about to describe the apparatus.

Chad hurried to forestall him. "I've got one I never use. Why?"

Pulver put out his cigarette. "Just an idea. What kind of person do you think your caller is?"

Chad shook his head. "I thought you'd tell us that."

"All right," Pulver said, laughing. "I'll try. But it's only guesswork, of course. Psychology is hardly an exact science. I think he's afraid of you, in a way. He knows he doesn't need to be. He has all the advantages—anonymity, for one thing. His telephone technique, for another. But he is afraid of you.

"Probably, the question of his sanity has occurred to you. That's always a difficult thing to be certain about—or even to define. But to me, he sounds quite sane. He's doing what we consider insane things, of course. But he comes across to me as being quite rational.

"There was no evidence of any sexual contact with Mrs. Koehler, and I haven't been able to discern any hint of anything sexual in his conversations." Lighting yet another cigarette, he smiled apologetically at Reason. "Except, of course, in his rather candid, and I might add, quite honest—albeit crudely phrased—comments about you." Waving that away with the smoke, he continued. "We could become quite Freudian, I suppose. He waits in a darkened room—a womb. He kills with a shotgun—a most satisfactory penis-object. Shooting the gun—ejaculation—sets him free to leave the womb. Et cetera.

"But I think that's taking the long way 'round. I think the most profitable use of Freud in this case is to look at it as a set of symbols which interlock in some way into a form which, to us, is both incomprehensible and insane, but which to him is quite clear."

He stabbed his cigarette toward Chad. "You are a symbol of something which is very important to him. As are his victims. As are the darkened houses, perhaps."

Chad rubbed at his jaw, pulled at his upper lip.

Reason started to speak, but Pulver cut her off. "What are you doing, Mr. Palmer?"

"I had a beard," Chad said, feeling caught in something

embarrassing. "I always messed with it when I was upset or thinking."

"A beard. Did this situation have anything to do with your shaving?"

Chad shook his head, chuckled. "Did this guy get me so crazy, I scraped my face? No. One morning, I just hacked it off for no reason at all." He dismissed the beard. "Look, Doctor, what do you suppose he'd have done, if the phone number he picked had been a woman's instead of mine?"

Pulver frowned at him, then turned toward Reason, seeming to ignore the question. "I'm sorry, Officer. I cut you off quite rudely a moment ago."

"You were talking about sexual things," she said. "There doesn't seem to be anything sexual with the victims, but I've kept wondering. What about something sexual with Chad?"

"Oh, come on!" Chad said.

Pulver waved his hand. "No, no, Mr. Palmer. That's a valid question. When Captain Hart first outlined the case to me and asked if I'd be interested in working with you, I wondered about that very thing myself. But the answer is no. I don't hear anything sexual. There is very definitely an intimacy, however—on the part of the caller."

For a few moments, it seemed the discussion was stalled. Then Chad said, "What I asked you before, what if he'd picked some other number out of the air, and reached a woman, instead? What do you think he'd have done then?"

Pulver studied him. Finally, he said, "What, indeed?"

Frustrated, Chad tried to joke. "Fine. Another mysterious symbol, I guess. But what are we going to do about him?"

"We are going to formulate a plan of action and have it

from another victim's house."

"A plan of action. All right. What plan?"

"One in which you act, instead of react, Mr. Palmer. So that you control the situation, instead of your caller."

"Control?" Chad asked. "How do I do that?"

Leaning forward, Pulver switched on his recorder.

Chad's voice, sounding thin and artificial, came from the machine. "Give me a chance at you, son of a bitch! Just show your fucking face to me, don't spy on me!"

There was the sound of the handset striking something hard and, immediately, Pulver stopped the tape. "This was recorded by the police when the killer called you at the store, the day after he shot the woman who did needlepoint."

"Do you think that really happened?" Chad asked. "They still haven't found her."

Solemnly, Pulver said, "From the sounds, it seemed quite authentic to me." He tapped the recorder with a fingertip. "That noise, I believe, was your putting the handset of your telephone down on the desktop. You were angry, and you refused to listen for a time, I would guess."

"Yeah."

"Why don't we listen to the part you didn't hear?" he said, and switched the recorder on again.

The man said, "What'd you do, Chad? Chad? Where'd you go? You can't do this to me! You can't just leave me alone!"

From the recorder, there came then a slight scraping noise, and Pulver pantomimed lifting a telephone receiver to his ear.

"Chad, where are you?" the man said. "Chad? Chad! Answer me."

"Yeah," came Chad's recorded voice.

Pulver switched off the recorder. "That was the portion of his conversation you didn't hear, Mr. Palmer."

Chad nodded.

"How did he sound?"

"Angry. Surprised, I guess."

"More than that," Pulver said, and quoted, "'You can't just leave me alone!'"

"Scared, I guess. That part of it."

"Quite frightened, in fact."

"Good," Chad said. "I scared *him*, for a change."

Pulver nodded.

Chad lifted his hands in futility. "I don't understand any of this. You ask about answering machines, you talk symbols, and there's going to be some kind of plan, and he got scared some. But none of it makes any sense."

Pulver rose and walked to the glass wall of the atrium. "Rather more than symbols, Mr. Palmer. At my suggestion, the case has taken quite a new direction."

Chad turned, frowned in bewilderment at his back. "What direction?"

Pulver moved again, to the fireplace, and stood in front of it, facing Chad and Reason. "I asked Officer Reason not to discuss it with you until we had this meeting." He smiled toward her. "But now, please do so."

"We've stopped working on Marian Koehler's background altogether, Chad," she said. "The only thing we're working on now is you. We've had no luck with the files from your store—as you know—but we're going much deeper now than that."

"Then you're sure he's somebody I know."

Pulver said, "Perhaps not exactly as you interpret that. You may not even have noticed him. Your knowledge of him isn't important; his knowledge of you is. The connective event between the two of you may have been so slight, in your eyes, that you don't even remember it. But to him, it's something worth attempting to exact a terrible revenge upon you."

Shaking his head weakly, Chad leaned back.

"You wondered how he might have reacted, had his 'random' phone call been to a woman, instead of to you."

"Yes."

"And yet, in the second call, he called you by name."

"He could have just found it out somehow. After the first call."

Pulver was shaking his head in negation even before Chad finished. "There was never a 'random' phone call. There was never any need for him to find out whom he'd called. From the very beginning, he was calling you, and only you, as difficult as it seems to be for you to accept."

"How can you be so sure?"

"You'd be sure, also, if you weren't so close to it. Don't you agree, Officer Reason?"

"It was obvious," she said. "He was calling you; he didn't just pick out a number that turned out to be yours."

Chad looked up at the ceiling. "You really did think I had something to do with it, didn't you?"

"It seemed very possible."

Pulver said, "It's exactly as you said early on, Mr. Palmer."

Chad tried to think what that might have been, but his mind was swimming. "What?"

"That you're the real object of his acts of violence. You, and you alone. His victims are innocent pawns. You were never any random phone call. From the first, he was specifically calling you."

"Why, for God's sake?"

"Why?" Pulver said. "When we have the answer to that, we'll know who he is."

"AM I ever going to be happy again?" Beth asked.

Dr. Wray looked blandly at her, kept his silence.

"When will I ever learn to stop asking you things? If I want an answer, you just sit there. If I don't, nothing could keep you quiet."

He chuckled. "Yes, you're going to be happy again. Why would you ask such a question?"

"Because I'm not. I should be getting better. You tell me I'm making good progress, and even I think I am. I don't even really think any more about letting Bill—or anybody else—hit me. But I don't get any happier."

"How are you unhappy?"

"How am I unhappy? My nerves are just as raw as ever. I go every which way, all the time. A shadow scares me to death one moment, and I want to run over and kick it in the pants the next. The telephone rings at the office—or at home—and I want to scream. The place where I'm living is so empty. I have twenty-one books, and I've had them in fifty different places. How many times can somebody strip and wax the kitchen floor? I'm jittery and lonely. I just don't know what to do."

"Have you thought of getting a pet?" Dr. Wray asked. "A kitten, perhaps. Or a dog."

"Oh my God!" Beth said, waving away the entire idea.

Dr. Wray shrugged. "Have you and your husband talked since the day of the lunch?"

"No!"

"You've had no sight nor sound of him?"

"No. And not much sight or sound of anyone else. Except Alma and Linda, and I've already imposed on them so much." She threw her hands into the air. "A pet! Good grief. That's what I'm getting to be. One of those silly, jittery women who spend all their time putting nail polish on some fat poodle."

"Are those women as jittery as you?"

Dejectedly, she said, "I don't know."

"Your uneasiness. Are there any grounds for it?"

"People call the office sometimes and hang up. Whether I'm the one who answers or not."

"But that's always happened, hasn't it? Businesses always have those calls from time to time, do they not? Are there more than usual now? Do you know they're from Bill? Isn't it possible you're just conscious of them now?"

"I don't know."

"Have you had any strange calls at home?"

Beth shook her head.

"Have you had any indication that your husband is still attempting to follow you home?"

"I don't know. Alma still follows me part of the way almost every evening, but we don't talk about it any more."

"You must continue to be on guard. But it mustn't take control of you."

With a bitter edge in her voice, Beth said, "Oh, of course not. Why didn't I think of that?"

Blandly, Dr. Wray said, "Perhaps you really want your husband to find out where you're living."

"No!" Beth cried. "Oh, God, no!"

"If it isn't wish-fulfillment, is it self-flagellation?"

"Am I just dreaming up punishment for myself, then?"

"Are you?" Dr. Wray asked.

THE TELEPHONE was ringing.

Chad kicked the kitchen door shut behind him and glanced at the wall clock. It was 6:02.

There was another ring as he hurried out of the kitchen and along the hallway, the bundle of plastic-shrouded shirts he carried rustling as he went.

In the study, he draped the shirts over the desk chair and stared at the red telephone as it rang yet another time. The answering machine sat on the desk now, also, along with the extension telephone. The machine was hooked into the line, but was not turned on.

As another ring started, Chad answered with a frowning "Hello."

"Ah, Mr. Palmer. This is Dr. Pulver."

"Hey, okay," Chad said, breaking into a smile now. "How are you?"

Pulver chuckled. "It's astonishing how much different your voice sounds now. Not anything like that gruff, guarded voice with which you answered."

"Lots of people are telling me that. I can't hear a phone ring any more without wanting to hit somebody."

"I certainly can't blame you. Actually, I'm calling in order to leave a message with your surveillance people." Pitching his voice as if he were calling to someone far away, he said, "Hello, Surveillance? Are you still on the line?"

There was an answering burst of static.

Pulver laughed. "Well yes, you are, aren't you? I've

been unable to reach Officer Reason, and I need to leave word where I'll be from now until about ten. Five-five-five—oh-seven-one-three. Do you have that?"

Another burst of static.

"I guess they got it," Chad said. "Does this mean you won't be able to get here, if he calls tonight?"

"Oh no, no. I'll be just down Bissonnet from you, and I'll break away instantly, if need be. I'll be at the television studio, but I wouldn't miss implementing our plan on your caller for anything."

"Television studio," Chad said. "You're darned-near next door."

"Yes. We're shooting a Crime Stoppers spot tonight."

"Ah. That ought to be interesting."

Pulver chuckled. "Even so, don't worry. If he calls you, I'll drop my camera and rush right over to your house."

"Drop it on that hammy consumer-advocate guy they've got. Mash his wig with it."

"Good idea," Pulver said happily. Then his voice changed to mock seriousness. "Except that then, I might find myself the subject of the next Crime Stoppers spot." He paused and turned serious. "There still hasn't been any word about the last victim, I take it."

"No," Chad said. "They still haven't found her."

"I see."

"Monday night. And it's Friday now. Why haven't they found her yet?"

"There are a thousand reasons why someone might not be missed for that long," Pulver said. "You know that."

Chad rubbed at his jaw. "Yeah. I know that."

IN THE middle of Friday afternoon, Beth remembered Dr. Wray's absurd suggestion that she get a pet.

"What's so funny?"

Half-startled, she looked up to find Alma standing beside her desk. She had worn a new green silk suit today, and now was carrying her purse and an attaché case.

"Oh, nothing," Beth said. "Looks like you're all ready to leave."

"Loaded the car this morning. I'll get out of town before the traffic gets too heavy." She checked her watch. "Still not too late for you to change your mind and come along."

Beth laughed. She loved real estate, but not meetings about it, whether in Houston, or in Austin, as was this one.

Alma's face went serious. "You be careful driving home. You feel like there's any problem at all, call Linda."

"I'll be fine."

"And don't stay around this office late tonight. I told Chuck not to leave until you do."

Beth waved away the concern. "If you don't get going, you're going to be late for the kick-off dinner. And drive carefully."

With a wave, Alma was gone.

A moment later, Beth found herself wishing desperately that she were going after all.

"Stop it!" she said to herself. "This is your chance to

prove you can get along without a baby-sitter for a couple of days. Now, do it."

She set to work trying to figure out some place to show the Thorntons Monday that they hadn't already seen. They were a pain in the neck and were never going to buy anything, but they knew so many people that they couldn't be ignored. There had to be something they hadn't seen.

In a little while, she found herself wondering what was on television tonight.

And she thought again of Dr. Wray and his absurd "Have you thought of getting a pet?"

Smiling wryly, she thought, "Maybe I should, after all. And I could be going home to an exciting evening painting his toenails."

She shook her head at her silliness.

But Dr. Wray's voice wouldn't go away. "Have you thought of getting a pet?"

Frowning, she pulled open the big drawer of her desk where she kept listings filed neatly by location. Where was that place? Memorial? Yes.

She pulled the photograph out of the file. The Doberman pinscher was just as majestic-looking as she remembered. He looked as if he were half cobra, half spring steel. He looked as if he owned the world.

They were supposed to be treacherous. But the woman who stood beside him, holding that frail-looking leash, didn't seem at all worried.

"This is silly," Beth told herself.

But what would it hurt, just to go look? What else did she have to do?

She pulled out the Yellow Pages. By the time she smilingly hung up the telephone, she not only had an appointment to look at Doberman puppies, she had decided on a name for her own puppy. She would name him Ajax, after the hero in the *Iliad*. Ajax!

Chuck was pleasantly surprised when she told him at four-fifteen that she was leaving early.

Traffic on I-10 was murder, as usual, but Beth didn't mind at all this afternoon. She hummed happily along with Willie Nelson on the radio as she coped with the madness on the freeway.

At the kennel, she found Ajax almost immediately. Or rather, he found her.

He came gallumphing up to the fence to try to lick and smell her through its links as soon as the owner showed her into the walkway between the rows of pens. She knelt down and he stood up against the fencing, his huge puppy feet trying to push the wire barrier aside.

Beth had no idea what differentiated this clumsy puppy, all feet and mouth, from any of the others. Maybe it was nothing more than his frantic interest in her. Whatever, it was enough. He was her Ajax.

When she left him, he stayed at the front of the pen, his mal-proportioned baby black-and-fawn face and wet pink tongue pushed against the fence, watching her for as long as possible.

In the owner's office, she wrote a check for him. His name was Ironclad Hieronymus, VI, but on the little line at the left bottom corner of the check, she wrote, "Ajax."

Glowing, she started home. She would read every word in the puppy-care magazines and pamphlets the owner had given her.

In the morning, she would rush out and buy a supply of food and toys and grooming supplies and whatever other magazines and books about Doberman pinschers she could find. And a collar and leash. And then she would return to the kennels to pick him up.

She was liltingly happy as she approached the freeway,

but as she fitted her car into the town-bound traffic, the
first fingers of worry began to tug at her. It was already
dark, although it was barely six-thirty. A greasy drizzle
was beginning, turning everything gloomy.

"For God's sake, stop this!" she told herself aloud.

She tried to keep her mind on Ajax. When the owner
brought him out onto the lawn, he had been so funny,
tripping over his big feet, running all around her, trying
to find out everything about her in a flash.

A rise in the freeway brought the Houston skyline into
view. Usually, it was awe-inspiring, a source of pride. But
in this drizzling gloom, it looked diseased and melting.

"I will not be like this!" she shouted.

A tanker-truck thundered past, throwing a blinding
scum of oily grit across the windshield.

She wrestled the car into the right lane, levered the
windshield washer again and again until the glass was
clear, and drove on, her heart pounding, her hands
clenched on the steering wheel, her bladder feeling
swollen and tender.

She left the freeway early, taking a side street over to
Memorial Drive, to drive through the park, among its
stands of majestic oaks. She almost went to Alma's house,
and probably would have, had Alma been home, but she
flinched from inflicting more of her wimpishness on
Linda.

"I'll be all right in a minute," she kept saying to herself.
But the farther she went, the more afraid she became.
The monster trees loomed ghoulishly in the damp
darkness. Gooseflesh pebbled her arms. Her abdomen
ached with fullness.

She circled her block three times, biting her lips, staring at every parked car she passed, shivering each time
headlights approached. So strong was her fear that, regardless of her earlier resolve, she almost drove away

from the area completely and fled back out Memorial Drive to Alma's and Linda's. Longingly, she thought of speeding away to the brightly lighted Galleria area and checking into a hotel for the night.

Finally, though, when there was no sign of approaching cars, she turned off the street. Her mind chattering, she crept the car along the drive and eased it around the corner into the alleyway that ran along the garage entrances of her row of town houses. Why weren't there some lights here?

She stopped the car, looked around into the night, trying not to think about the thick bank of oleanders that towered over the alleyway opposite the garages. With cold fingers, she triggered the garage-door opener.

Ponderously, the wide door lifted up and back. The car lights showed the garage interior to be empty and safe.

Even so, spiders of panic skittered up and down Beth's back as she drove inside. All she could think of was running into the town house and turning on all the lights.

Impatiently, she sat in the locked car, its motor still running and its headlights glaring, and waited for the door to thunk down securely closed and locked. Then she would bolt for the kitchen door only a few feet away, and run inside and be safe.

"How stupid!" she thought suddenly. "I'm safe now."

The door thudded shut.

She laughed at herself, pulled the key from the ignition, unlatched and pushed her door open, and with one foot out on the concrete, reached over for her purse and the magazines and pamphlets, gathered them up, and started to step out of the car.

The headlights.

Shifting the purse and magazines to her right arm, she leaned forward and punched inward on the headlight switch.

And was plunged into darkness.

SHE SCREAMED. The magazines and purse slithered away from her as she tried to grasp the steering wheel to keep from falling headlong into the car. With her left hand, she yanked viciously to close the door, and felt its bottom edge smash against her ankle. Her belly felt weak and loose; she was sitting in warm wetness.

Darkness! The maplight pooled only around her, showed her nothing.

She moaned, pulled her leg up into the car now, and gasped with relief to hear the door close. Pulling herself more upright, she found the lock button, jammed it down.

Squirming disgustedly in the wet seat, she jerked at the headlight switch, and bright light exploded all around her.

The garage was still empty.

She had wet herself!

"Ugh!" she cried. "Oh, goddamn it! Ugh!"

She remembered the door at the side of the big one, turned to stare at it. But it was secure. She could see the brass-colored bolt extending across the space between the lock and the catch. And the chain on the door was in place.

Frowning upward through the windshield, she switched the headlights off and then back on. "It's just a burned-out light bulb," she said angrily.

Leaving the car lights turned on, she pushed open the

door and gathered up her things again and stood out into the garage. Again, she said, "Ugh!"

At the kitchen door, she started rummaging in her purse for the key but stopped, and gave the knob an angry twist. The door opened. She had forgotten to lock it this morning.

"Damn it!" she said, and stamped inside.

Slapping the kitchen light switch on, stepping forward a little to throw purse and magazines onto the sink counter, she kicked out of her shoes. With one hand, she pulled her belt open and off while she slammed open the lid of the washer with the other. The belt, she threw onto the floor with her shoes. Unzipping her skirt, she hurled it into the washer. Her half-slip and clammy panty hose followed it as she muttered yet another "Ugh!"

Yanking open the pantry door, she seized a spray can of room deodorant and rushed back out into the garage with it.

Leaning into the car, she exhausted the deodorant on the driver's seat. After that, she rolled down the window, slammed the door shut, reached in to switch off the lights, and went back into the kitchen.

Kicking shoes and belt aside, she stamped out, through the dining room, started to cross the living room.

But her reflection in the antique mirror stopped her cold. She stared at the image of a furiously frowning, half-naked woman, hair frowsed all to hell.

"And you think you've got sense enough to housebreak a puppy!" she said angrily.

Then she laughed. She did a mocking, giggly curtsy to herself and said, "Just one thing you'll have to learn, Ajax. Whatever you do, do as I *say*. . . ."

ALL THROUGH Friday evening, Chad was on edge, certain that it was time for the man to call him again.

He had brought home a thick envelope of ad ideas to cull through before Monday so that the agency could have finished products ready for the approaching deadlines of *Ultra* and *Texas Monthly* and *Houston City*. Usually, he enjoyed going through the often zany brainstorms of the ad people. But tonight, he couldn't generate interest in cartoons of talking track lights or photographs of blue-haired, sable-clad women perched on stepladders, proudly polishing their Lalique chandeliers.

He turned on the television and flipped from channel to channel, then turned it off.

He called Reason's work number. She was out, Sergeant Andrews told him, but could be beeped for an emergency.

His nerves seemed shot, but he didn't think that, in the larger scheme, that would qualify as an emergency.

He tried to read.

He tried to talk himself into taking the clogged-up coffee maker out into the garage and running vinegar through it where it wouldn't stink up the whole house.

He thought about going to Gilley's, but a look outside at the drizzle slicking the streets discouraged him.

He thought about calling Officer Reason again, and did, and got the same information as before. This time, he left word for her to call him, but carefully specified that it was no emergency.

Tactfully, Sergeant Andrews suggested it might be as well for him to call Dr. Pulver. Chad thanked him politely, but didn't.

He waited for the telephone to ring.

He checked to make sure the answering machine was plugged in, turned it on, and turned it off again.

Finally, he tried television once more.

A Crime Stoppers spot followed the "Ten O'Clock News." He watched it because of Dr. Pulver's involvement with the organization.

The spot was the reenactment of the killing of a man who walked in on a liquor-store holdup. When the quick violence was finished, the anchorman from Channel 13 News told how you could make a thousand dollars by calling in, if you had information that led to the arrest of the killer.

Chad watched the spot carefully, trying to find any evidence of Dr. Pulver's psychological expertise.

He couldn't. But who was he to judge?

Next came "Nightline." He listened to Ted Koppel appreciatively and found himself chuckling over a fantasy of turning him loose on his caller—Koppel could handle the bastard, if anybody could.

The Crime Stoppers spot ran again before the late movie began—the station must be trying to catch up on Public Service Time. Again, he watched it, forehead wrinkled with interest.

And now, the "Friday Night Movie" began, and he settled back to watch it, telling himself to enjoy it, whatever it was.

It was *Dial M For Murder*.

He switched off the set, hid it away in its cabinet in the side wall, and went upstairs to bed.

SATURDAY BEGAN with fog that closed the airports until it burned away at midmorning. There was an hour of sunshine then, but it gave way to overcast that thickened into drizzle and finally to real rain that continued late into the night.

At a few minutes after eight, Officer Reason came running through the rain to Chad's front door.

"We still haven't found her," she said, watching rain fall onto the ficus tree in the atrium.

"Monday night to Saturday," Chad said. "Five days. A dead woman in a house full of needlepoint."

Reason was dressed in another of her policewoman outfits, a severe navy blue skirt and a blazer-cut jacket over a frilly white silk blouse. A few raindrops still sparkled on the golden helmet of her hair. "She may have been on vacation from her job. Whatever, it's just that no one's missed her yet."

Chad had finally finished going over the ads and now he started pushing them into a neat stack. "I wish to hell he'd hurry up and call one more time, so we can get this finished with."

"It'll come soon enough," Reason said.

She watched him push the ads away, toward a rubber-banded jumble of magazines and circulars and letters that sat near the automatic dialer.

"What's that?" she asked.

"My next-door neighbors' mail. They're off somewhere,

and their mailbox was overflowing—the top wouldn't close any more. I brought the stuff in before it got ruined." He looked around at the atrium. "They'll have a bunch of wet newspapers, though. I've just been tossing them through the gate."

He waved away the whole idea of the neighbors. "I guess you're working all night tonight. I guess you're not going to get off any time soon."

"Not any time soon. This is my lunch hour. I got your message late last night. Andrews said it wasn't an emergency."

Chad stood up and went to look out into the atrium, at the falling rain. "Yeah, it wasn't. Don't you ever get any time off?"

Reason chuckled. "Sure. The last time was last Monday night."

Shifting his vision to look at her reflection in the glass, Chad said, "Why don't you get a geology job? A day geology job. So a guy could see you without its being business?"

She was smiling, but she was standing up, getting ready to leave. "I've got to be going," she said.

CHAD GOT up late Sunday morning, showered, and put on a pair of old, soft, faded jeans. After starting the coffee maker, he went out front to get the newspaper. The rain had passed, leaving the world bright and clean. Stretching, he breathed the fresh-smelling air, enjoying it now, knowing that, in another hour, it would be steam.

The fat Sunday paper, in a Day-Glo orange plastic sleeve, was almost halfway up the walk. As he picked it up, a cab stopped at the curbing, and Dr. Mullins stepped out, his fringe-bordered scalp glistening in the sunlight.

"Good morning," Chad called.

Dr. Mullins looked over at him, frowned, placed his face, and nodded. "Ah, yes, well, good morning." It was probably the third time they had had occasion to speak in the two and a half years they had been neighbors.

'So, Mrs. Mullins stayed over for another day or two on the Riviera,' Chad thought, with a recurrence of his envy. Aloud, he said, "I'll run in and get your mail."

When he came out front a few minutes later, Dr. Mullins was nowhere in sight.

Going across the lawn, he found the front gate standing open. Beyond it, past the pile of newspapers, turned gray and sodden by the rain, the front door was open, also. Dr. Mullins' luggage sat just inside the foyer.

Pausing at the gateway, Chad pushed the button set in the bricking, and chimes echoed inside the house.

When there was no acknowledgment in a minute or so, he went on to the doorway. "Dr. Mullins?" he called. "Hello?"

The air in the doorway was cool enough from air conditioning to raise gooseflesh on his bare shoulders, but it smelled stale and thick.

"Hello?" he called again, realizing that his body seemed to be urging him not to breathe the air spilling from the house.

There was sound then. Stepping slowly forward, to the end of the foyer, he saw Dr. Mullins stumbling down the staircase from the second floor. He was coughing, almost falling, moving so heavily that the Waterford chandelier in the two-story-high formal living room was set swinging at the end of its heavy gilt chain.

138    His shoulder struck the wall, dislodged a picture frame that bounced on one carpeted riser and broke on the next, the glass over the needlepoint lilies splashing away.

At each end of the blue velvet sofa to Chad's left were fat pillows, their covers showing off panels of intricate needlepoint.

Drawing back involuntarily, the air of the place beginning to stick chokingly in his throat, he saw, on the foyer wall, not a foot from his face, a silver-framed mountain scene done in needlepoint.

Dr. Mullins reached the foot of the staircase and fell to his knees. He vomited rackingly, violently.

"ISN'T HE darling?" Beth asked proudly.

Alma rolled her eyes. "Darling! He looks like something that escaped from the Muppets."

The puppy was across Beth's living room, chewing on the remains of a fluffy pink bedroom slipper he had found under the bed last night and ruined before she woke up.

Beaming, she said, "My own Ajax."

The puppy looked up, electrified.

"See, Alma? He already knows his name."

Alma shook her head. "That's going to be the most thoroughly spoiled animal in Houston. But you just make a note of this right now, Beth Rhodes. The minute you start showing pictures of that creature around, I stop speaking to you."

Beth laughed.

Alma leaned forward and peered across at the puppy. "What in the world's wrong with his ears?"

Instantly, Beth was up and across the living room, kneeling down. "What do you mean? What do you see?"

"I never saw a Doberman with big floppy ears like that."

Laughing, Beth patted Ajax's rump and returned to her seat on the sofa. "Don't be silly. They have to clip them. That's what they do to Great Danes and boxers, too. He'll be old enough to get them done in a couple of weeks."

Alma sighed. "Plastic surgery. My God, I won't be surprised if you get his teeth capped."

Ajax abandoned the slipper and romped across the room to Beth. Pink fluff was stuck to his wet muzzle, and lovingly she wiped it off.

"You'll be burping him next," Alma said.

Ajax danced disjointedly around in front of them for a moment. Then suddenly, he stopped near Alma's leg, sniffed at it, and started to squat over her foot.

Whooping with laughter, Beth scooped him up. "Oh no, you don't, big boy! Come with Mommy."

Alma heard the sliding glass door of the walled-in patio off the bedroom open and close, and then Beth returned.

Wrinkling her nose, Alma said, "Does he do that on the bed at night?"

A picture of her awful reflection in the antique mirror flashed across Beth's mind. Stifling laughter, she said, "Of course not. He gets restless first. That wakes me up, and I put him out. Well, usually. I've only had to change the bed a couple of times."

"A couple of times," Alma repeated dryly. "You've had him three days. How about tonight?"

"He's only a baby."

Alma laughed. "I think it's wonderful. I think he's wonderful."

Beth smiled, and then remembered the garage. "I meant to tell you all day, but we were so busy. There's something wrong with the light in the garage. Every time the door opener runs and switches on the light, the bulb blows out."

"Sounds like a short. I'll get Harold over tomorrow to check it out."

Beth looked toward the bedroom and the muffled sounds of Ajax's yapping and scratching at the glass door. "You don't think I've just gone silly, do you?"

Alma smiled warmly. "Of course not, honey. I just can't help wishing he was already big, and mean as hell. But I guess that'll come soon enough."

Standing to go let Ajax in, Beth paused. "I haven't heard a word from Bill. Since that day at lunch. Last week."

"Good," Alma said. "But don't you get careless. He's just trying to figure out something else."

JAWS KNOTTED, Chad frowned at the telephone for a moment, then picked it up.

"Hey, buddy. How're you doing?"

Pulling the handset from his ear, holding it as if it were a club, Chad stared at the answering machine, the man's voice only a distant buzzing.

"Hello? Where are you?" he was saying when Chad put the handset to his ear again.

"Where are *you*?"

The man chuckled. "You sound tense."

"Where are you?"

"Come on, Chad. Loosen up."

The clock showed WED 27 MAR 7:14 PM. He said, "Are you hiding in some woman's house again?"

"Of course, I am. You're pissed-off, aren't you?"

"That doesn't even come close."

"I embarrassed you, didn't I?"

"Embarrassed me?"

"By using that woman right next door to you." His voice changed, went lower, softer, as if he were hurt. "And you kind of let me down."

Chad shoved the desk chair back, dropped into it. "How the hell could I let you down?"

The pain was still there. "I thought maybe you'd hear the shot. Come running over." A pause, and then he chuckled and sounded as always. "You could have joined the party."

Chad frowned in confusion. "These places are insulated. There's a fire wall. Did you want me to hear it? Besides on the phone?"

Laughing, the man ignored the question. "I saw you on TV. When they came to pick her up." Mockingly, he imitated a reporter's voice and accent. "'Mr. Palmer, how did you feel when you found out about this terrible crime in the house next door?'" Then he burlesqued Chad's angry answer, "'How the hell do you think I feel?'"

"Damn you!" Chad said.

"And then you stomped in your house and slammed the door in their faces."

Chad picked up the telephone and walked stiff-legged to the study doorway and looked along the hallway at the front door. Where the hell were Reason and Pulver?

"The cops've really kept you out of it," the man said.

"The Rose Lady and the Needlepoint Lady are big-time news, but except for your little walk-off part, they've kept you out of it."

"I wish to hell *you* would."

The man laughed.

Chad took a deep breath, told himself that anger was futile. "Tell me about yourself."

"Why?"

"Why not?"

"What do you want to know?"

Out on the street, a truck rumbled past. "You mean, what do I want to know, besides your name, and where you are right now?"

"Yeah."

"You must have really got your rocks off, being not even thirty feet away from me, over there with Mrs. Mullins."

"It was okay."

"You piece of shit!"

The man laughed.

"I keep trying to recognize your voice," Chad said. "God help you if I ever do!"

The only answer was more laughter.

Biting back anger again, Chad said, "Don't you find it difficult, remembering all those phone numbers and code numbers and access numbers you have to use to do this roundabout calling?"

"No. Not particularly."

"You're good with numbers, then."

"Yeah, I am. Kind of."

Chad leaned against the side of the doorway, willing Reason and Pulver to arrive. "Who are you pretending that I am?" he asked, pulling the question out of the air.

The man sounded as if the question caught him by surprise. "What are you talking about?"

There was a key-sound.

Quickly, Chad said, "About your twisted brain," and stepped forward and opened the door.

Reason and Pulver quietly came inside.

Leaning close to Chad, Reason whispered, "Everything's set. Everybody's ready."

"My brain's not twisted," the man said.

Chad led the way back into the study.

"What's in the house where you are now?" he asked, watching Pulver go to the desk to stand looking down at the answering machine while Reason rushed across to the automatic dialer, punched a button, impatiently waited for an answer.

"What do you mean?" the man asked.

Pulver depressed a button on the answering machine. The "on" light glowed red.

Chad said, "The Rose Lady. The Needlepoint Lady. What are they going to call this one?"

At the automatic dialer, Reason was listening frowningly.

"Well, this one's kind of nondescript," the man said. And then his voice brightened. "Winberg prints, maybe. There's a couple of 'em here in the bedroom."

Reason hung up from her call. She shook her head, mouthed to Chad, "They still can't trace it."

"I wonder what we'll find in your place," Chad said.

"My place?"

"What kind of silly thing are we going to use to characterize your place, after you're caught?"

Coldly, the man said, "She'll be home any minute."

"So?" Chad said, turning toward Pulver.

"What do you mean, 'So?'" the man asked.

Pulver lifted his hand, knifed it across his throat.

"Don't be so damned dense," Chad said. "What I mean is, 'So, who gives a shit?'"

Then he hung up the telephone.

The clock showed 7:33. The room seemed hollow with silence. "Well, that's it," Chad said.

Pulver went meticulously into the business of extracting a cigarette from his pocket and lighting it.

"God!" Reason said. "This is worse than listening to him."

"Not from here, it isn't," Chad said.

He bolted from the study, went to the bar, and poured shots of bourbon into three glasses. When he returned, both Reason and Pulver were standing at the desk, looking at the answering machine. Handing the glasses around, he joined them.

He was just starting to take a drink when the telephone rang.

"It takes him a while to go through all his numbers, doesn't it?" Pulver said.

Chad emptied his glass all at once.

The telephone rang again.

And again.

Again. But this fourth ring was broken off and Chad's recorded voice came from the answering machine. "Hello. You've reached five-five-five—three-one-five-five. After the beep, you'll have thirty seconds to leave a message."

The beep sounded, and then the man's voice. "Chad, what are you trying to do? This isn't funny! Chad? Chad! You pick up this phone and answer me! She could walk in the door any second. You pick up the phone and talk to—"

Its timing cycle finished, the machine disconnected the call, cut off the man's voice.

Three and a half minutes later, the next call came.

"Stop it, Chad!" the man shouted. "I want to talk to you. You pick up the phone! Now! You'd better pick up this phone, Chad! You've got to talk to me! I've got to—"

Chad reached out, savagely twisted the volume-control **145**
knob to "off."

"I'm going to get out of here," he said. "You people stay around and listen to this, if you want to. But I'm going to go someplace loud, and drink. Let him talk to the goddamned machine."

The next ring of the telephone came as he was closing the front door. Angrily, he pulled it shut, cutting off the sound, and went down the front walk, hurrying Reason and Pulver along with him.

"BETH! I'M so glad you called. I've missed talking to you so much, and I've been so worried."

Beth smiled into the telephone. It had taken a lot to work up the nerve to make this call, but now it was all worth it. "I've wanted to call you, Mother Rhodes, but I just wasn't sure."

Mrs. Rhodes sounded exactly as she looked—solid and motherly. At this moment, she would be brushing a tear from her eye, even though her face was creased with smiling. "What in the world has that boy of mine done to you, Beth? I can't get anything out of him."

"It's awfully complicated. I can't tell you how much I didn't want anything like this to happen. Or how much I don't want it to go on."

"Another woman? Is that what happened?"

In Alma's office, the clatter of adding machine keys broke off. There was a muttered curse and the sound of paper tearing.

"Oh no, Mother Rhodes. Nothing like that."

"Well, not another man, surely. I wouldn't think that of you for a minute."

"Of course not," Beth said.

"Can't I help some way? Just out of pure selfishness, I don't want to lose you. When I think of some of the daughter-in-laws some of my friends have to put up with . . . If Bill's father was still alive, maybe he could put some sense into that boy."

"I don't want to lose you, either," Beth said. "I'm doing all I know how to. I've been going to a therapist. A psychologist. He's helped me so much."

"Well, that's good."

"But Bill has to do it too, Mother Rhodes. And so far, he's just refused to. He won't even talk about it."

"Why won't he, for heaven's sake? Marriage counseling, is it? Why won't Bill go to a marriage counselor?"

"Not exactly a marriage counselor."

"What then?" Mrs. Rhodes asked. And then her voice went low and breathless. "Is it some kind of . . . well . . . sex counseling? One of those sex-counseling things I see about on the TV?"

Beth smiled. "Oh no. Nothing like that."

There was a fluttery breath of relief. "Well, any case, I can't see Bill not wanting to do what he can to keep his marriage going."

"I don't know quite how to explain it."

Softly, Mrs. Rhodes said, "If there'd of been children."

"We went through that long ago, Mother Rhodes. I can't, and that's all there is to it."

"But you were talking about adoption."

"I was. Bill wouldn't hear of it. The idea just made him mad."

"That temper of his," Mrs. Rhodes said. "Well now, honey, you just say it right out, what's wrong. You may be a long way away, down there in Texas, but you and I've always been real close. Don't let that change now."

Beth looked out at Kirby Drive. There was no traffic at the moment. It was just dark. "It's Bill's temper," she said.

Mrs. Rhodes sounded bewildered. "His temper? What's that got to do with anything?"

Beth took a deep breath. "He's been beating me, Mother Rhodes. It's always happened. But it's gotten worse. And I was letting him do it. But not any longer. He's got to get help for himself. He's got to get therapy, too, or . . ."

She broke off, frowning at the telephone. Dial tone hummed in her ear.

She redialed.

There was part of a ring, and the telephone was picked up on the other end.

"Mother Rhodes? We were cut off," she said, and realized she was speaking to the dial tone again.

Once more, she dialed the number. This time, there was a busy signal.

Hanging up the telephone, she rose and went to the doorway of Alma's office. Almost crying, she said, "She hung up on me."

Alma frowned.

"As soon as I started telling her, she hung up. Now, her phone's off the hook."

Shaking her head sadly, Alma said, "The sins of the fathers . . ."

THE NEARLY empty parking lot showed that this wasn't throng night at Kitty's Pistol Tavern, but Reason refused to go any farther.

Just inside the entrance, the three paused, looking around.

It wasn't much. The decorations were neon and plastic beer signs and a few dusty six-guns in frames. The patrons were a couple of office-dressed women sitting at a table and, at the bar, a pudgy little man with pompadoured hair who wore a green double-knit suit and a string tie. He daintily sipped beer and sneaked beady-eyed looks at the waitress who wore an Astros T-shirt and sneakers and a miniskirt that had been popular back when she was.

"Nice place," Reason said.

Chad cocked his head toward the jukebox which was knocking out "Mommas, Don't Let Your Babies Grow Up To Be Cowboys," and said, "Damned right it is. That's Waylon Jennings you hear. Not some son of a bitch hassling me on the telephone."

They sat at a table near the wall away from the counter. When the waitress walked away to get their drinks, Chad said, "So, what's he doing right now?"

Reason pulled at the drawstring top of her purse, checked the beeper inside. "I thought you came to this place to get him off your mind."

"It hasn't worked completely yet."

Toying with the ashtray, Pulver said, "We think he's feeling abandoned. Lost. Set adrift. We think we've de-

stroyed whatever symbolic construct it is he's set up
around himself and you and his victims."

The waitress returned. Chad set a bill on the tray and
picked up his bourbon and water and drank it down while
she was setting out Reason's club soda and Pulver's beer.

"You can go ahead and bring me another one," he said,
returning the glass to the tray.

Reason said, "You're drinking awfully fast."

"I'm not driving."

He smiled up at the waitress as she set down his second
drink. When she walked away, he said, "There's a cop
hiding behind every bush in my entire neighborhood
right now. Let them do the worrying for a change."

He waved the subject away, took only a tiny sip of his
drink, and grinned at Reason. "We should have gone to
Gilley's. Lots of people. We could dance."

She smiled.

"We could teach Dr. Pulver, here, to kicker-dance," he
said, laughing.

Reason and Pulver smiled politely.

"Okay. That's it," Chad said, drinking off most of his
drink and signaling for another one. "This is supposed to
be a celebration. You people've got to loosen up some."

To Reason, he said, "See that little guy over there at
the bar? In the last Kelly-green double-knit plastic suit in
North America? Well, he's uncomfortable as hell, trying
to do some serious drinking in the same place with a
beautiful woman with her hair done up like a Viking."

Reason laughed, hesitated, put her hands up to her
head, and started removing hairpins.

Giving her a grateful nod, Chad turned to Pulver. "And
you, Dr. Pulver, sir. We've got to ashcan that doctor-
stuff. Those two nice ladies over there, trying to unwind
after a tough day with the Liquid Paper, don't want to be

drinking with some doctor. So, cut yourself some slack, J. L. And I'm Chad."

He saw the waitress approaching and hurried to finish his drink. Smiling, he received the new one.

Pulver grinned, said, "My nickname's Pulley."

Chad extended his hand. "Well, howdy there, Pulley." They shook hands and he said, "And meet my friend Sharon."

She shook her head, holding one hand up to keep any more of her hair from coming loose. "I'm letting my hair down," she said. "And he's Pulley. Well, I've got one for you."

"Sure."

"Switch to beer."

He looked at his fresh drink. "I'll take it easy."

"Fine." She leaned toward Pulver, turned the back of her head to him. "Dr. Pulver, will you help me get this stuff back up and pinned down, please?"

Chad threw up his hands in surrender. "Okay. That's it. I give up. After this one, I switch to beer."

She smiled and sat straight again, shaking her head so that her hair massed out around her face.

"I wish you weren't a cop," Chad said softly. "On my case."

Reason smiled and then stood up, picked up her purse. "Excuse me for a moment."

"Some lady," Chad said, as she walked away to the ladies' room. Then he lifted his glass to Pulver. "Well, here's to answering machines."

Pulver pushed back his chair. "I'll go, while she's in the ladies' room, Chad."

"Go?"

"Back to your house to wait. It's only four or five blocks. I enjoy walking. Actually, I shouldn't have tagged along at all."

"What the hell are you talking about?"

"Well, you and the young lady. You should be alone. To enhance your personal relationship. It's perfectly obvious. I'm just in the way."

Angrily, Chad said, "What the hell kind of psychologist are you anyway? 'Enhance our personal relationship!' While that maniac's out there doing God-knows-what? What the hell did you think I ought to do? Hang up on that bastard, and grab her and run over to the Holiday Inn and jump into bed? For Christ's sake, I don't know what you do with your 'personal relationships,' but mine don't work worth a shit while something like this is going on."

"I'm sorry. I didn't understand."

Chad's anger was gone as quickly as it started. Leaning over, he put his hand on Pulver's shoulder. "No. I'm the one that ought to be sorry. I had no right to go off on you like that."

"I just thought it was what you wanted."

"Just please forgive me," Chad said. "I didn't mean all that."

"It's all right," Pulver said.

"She's terrific. But this is the worst time in the world for me to even think about anything like that." He shook his head and grinned. "Listen, if this idea of yours shook that son of a bitch out of his tree tonight, well, next time, you better leave a lot quicker than this."

Pulver grinned and nodded.

"But right now, I just want to sit here and wait it out with my friend Pulley, and my friend Sharon, and act like everything's a joke. Okay?"

"Okay," Pulver said.

"What's okay?" Reason asked, sitting down. She had brushed out her hair while she was gone.

"Oh, boy!" Chad said admiringly. "That guy at the counter can really get bombed now."

Reason laughed.

"We were drinking to answering machines," Chad said. "What do you really think? Is this plan going to work?"

Reason frowned. "It's as good as anything. It sounded good to me, and to the higher-ups, which is what counts."

Pulver said, "His fixation's on you, Chad. You brought up being an accomplice. And that's what you are, no matter how unwilling. Without you, he can't proceed. You've cut yourself off from him, so he'll come after you."

"I hope they've got him down on my front walk right now, beating the crap out of him," he said, looking into his drink.

The pay telephone rang.

His hands convulsed on the glass, sloshing most of the liquid out onto the table. "Reach out and crush someone!" he said shakily.

The waitress came with a bar towel and wiped up the mess. As Reason lifted her purse out of her way, she said, "Hey. You a cop?"

"She's a geologist," Chad said, drying his hands on a napkin.

She pointed into Reason's purse. "There's her badge. And her beeper."

"That's a Geiger counter. She's a geologist."

The waitress laughed. "Okay by me. You think you can handle another one?"

Chad shook his head. "No. Just a Lite."

When the waitress left, he said, "What's he doing right now?"

"He's lost without you," Pulver said. "Frustrated. He's getting all his numbers confused and calling you direct, and they're tracing him. Or he's come to your house, and they're picking him up."

there all right, huh?"

"We hope so."

"God! I guess we hope so. It's got to work. I know what you said—that I just talk to him, I don't get shotgunned— but I don't know if I can take much more of it." He looked angrily around. "Christ! A pay phone rings, and I go crazy."

"Have confidence," Reason said.

Pulver nodded.

Chad forced a laugh. "What's wrong with me? I'm the one that tore your head off a minute ago for being too serious."

The beeper went off.

LIEUTENANT ROSS Burke and a gray-haired man in a pin-striped suit were waiting at Chad's front door.

Burke's lips were a thin white line. "Palmer, get this goddamned door open!"

Chad shouldered between them and turned to face them from the doorway. "What the hell's going on? What's this hard-line stuff?" He looked at the gray-haired man. "Who the hell are you?"

"He's Captain Hart," Reason said, looking at Chad as if imploring him to temper his reaction.

Burke stepped toward Chad. "Open the door, or I'll break it down!"

With a peremptory gesture, Hart silenced him, made him take a step back. "Mr. Palmer, you don't have the least idea what's been happening while you and this police-person and this psychologist have been out playing." He ran a hand over his pewter hair. "You can let us in your house, or we can go down to the station. I don't give a damn which, but we're going to do something, right now."

Chad unlocked the door.

Hart stepped inside. "Where's this answering machine?"

Burke shoved past Chad, hurried along the hallway. "This way, Captain."

"We'll find it," Hart said. "Go make us some coffee."

"Coffee! Me?" Burke said, and then folded, went reluctantly off along the hallway toward the kitchen.

In the study, Hart went directly to the desk. The counter on the answering machine showed eleven calls.

Pulver said, "Did something go wrong, Captain? We had approval to shut him down like that, all the way up the Police Department."

Hart ignored him. "Palmer, play back what's on this machine."

Chad was about to depress the "rewind" button when the captain's voice stopped him.

"Wait a minute. I don't know how this thing of yours works. Is it hooked up so you can answer a call coming in while it's playing back?"

"Sure."

"All right. If he calls, even if it's while we're listening to these recorded calls, you're going to answer and talk to him. For just as long as he wants to talk. Understood?"

Chad looked toward Pulver, and Hart's face twisted angrily. "The hell with psychology. We're doing this now, like we have to do it. This isn't mind-games any more, it's what we have to do. Now, play those back."

Chad worked the machine through "rewind," and then turned up the volume and hit the button for "play."

The man said, "Chad, what are you trying . . ."

"Captain, we heard the first two," Reason said.

"Skip 'em."

Chad fast-forwarded to the third call.

"You're going to be sorry for this, Chad! I thought you had better sense. And I thought those cops'd have better sense, too. Wait a minute! I hear something. She's coming home! Where are you, Chad?" The man's voice dropped to a whisper. "Yeah! She's here. Where are you? We . . ."

The machine ended the call and Hart said, "He called back about fifteen minutes later."

In a moment, there was the beep and another thirty-second recording started. In this one, the man didn't speak at all. The entire time was filled with a woman's screaming against a gag over her mouth.

Chad went away, across the room, dropped down onto the sofa, bent his upper body forward against folded arms. And listened. There was no escaping that.

The recording of the next call was the same, except that the woman's voice had grown hoarse and hopeless.

The next one started with the man saying, "This is for you, Chad-buddy."

The woman was only moaning now, but she turned that abruptly into a scream.

The sound raked at Chad's belly. Almost, he could see the muzzle of the shotgun shoved at his own face.

The blast of the gun thundered from the answering machine, cutting off the screaming. The man said, "Talk to you again in a little while, Chad."

Unfolding his body, Chad pushed himself up from the sofa. "It didn't work at all," he said. "He didn't just leave her there, and come after me."

Pulver was chewing at a thumb. Reason's face was waxen.

Chad started toward the desk. "What are we going to do now?"

In a hard voice, Hart said, "It isn't over yet. The next call came eight minutes later."

Chad couldn't breathe. He dropped onto the sofa again as another call began.

A very frightened young man was saying, "Listen, mister, I don't know why you busted in here. Or what you want. But you can have it. Just don't hurt Eileen. Let her go, can't you? She won't say any—"

The shotgun blasted. As its echo died, a woman's screaming replaced it, along with floundering sounds, and the sounds of kitchen things—dishes, kettles—being knocked to the floor.

"You killed him!" she screamed. "You—"

There was another gunshot. "You did that to them, Chad, when you cut me off," the man said.

Chad stared at the glass wall of the atrium.

"The next one took about ten minutes," Hart said.

Talking very fast, a man said, "Hey, take anything you want. And use the phone—s'okay. Just take it easy with that gun. I'm cool. You be cool. Here's my watch. Ring. I'll just put 'em here on the washer. I got some money in the other room."

Then came the voice Chad knew so well. "Mister, I don't want that stuff. This is for my buddy." The gun thundered. The man hung up the phone and there was droning dial tone for a few seconds until the answering machine timed out.

Chad tried to trick his vision to see into the dimness of the atrium where the delicate leaves of the ficus shivered in the slight movements of the night air. But he couldn't penetrate his own reflection.

Hart's voice came from somewhere. "Took him six minutes, this time."

The woman's voice was high, thin, shivery with fear. "What do you want? You broke my door."

"Gee," the man said. "You should have worked late, or something, tonight."

The shotgun blasted.

The man said, "Object lesson for you, Chad. For bugging out on me when I needed you. These are all yours. You turned on me, and this is what you got."

The recording ended.

Chad stared at his reflection, waited hopelessly for the next recorded call.

But the machine was clicked off. Hart said, "The rest of them are hang-ups." He looked around at Reason, at Pulver, and finally, at Chad, and kept staring at him until he looked up, as if startled by the silence.

"He killed the first one—the woman—after she came home to the house he was waiting in. After this 'plan' was put into effect to turn him over to the answering machine.

"And then, when he still couldn't reach you, he went door-to-door. To the next three houses. One right after another. Breaking in the back. Killing whoever was there. Four, besides the first woman. Five dead, altogether."

The telephone rang.

Chad's body convulsed with the sound. His jaws creaked with sudden pressure.

Hart picked up the telephone, jerked at the cord so that it looped out in front of him, and went to Chad. Lifting the receiver, he held it out.

Chad took it, said, "Hello."

"Hi, buddy," the man said. "So, you're answering your phone again."

Chad tasted blood. "Yeah."

"That's good. That makes me feel a whole lot better."

"Fine."

"So, good night now, buddy. I've got to hit the sack. It's been a rough day. You put me through hell."

Chad tried to force himself to say something.

But the man didn't wait. He chuckled, said, "Good night. Talk to you soon," and hung up.

"THIS IS Rhodes."

"Bill, it's Beth."

"Hello, baby. Hello!"

"Can you talk?"

"Uh, sure. Let me shut the office door. Yeah. How are you, Beth? Damn, I'm glad you called!"

"I'm fine. How are you?"

"Great! Particularly, now you've called. I can't believe how great it is to hear your voice."

"We have to talk."

"Sure, baby."

"I mean, we have to talk seriously."

"Well, sure."

"Bill, I don't want us to lose each other. I die when I think that may be happening."

"We'd be in Puerto Vallarta—with each other—right this minute, if you'd been thinking straight."

"I was thinking straight. That trip would have been the worst thing we could have done."

"What? Being together?"

"No. Going off together, with things like they are."

"You're still going to that shrink, aren't you?"

"Of course I am."

"That's your whole problem. He fills you full of complexes and neurosises and penis-envy, and crap like that. You stop listening to him, you'll feel better. You'll know what your own mind is."

"I'm getting to know my mind, Bill. And I'm going to keep on seeing him—and listening to him—for as long as I need to. Until I know enough about my life and myself to live without being abused."

"Oh, baby. That guy has put the brainwash on you."

"Bill, will you start seeing a therapist yourself?"

"You know goddamned well I won't."

"I have something very important to say to you."

"Baby, everything you say's important to me. You know that. Just as long as it's you saying it, and not some phony, brainwashing creep."

"What I have to say is out of my heart. Nowhere else. It's straight out of me."

"All right, baby."

"I want to keep on loving you. I want to live with you again, and be your wife, and love you. More than I can even say."

"Well, all—"

"Wait, Bill. It's like I've said to you again and again. I cannot be somebody any longer that lets her husband beat her. I will not. I *won't*! And you're a wife-beater. You'll be one until you want to get help and actually do it. And it comes down to this. If you won't even make a move toward getting yourself straightened out, I'm going to go ahead and file for divorce."

"Divorce! Did you say 'divorce'?"

"Yes. I said it. I mean it. You have to get help to get yourself straightened out, or we're finished. I mean that, Bill. Much as I don't want it this way, I mean it."

"That goddamned shrink and that old slut you work for've put you up to this."

"No. They have not."

"You can't pull this crap on me. You're my wife. You need some sense put into you."

"Like your father used to 'put sense' into your mother?"

"What? Goddamn you! What'd you say?"

"Did you like it, watching your father beat your mother?"

"Goddamn you! Don't you talk about my dad!"

"Oh, Bill."

"I swear to God, all you try to do is make me mad. Why the goddamn hell can't you see some reason?"

"You curse one more time, and I'm hanging up this phone."

"Now, listen— Oh, boy. You just shut me out any more. Why won't you listen to me, baby?"

"You call me 'baby' again, and I hang up."

"Oh, for— You've changed. they've changed you all around."

"You think it over, Bill. You start therapy. You really start it, or I go to the lawyer a week from Friday."

"Don't you try bluffing me."

"It's no bluff. I've made my appointment. It's up to you whether I keep it or not."

"You went completely off the bend! You're talking crazy! I wish I had ahold of you right now!"

"This is the way it is, Bill."

"You're not seeing any lawyer. You're my wife. Don't you try it! I won't have it! I'll stop you, goddamn you! You're not going to—"

"I'm hanging up, Bill."

"You listen to me! You try an' see any goddamned lawyer, I'll fix you! By God, I'll stop you! Beth? Beth! Don't you be hanging up on me! Beth?"

PULVER ARRIVED first, barely greeted Chad, rushed past him into the study, his recorder tucked under his arm. "If only I could have heard last night's conversation," he was saying as Chad caught up to him. "It puts an entirely different light on the situation."

He sat on the sofa, set the recorder on the coffee table. "Just listen to this." He depressed the "play" button.

Chad heard his own voice, recorded by the police wiretap during his conversation with the man last night. "How the hell could I let you down?"

And then, the man's hurt-sounding voice. "I thought maybe you'd hear the shot. Come running over."

Pulver stopped the tape. "You see? That meant our plan was no good. That one line changes my entire profile on him."

Chad glanced at the clock.

"I'm sorry," Pulver said, moving his hands away from the recorder. "You asked me to stop by for a talk, and I've just been running on."

"No," Chad said. "What else have you figured out?"

Pulver fast-forwarded, played.

The man laughed.

Chad said, "I keep trying to recognize your voice. God help—"

"That's too soon," Pulver said, cutting off the rest of it, fast-forwarding some more.

Now, Chad heard his recorded voice saying, "Who are you pretending that I am?"

Sounding surprised, the man said, "What are you talking about?"

Pulver hit "stop," leaned back into the sofa. "You started something important there. But that's when Officer Reason and I arrived, and you had no opportunity to go on with it."

Chad nodded.

Pulver worked the machine's controls again. "Let's just listen some more."

The recording of the conversation began again, from the first, and Pulver leaned forward over the recorder, so intent that he forgot to smoke his cigarette.

But Chad didn't really listen. He didn't need to. Maddeningly and incessantly, it seemed, last night's conversation had run through his mind, disrupting sleep and making wakefulness ugly.

He checked the time again, heard a few words from the recorder, enough to know from memory that coming up was himself, saying, "I keep trying to recognize your voice. God help you if I ever do!"

Pulver was paying no attention, used these unimportant moments to smoke his cigarette.

The doorbell chimed.

Pulver looked up, stopped the tape, and Chad said, "Be right back," and hurried out to answer the door.

Captain Hart wore the same pin-striped suit. Gray stubble showed on his face, and his eyes looked watery. "This better be important, Mr. Palmer," he said, as he stepped inside. "I've got a tight schedule, explaining how we wiped out an entire block of Bellaire last night."

Chad followed him into the study and found him and Pulver glaring at each other.

"You didn't tell me he was coming," Pulver said accusingly.

Hart was no more pleased. "Look here, Palmer. I've had a bellyful of mind-games."

Pulver's eyes flashed. He jabbed at the air with his cigarette. "That 'mind-game,' as you so ignorantly call it, was a joint project of Police *and* Psychology. And you seem to overlook the fact that the police were pushing me all the way—wanting something immediately. Regardless, what we did was approved by everyone."

"What did it get us? A slaughterhouse!"

"Goddamn it!" Chad said. "Knock it off. Both of you."

Hart wheeled on him. "Now, you look here. You aren't going to talk to—" Breaking off, he swallowed and rubbed at his eyes. "Sorry, Palmer. I stand corrected."

Pulver seemed to shrink inside his jacket. "I'm sorry, Chad."

"Just sit down, please. I want to talk to both of you."

Pulver took his original place. Hart looked at the empty space on the sofa and chose to sit in a chair on the other side of the coffee table.

Chad remained standing. He said, "Neither one of you is doing any good on this, it looks like, to me."

Hart bristled. Pulver stabbed out his cigarette.

"Psychology's struck out," Chad said. "So has good old-fashioned police work."

"Random killings," Hart said distastefully. "Kill somebody you hate, and all we have to do is find out who hated the dead one. But kill somebody because he—or she—happens to be some place at the wrong time, and we have a problem."

Chad said, "You've been through my life upside-down and backward. Guys I've fired, had fistfights with in the fifth grade, had accidents with, unhappy customers—you've hassled them all. And you don't have a start on him yet."

He looked at Pulver. "And every time you get a profile worked up, he says something else, and it's no good any more."

Pulver and Hart suddenly found themselves comrades. Hart smiled sympathetically at Pulver; Pulver shook his head mournfully at Hart. Then he turned toward Chad, jutted up his chin at him, the extension of his neck making his shirt collar seem absurdly oversized.

Sarcastically, he said, "But you have a brilliant solution, I presume."

"I don't know how brilliant it is, but it's as good as anything you all are doing."

Hart stood up, angrily waved everything away. "I don't have time for this," he said, and started toward the doorway.

Chad said, "You'd better make time, Captain. Or, whatever you try to do about this son of a bitch, you're going to be doing it without me."

Hart stopped short, wheeled. "What did you say?"

"Without you!" Pulver cried. Frantically, he punched at his recorder. "But more and more is coming out about the killer. We're getting closer to a breakthrough."

Chad's voice blared from the recorder. "I keep trying to recognize—"

"Not that!" Pulver cried, stopping the tape, fumbling at the "rewind" button.

Chad stepped forward, leaned down, pressed the "stop" button. "Please, Doctor," he said, pulling the recorder from his hands, standing away with it.

Hart stared belligerently at Chad. "What are you trying to pull? Just who the hell do you think you are, to be telling us our job?"

"Your only contact with him. That's who."

Pulver stood up, looked at Chad with horror in his face. "You wouldn't, Chad! You wouldn't stop talking to him."

Hart said, "Now, goddamn it, Palmer!"

"What the hell are you going to do?" Chad said. "Put a gun at my head, and make me answer the phone?"

"Chad!" Pulver cried.

Hart rubbed at his face. Finally, he said, "What is it you want?"

"Use Crime Stoppers."

Pulver's eyes went wide. "This isn't the type of crime that's been effective with."

"For Christ's sake, Palmer," Hart said. "This isn't some punk blowing away some cashier at a Seven-Eleven."

Chad set the tape recorder on the coffee table. "Does either one of you have a better idea?"

BETH'S RED Firebird disappeared around a curve ahead, and Bill accelerated to keep her in sight. "Divorce!" he muttered.

He passed a young woman in a Maserati, pacing an elderly woman who jogged stiffly along the walkway. On his right was the wall behind which sprawled the palace of an heiress to a trash-collecting fortune. But on the left was a relatively low-income area of unwalled houses, more than one to a block.

There was Beth's car ahead, winding on along the street

Bill glanced left, pitied the owner of the cheap Cadillac parked with only its nose showing, and stepped up his speed just a little more.

The Cadillac was moving!

Even inside his closed car, Bill heard the scream of its tires and the roar of its engine. It was hurtling directly across the street at him!

He panicked. Everything left his mind except steering away from that hurtling machine. His right front tire slammed into the curbing, lurched grindingly over it, while the steering wheel spun out of his grip, and he was bounced across the seat.

Yelling, pushing one hand out against the glove-box to try to avoid being thrown into the floor, he waited for the inevitable crash.

It didn't come. His car only lurched alarmingly and then came to rest, its motor dead.

Raising up from the car seat, he saw through the windshield that his car was stopped against the embankment at the base of the trash heiress's wall, its right front fender only inches from the bricks. And he saw that the Cadillac was parked neatly at the curbing just ahead.

A pale blue Seville! He recognized it at the same instant as there came sharp rapping at his window.

Alma Henderson! Knocking on the glass with the muzzle of that squat, ugly pistol of hers.

Bill pulled himself over behind the wheel, paused only to give Alma a dirty look, and reached for the key to restart the car.

"Open it up, or I'll break it in!" Alma shouted. She looked as if she meant it.

He buttoned down the window and tried not to look at the pistol. He hadn't been sure that day in the office, but now he was. It was a .357 Magnum.

But so what? This was River Oaks. It was still daylight.

"You're crazy!" he said.

"Not half as crazy as you are, trying to follow Beth home."

He blustered, "You already mixed in too much with us. She's my wife."

A smoke-gray Mercedes was approaching.

Bill said, "You better put that thing away and get out of here before you get in trouble."

Very calmly, Alma said, "I guess I'm just going to have to go ahead and blow your goddamned head off, you won't be reasonable."

The Mercedes slowed, stopped, and the driver's window slid down. Bill allowed himself a small grin because Alma's pistol was in plain sight of the man driving.

He wore a Western-style shirt. A Stetson rested on the pearl-gray leather of the passenger seat. "Anything wrong here?" he said—to Alma!

She turned toward him, but kept the pistol on Bill. Smiling, she said, "Thanks. It's just a little personal matter."

The man looked coldly at Bill and then smiled at Alma. "You sure everything's all right, ma'am?"

She nodded. "Well in hand, but I appreciate your interest."

The man nodded. "Just the same, if you don't mind, I think I'll just stop a little way down the street. In case he gets out of hand." With a quick tip of his absent hat, he started his car forward.

Alma turned back to Bill. "Tell me chivalry is dead, you son of a bitch."

Bill's heart was pounding now.

"You listen here," Alma said. "If you can't do right by Beth and get yourself straightened out, well, you better just leave her the hell alone."

His stomach was starting to hurt. In the rearview mirror, he saw the Mercedes waiting a hundred yards away. Waiting to come to Alma's aid, not his.

"I had one just like you once," she said, waving the pistol in his face. "He couldn't understand anything but gunpowder, either."

Bill licked his lips. The pain in his stomach was going over into nausea now.

"You going to bother Beth any more?"

He shook his head, forced out, "No."

Alma lunged at him with the gun. "I don't hear you!"

"No!" he shouted. "No. No! I promise I won't!"

"See that you don't," Alma said, and started backing away.

Bill held desperately to the steering wheel.

Alma reached her car, pulled open the door. Over the roof, she called, "You better try and get that thing started and move it out of there, before you get your ass hauled off to jail."

"WELL, HI, buddy," the man said. "How's it going?"

"Yeah," Chad said. "It's going fine."

"What are you doing home in the middle of the afternoon? How come you're not over at the store, making bucks?"

"What are you doing? Have you sneaked into somebody's house in broad daylight?"

A chuckle. "No. This is just a social call."

"Meaning you're not on a kill right now."

"Yeah. Meaning that." He laughed. "I just called you up to shoot the shit with you."

"How many did you kill before Marian Koehler?"

"She's the one I started with."

"Are you sure of that?"

"Sure, I'm sure."

"Why did you start with her?"

"Her house was the first one that came up dark and waiting for somebody to come home."

"That's not what I mean. I mean, why did you start all this then?"

"Well . . . you didn't come back until then."

"Come back? What do you mean? I hadn't been anywhere."

"Yeah, well, hey, Chad, I couldn't believe it a couple of weeks ago, when my Brigatti chandelier turned up on sale."

"You didn't answer my question."

"I got real excited when I saw that red tag. Damn! That would've saved me three hundred and eighty bucks."

"Where did I come back from?"

Chuckling, the man said, "You just grab hold like a bulldog, don't you? Well, I sure would have liked to fall for that red tag. But it was too obvious it was a put-on. That one must have been a cop trick."

"Somebody doesn't just start killing people for no reason."

"Boy, you got that right!"

"What started you?"

"It was a cop trick, wasn't it? 'Forty-eight Hour Sale,' it said all over your windows."

"It was their idea," Chad said, staring at the happier one of the Roel Peña paintings, trying to fold its bright colors around himself. "I didn't much want to do it. The Brigatti lights are the best things going, you know. We never have to mark them down."

He fixed his eyes on the colors, tried to bore into them. From far away, it seemed, he heard himself saying, "What that sale did was just cost me money. But the cops said that my turning up like that—coming back just then—got you started off killing those women, so I shouldn't bitch too much about it."

There was silence from the man. Chad's eyes ached from strain and he closed them, lost the colors.

He didn't hear Reason unlock the front door and come into the study. But a sudden wash of air brought the faint, soft scent of her perfume to him and he opened his eyes to see her standing near the desk.

The man finally spoke again. "You're trying to play tricks on my mind, aren't you?" Reason started to pick up the handset of the extension, but Chad put his hand on it, shook his head urgently.

"Who are you playing like I am?" he asked the man.

After a long time, in a low, uncertain voice, the man said, "Maybe I ought to hang up now."

"No. Don't hang up. Who am I to you?"

"Stop it, Chad! You're trying to confuse me. Trying to play around with my mind."

Reason watched, biting her lip.

"I've been playing around with your mind for quite a while," Chad said. "That's what I came back to do."

The man said, "You came back to . . . No! Listen, I've got to go now."

"You've always been like that."

"I don't want to talk to you any more right now."

"Fine," Chad said, watching his hand clench until the knuckles went white. "I'm used to that from you."

The man hung up.

Slowly, Chad replaced the receiver of his telephone.

Reason asked, "What was going on?"

Now, he let his fingers relax. "I don't know."

BILL WAS very happy with himself.

All this time, he'd farted around, trying to follow Beth home *from* work, when that was completely the wrong way to go about it. Kind of dangerous, too.

But now, he was going about it the right way. He was following her *to* work. Or maybe the right word was "backtracking."

Last Friday morning, just two days after that old bitch had got the drop on him right there in the middle of River Oaks—just a week from the time when they had Beth brainwashed to go to the lawyer—the idea had flashed on him while he was in the shower that was getting eaten up with mildew. And it hadn't been more than twenty minutes later when he put it into effect.

At fifteen minutes before eight, he was parked in the driveway of a vacant house about a block and a half north of Westheimer on Kirby Drive. At six minutes until eight, he saw Beth's red Firebird turn onto Kirby and drive south, in the straight shot to the office. The street she'd turned off was West Gray.

Monday morning, at twenty minutes before eight, he waited on West Gray and saw her turn off South Shepherd and head for Kirby.

Tuesday was South Shepherd day.

Wednesday—today—he saw her car emerge from the drive at the end of a row of town houses.

Tomorrow morning, he was dead certain, he'd see which one of those town houses she was hiding out in.

And tomorrow night—Thursday—he'd just drop in and they'd have a nice little reunion.

Friday morning, he'd wake up and look over at her, and say, "Hey, baby. Didn't you have some kind of appointment, or something, today?"

And she'd say, "Oh, that. I forgot all about it, darling. I'll call and cancel it. Pretty soon."

"CHAD. I called to tell you they're shooting the Crime Stoppers spot tonight."

"God, Sharon! That's wonderful. That's incredible! I just wish I could be there."

"Oh, sure. The TV people already went crazy when they saw our script and found out the killer used the phone. All you need is to show up and let 'em figure out it's you he talks to."

"Yeah, well. I just can't believe it's finally happening. Now we can stop this crap."

"Chad, just don't get your hopes up too much. Everybody but you is convinced it's only going to bring out the cranks. You know what's happened the other times we thought we had the answer."

A GARAGE door started to open.

Bill's pulse quickened and he pushed farther back into the bank of oleanders. His watch showed 7:29 A.M.

A green Porsche drove out.

His pulse settled.

At 7:32, the garage door of the nearest town house—the end one—opened.

His pulse kicked again, started to race, as a candy-apple-red Firebird emerged.

He was a little too far away to make out Beth's face, but that was her car. And that was her mass of silky hair, glowing like copper in the morning light.

He stepped out of the oleanders and lifted his hand toward the back of the car as it disappeared off toward the street.

"Gotcha, baby!" he whispered hoarsely, clenching his fingers as if he were crushing a baby bird.

BETH SAID, "If it's okay, I'm going to leave a little early and let Ajax out for a while, since there's that meeting tonight."

Alma smiled. "I thought you'd get a baby-sitter for him."

"Oh, stop. It's just that he's gotten so good about trying not to go all day while he's locked up in the bathroom. Not even on the newspapers. So I hate to upset him by abandoning him until late."

"Tomorrow's Friday. You haven't heard from Bill, have you?"

"Bill who?" Beth said, picking up her purse and starting out.

Alma walked with her. "Don't give me that 'Bill, who?' stuff. And you keep on being careful."

Beth laughed. "I'll see you at about six. And I'll be careful."

"You tell Ajax, Auntie Alma said hi."

THE CLOCK in Chad's study showed THU 04 APR 5:06 PM. The television set was rolled out of the cabinet. The sound was off, but on the screen, a thin-faced young woman was bobbing her head vivaciously as she talked her way through "Live at 5," the half-hour local news teaser that preceded the network news.

Reason sat on the sofa, drinking a Coke. Chad was across from her, holding a can of beer and the television remote control.

"I love the local news," he said.

Reason raised an eyebrow.

Chad laughed. This was one of the happiest days he could remember. It had gotten that way this morning when Pulver called to tell him that Channel 13 was break- ing precedent and would immediately run the Crime

Stoppers spot taped last night. "The first airing of it will be today, between five and six," Pulver had said. "Usually, they start a new Crime Stoppers spot only on Mondays, but they're rushing this because the police won't tell them who you are, or anything about you until the killer's caught."

Pointing at the television screen, Chad said, "What she's saying right now is something like, 'Today, Houston Mayor Kathy Whitmire said that, contrary to vicious rumor, she has no intention of playing Dustin Hoffman's sister in the sequel to *Tootsie*.' And then we'll go to a shot of the mayor herself, with her cute glasses, saying, 'Contrary to that vicious rumor, I'm not going to play Dustin's sister or anything else in the sequel to *Tootsie*.'"

Reason laughed.

"That's not all. Then we'll come back to What's-her-face, there, and just in case we didn't understand, she'll tell us, 'That was Mayor Whitmire, denying that she has any interest in playing with Dustin Hoffman in the sequel to *Tootsie*.'"

"I haven't seen you like this before," Reason said. "Except for that evening in the bar."

"Yeah. That evening. When I was ripped. Or trying to be."

"Well . . ."

"You haven't known me during any good times."

Reason said, "You seem to be hoping for some improvement."

Chad sat up, smiled hugely, fluffed imaginary curls, and, in falsetto, said, "And today, Chad Palmer, the foil of the Houston Telephone Killer's Reach-Out-And-Crush-Someone campaign, said he's hoping for some improvement."

Sitting back, scowling, pulling his tie a little looser,

using a gruff voice, he said, "I sure as hell do hope for some improvement."

Reason laughed.

Chad pulled the tie the rest of the way off and started to toss it onto the other end of the sofa from Reason. But he let it drop on the coffee table, grabbed up the remote control, punched at the volume button.

Television sound came up. ". . . bringing you now a new, and very important Crime Stoppers."

The "Live at 5" set was replaced by the station's news anchorman sitting on a stool on a blank set. Looking seriously into the camera, he said, "At about eight o'clock on the evening of March eighteenth, an intruder stealthily entered the home of a prominent Houston doctor."

His voice continued while, on the screen, a man carrying a shotgun slipped through a garage doorway. There were then shadowy cuts showing him moving through a residence, up a stairway, into a dimly lighted bedroom.

"The physician was out of the country. His wife was at a meeting of the Opera Society."

The shadowy form of the intruder sat on the foot of the bed and dialed numbers on a telephone.

"While he waited for the woman to return home, the intruder, using a clever technique to circumvent tracing, dialed the number of a man living in Houston—a man who did not know the intruder.

"The following is made up of excerpts from actual, legally-obtained wiretap recordings of the intruder's telephone voice. We have blocked out the called person's responses and replaced them with subtitles. Listen carefully, please. The voice you are about to hear is the actual voice of the intruder."

"WHERE ARE YOU?" read the subtitle below the dark form of the man with the telephone.

The light on the scene was so dim that the man could not be seen to be speaking. "In a house, waiting."

"Waiting. In the dark."

"WHAT DO YOU MEAN?"

"You ought to see this place. Needlepoint stuff every-where."

"WHY DO YOU KILL?"

"Because I like to."

"LIKE TO!"

"It makes me feel like I've made things be okay. Kind of like you feel when you start feeling good again after you've been sick. Alive and well."

A woman walked into the bedroom. Unconcernedly, she flipped on the light, and then turned and saw the man on the bed. She screamed, threw out her hands in terror.

The bedroom blacked out, and the anchorman reappeared. "The intruder bound and gagged the woman. The telephone carried the sounds of her ordeal to the man on the other end of the line while the killer continued to talk to him."

Cuts from the recording began again, and the awful scene in the bedroom returned. The woman struggled in the chair to which she was bound while the killer, shown only from behind, threatened her with the shotgun.

"She's a good one. You should see her eyes."

"STOP THIS! LET HER GO!"

"That'd spoil everything."

The camera moved around to go close-in on the woman's face and the shotgun muzzle, and the anchorman's voice replaced the recorded sounds. "Finally, after almost two hours, the intruder fired his shotgun."

On the screen, the camera moved even closer, until it showed only the gaping muzzle of the shotgun as it fired.

Blackout. The anchorman returned. "You have heard an actual recording of the phone voice of the intruder. He had killed before this, and has since killed again.

"If you recognize his voice, call Crime Stoppers. Crime

Stoppers will pay a one thousand-dollar reward this week for the identification and arrest of the man whose voice you heard. If you think you recognized that voice, call 222-TIPS. Your identity will never be revealed. Call now."

BETH PRODDED at something on her plate, hoping that it was intended to be a veal cutlet.

Around her, most of the real estate people of the Houston area were gathered at long, crowded tables, talking to each other about their latest victories in the property wars.

Well, she had her victories, too. Her session this afternoon with Dr. Wray had been the first one in which she had remained really comfortable, and she looked forward to those ahead.

"You're looking a little smug today," Dr. Wray had said, smiling approvingly.

"I think I have a right to. My emotions have leveled off. I'm not miserable all the time I'm home now—at least partly because of Ajax, of course. I don't think about Bill all the time. In fact, not very much at all. The only time I've been close to hysterics lately was when I sold the Tierney place right out from under that awful man at Red Carpet."

"No recent problems with your husband?"

"No. I think he's lost interest. Oh, he got in a rage when I told him I was going to file, but he gets in a rage about everything. Actually, I hope he has lost interest.

Because, if he's not going to change, I can't spare any in-      *179*
terest in him."

"So he's stopped harassing you?"

"Not a sign of him, phone or otherwise, since that
phone call."

"But you're keeping up your guard, aren't you? You and
Alma."

"Oh yes. But I think it's silly. She still insists on following me partway home, looking out for Bill, but I'm getting
a little tired of her mother-henning me. She was very
worried right after I called him about the divorce, but
there was no reason."

"Don't get too complacent. You're still learning about
independence, you know."

"I won't be complacent. But I won't be afraid all the
time, either, Dr. Wray. I'm just not going to be like that
any more. I think that night I just came apart over a silly
bulb blowing out in the garage was my last straw. I
haven't been really afraid since then."

"Tomorrow is when you see the lawyer."

"Yes."

"You're still determined to go ahead with starting divorce proceedings."

"Yes. I've wasted too much time already. Unless Bill
should call me between now and then. And be in therapy.
And do a terrific job of convincing me that a divorce isn't
necessary, after all."

"You don't think that, perhaps, you're moving just a little too fast?"

"Not fast enough, actually. Good grief, you sound like
Alma. She's been more down on Bill than anyone, but she
thinks I should wait. Or at least, just file for a separation
now, not a divorce.

"I've wasted enough time. I'm not wasting any more.
I've stopped worrying. I wish everybody else would."

She was startled out of her reverie by Alma's urgently whispered "Beth!"

Turning, she said, "Yes. What is it?"

Rolling her eyes, Alma said, "What has the mind of a bee, the emotions of a wart hog, and the mouth of a chain saw?"

Beth followed Alma's gaze, saw an entourage entering the banquet room, led by a stick-legged, potbellied woman resplendent in chartreuse silk, her hair looking like swirlingly-sculptured, plasticized vanilla taffy.

"Oh my God," Beth said. "Hilda Dott."

"I hope you put out some extra goodies for Ajax," Alma said. "This is going to be a long meeting."

"Maybe we'll be lucky," Beth said. "Maybe she'll eat the broccoli."

CHAD HAD just stepped out of the shower and was toweling his head dry when the telephone rang.

Pulling away the towel, he scowled. But then, a huge grin broke over his face. "Yeah!" he said.

Hurrying out into the bedroom, he grabbed up the receiver and answered as the second ring started.

"It's Sharon."

The note in her voice told him that his wild surmise had been correct. "I knew it was you! Somebody called Crime Stoppers, didn't they?"

"Yes! Several. The first was a girl he used to date."

Chad's eyes stung. He wiped at them with the towel and said, "Jesus! What'd you find out?"

"We've got his name. Address. Everything! Bart
Braden. Does that mean anything to you?"

"No. I never heard of him."

"I've got to hang up. Hart and Burke should be getting
to his house right now. I'm going over there, too. But I
had to call you."

Grinning, Chad imitated Hart's gruff voice. "'This isn't
some punk blowing away some cashier at a Seven-
Eleven!'" In a higher tone, he burlesqued Pulver. "'This
isn't the type of crime that's been effective with.'"

Reason laughed. "What are you talking about?"

"Nothing! And all it took was a couple of hours!"

"You're not making any sense at all, but I think it's wonderful. I've got to go, though. And get over to his place
myself."

"Call me," Chad said. "As soon as you can. No! Wait a
minute. What am I talking about? Come over. We'll celebrate! Now, we can celebrate."

"We'll see," Reason said, laughing.

After he hung up, Chad stood, smiling hugely. He was
still wet. So what? "They've got him!" he yelled.

He jumped, tried to hit the ceiling with a fist, missed it
by a couple of inches, and came down laughing, hitting
the floor hard enough to rattle the bed lamp.

He felt crazy, and he loved it. Laughing aloud, he
started toweling himself again. "'Palmer, don't give me
that Crime Stoppers shit!'" he said.

He made another jump, laughed, said, "Now's the time
to enhance that personal relationship, Pulley, old buddy!"

Wrapping the towel around his waist, he headed for the
stairway, saying, "Now, we can celebrate!"

In the dining room, he picked up the enamel-decorated
bottle of Perrier-Jouet champagne he'd bought once to
save for the Event of the Century, whenever it came
along, and hurried into the kitchen.

Grinning, he wrapped the bottle in a clean dishtowel. He saw himself easing out the cork, pouring, handing a glass to Sharon. As if rehearsing, he said aloud, "Nothing much. Just a little something I've had around, waiting until it was time to really enhance a personal relationship."

He pulled open the freezer door, glanced at the wall clock, reminding himself to transfer the bottle below after about an hour, and started to set it inside.

In his mind now was a picture of Sharon, her hair tossing around her face, as she directed a gang of cops to smash in a door and flatten the son of a bitch who cowered inside.

And then, the telephone rang.

He started to shove the bottle on into the freezer compartment and then hurry to answer it.

But he stopped in midmovement. Chill washed over his bare chest.

The second ring came.

He set the bottle on the counter, pushed the freezer door shut.

In the study, his upper body rough with gooseflesh, he stood and watched the telephone ring the third time.

And the fourth.

Finally, he answered.

"Hey, buddy. How's it going?"

"Where are you?" Chad said.

"WELL, HI, there," the waitress said. Flouncing her miniskirt, she went around behind the bar. "What'll you have?"

"How about a Wild Turkey and Coke?" 183

"Sure thing."

"Not much of a crowd. You take care of the whole place by yourself?"

She grinned at the three women who sat at a table near the ladies' room, and the middle-aged man and woman near the juke box. "Sam's in the back, watching the TV. He comes out when there's a rush."

"When's that?"

She set out the drink and chuckled. "Next Livestock Show and Rodeo, probably. That'll be two seventy-five."

"Sure."

"You probably get told this all the time, but you look just like Pernell Roberts."

"Yeah, I get told that. Listen, you make a good drink. Why don't you have one of those for yourself? On me."

"Sure!" she said. "Only you mind if I have it with water? Coke's not on my diet."

"Suit yourself."

She poured, took a drink. "Nice stuff!" Starting to propose a toast, she said, "What are we celebrating?"

He lifted his glass also. "Me getting back together with my wife."

The waitress looked disappointed. But a free drink was a free drink. "Well, okay. Terrific. Here's to the happy reunion."

CHAD SANK into the desk chair. "Why now? Why the hell now?"

"Well, gee, Chad," the man said derisively. "Why not?"

Chad forced himself to sit up straight. "You're in some woman's house, aren't you?"

The man laughed. "Sure. Where else?"

"Oh, God!"

"What's wrong?"

"Nothing."

"You don't sound very good, Chad."

"You're waiting right now, in somebody's house."

"Sure."

"Get out of there. Can't you just get out of there? Please."

"You're kidding! Why should I do that?"

Gooseflesh again crawled over Chad's body. The wiretap! They couldn't already have stopped surveillance, could they?

"You're doing wrong," he said. "You know that."

"Maybe you think so."

"I know so. It's wrong. I ought to just say the hell with you, and go away again."

There was a beat of pause, and then the man said, "You won't, though. You won't really go away." His voice went sad. "I wish you could. I've thought about that a lot. It'd be so much better if you'd stayed away. But you didn't."

Another pause. Longer. Chad tried to think whether he should break it, but the man finally said, "Wow! You're doing it again, aren't you?"

"Doing what?"

"Trying to get me confused."

Chad heard odd, scuffling sounds in the background.

The man chuckled. "I found a little friend here, waiting for me."

Chad's eyes widened. "A little friend! Is there a child there?"

The man was offended. "A child? Hell, no! I wouldn't go in some place where there was a child. What the hell do you think I am? No. It's a puppy."

Relief showing in his voice, Chad said, "A puppy. A
puppy, huh? Well, great."

"Yeah. He's terrific! Cute as hell. I think I'll take him with me when I'm through here."

The wiretap! Chad frowned across the room at the automatic dialer. Maybe he could get the man to hold on and give him time to get on the automatic dialer and punch its stored-number buttons until somebody answered who could tell him if the wiretap were still being monitored.

"What kind of puppy?" he asked, standing, cinching the towel tighter around his waist, pulling the telephone cord around, getting ready to cross to the sofa.

"A baby Doberman. Hasn't even had his ears trimmed yet."

Chad stepped away from the desk, but stopped short, made a tight smile of relief, as Reason stepped through the study doorway. Checking the towel, moving back to the desk, he said, "So, you think you're going to take him with you, huh? After you kill his owner. And then what?"

Turning to Reason, he motioned upward, mouthed, "Get me some clothes."

As she hurried out, the man answered, his voice sounding defensive. "I can take care of him."

"How can you take care of a pet? You can't even take care of yourself." Opening the middle desk drawer, he pulled out pencils and the yellow pad.

His voice even more defensive, thinner, almost child-like, the man said, "Yes, I can so!"

On the pad, Chad scribbled, "Doberman puppy. Male. Ears not trimmed yet," and said, "When did you ever show you could be trusted with a pet?"

The man's voice seemed very childlike now. "I had those hamsters."

Chad frowned. "Hamsters? Oh, sure. Those hamsters. Well, you know what happened to them."

He flinched away from the handset as the man shrieked a child's anger at him. "It wasn't my fault! It was—"

In the silence, after the man suddenly broke off, Chad wrote, "He had some hamsters. What happened to them (?) gets him *upset*."

When the man spoke again, his voice was hard. "I told you not to try to mess around with my mind."

"Fine. I'll hang up."

"No! Don't you hang up on me!"

"Is the puppy a real Doberman, or a mutt?" Chad asked.

"Listen, this guy's no mutt. He's a thoroughbred, all right. You ought to see him."

"What's his name?"

Reason returned with a pair of jeans, a red T-shirt and a pair of Jockey shorts.

"Name?" the man said. "How would I know what his name is?"

Dropping the clothing on the end of the desk, Reason hurried over to the automatic dialer and made a call.

"Well, then, name him," Chad said. "You're going to kill his owner and steal him, you're going to have to name him."

He motioned for Reason to turn away. She smirked, and then did so, as she began a low-toned conversation.

"Yeah, I guess I'd have to name him something," the man said.

Picking up the jeans, Chad swiveled his chair around, bent forward and bunched them so that he could get his feet into them. "So, what are you going to call him?" he asked, and pulled them over his feet. Giving a quick look around to make sure Reason was still turned away, he dropped the towel and pulled the jeans all the way on.

"I don't know," the man said. "What do you name a dog? All I ever had was those hamsters—Adam and Eve. You can't stick hamster-names on a dog."

Chad checked the T-shirt, found the Alley Theatre logo, turned that to the front, and pulled it over one arm, switched hands with the telephone, and got it the rest of the way on.

"What are you doing?"

"Just stretching. How about that name?" On the pad, he wrote, "Adam & Eve," and drew an arrow to "Hamsters."

The man hadn't answered, so Chad said, "If you can't even name him, how are you going to take care of him?"

Sounding as if he were afraid the puppy would be taken away from him if he didn't immediately name him, the man said, "Dobie! I'll call him Dobie. He's a Doberman."

Chad laughed derisively. "Dobie? What the hell kind of wimp name is that for a tough animal like a Doberman pinscher? That's a sissy name. You can't hang a sissy name on a stud animal like that."

Finished with her call, Reason came to the desk and read Chad's notes.

The man's voice was calm and cold. "You're doing it some more, aren't you? You're trying to get me to come up with some kind of name that'll get you in my head."

Reason picked up the shorts, made a disgusted face at Chad.

"Not with jeans," he mouthed to her and, into the telephone, said, "I don't have to go to much trouble." He chuckled, watched Reason toss the shorts over onto the credenza, and added, "Ever since I came back, your head's been like Swiss cheese to me."

The man spoke as if he were thinking out every word. "I think that, after this one tonight, I'll have to do something different. I think you're getting ready to act just like you did before. I think I'll have to do something about that."

Chad hardened his voice. "What are you going to do?

You can't even name a puppy. You couldn't even keep those hamsters alive."

The man shouted, "That wasn't my fault!" He broke off, and Chad heard scuffling sounds again. "Damn it. You made me scare this puppy."

"Fine. The hell with you. I'll get out of your life again."

"No, you won't!"

"I should have been harder on you. Maybe then you'd amount to something."

The man made an ugly laugh. "You tried. You showed me what you were like. Everything would've been okay, if . . ."

Chad waited. But finally, he said softly, "If?" And in a moment, after still more silence, said promptingly, "'Everything would have been all right, if . . .'"

"You're good at this, Chad. You pry in and ease around, trying to get at me. If-something you'll never know, old buddy. And you can quit pulling that easy, friendly voice on me."

Chad laughed. "What the hell would you do with a friendly voice? You'd turn it around and use it like a club. Like, you'll kill that woman, and take her puppy with you, and figure out a good, tough name for him. And then, one day, you'll pat him on the head, and he'll love you to death, and you'll feed him broken glass."

That angered the man. "I don't want you talking to me like that."

"I don't want to talk to you at all."

"You have to."

Chad said, "Take that puppy and get out of there. And come here, and we'll talk."

There was no answer.

"Are you going to say something?" Chad asked.

"You almost make me think I could get out of here," the man said sadly. "You almost get me thinking there's hope."

"There is."

"No, there isn't. No hope at all. It's all gone. The day I saw you when you came back, I knew that. Everything'd been okay for so long. I hadn't even thought about something being wrong again. And then, there you were."

Chad heard the sadness, listened frowningly and found himself trying to rub at his beard and pull at his mustache. Moving his hand, he bit at the knuckle of his index finger.

"Sometimes, I almost think that . . . well, you're Chad, and you could be my buddy. And listen to me. And talk to me. And be my friend. And you sound like you could really be my friend. I get myself sold on you being my friend, Chad.

"But that's not who you are, way down in my head. And that's what has the fist."

There was silence. There was sharp pain in Chad's hand, and he moved it away, set it open on the yellow pad, saw that he had bitten almost hard enough to bring blood.

The man's voice grew even sadder. "I'm going to kill another one in a little while. I get to thinking I can kill enough to fix it. But I can't. I can't."

Very softly, very gently, Chad said, "If I went away, would you leave that woman's house? Right now. Before she even finds out you've been there. Take the puppy, if you want to. But leave. And I'll go away. For good, this time. If only you'll come away from there. I mean it. I'll go away. Forever, this time."

"I don't know if that would work."

Chad stared at his outspread hand, the fingers under more tension than if they were clenched into a fist. "We could make it work. I promise you."

"How could I trust you? I found out I couldn't trust you before."

There were small sounds around him, and Chad looked

up, saw Reason, with a shushing forefinger at her lips, coming into the study with Captain Hart and Dr. Pulver and Lieutenant Burke. He hadn't even been aware that she had left his side.

He said, "We'll work out some way for you to make sure you can trust me."

Hart carried a flat box that looked as if it must once have held stationery. He came to the front of the desk, peremptorily made a cutting-off motion with a finger across his throat.

Chad shook his head, mouthed "No."

Suddenly, the man began laughing. "You're doing it again. Tying my mind up in knots. You just ease right in and stir things around, don't you?"

Impatiently, Hart set the box on the corner of the desk, pulled off its top, began taking photographs from it and laying them out face-up.

There were wallet-sized photographs. Three-by-fives. Color and black-and-white. An eight-by-ten sepia-tone portrait in a gray cardboard presentation folder. All were of the same man. Some of them were cut zig-zaggedly across to excise as much as possible of someone who had stood close to the man when the photographs were taken.

Chad stared at them.

"What's going on?" the man was saying. "Are you there, Chad?"

He moved angrily, covered some of the photographs with his hand, shoved them away from him.

"I'm here," he said, swiveling his chair away from the desk, turning his back on the photographs.

"What's going on?"

He breathed deeply. "Nothing. Listen, I've got to go for a minute. Hold on. Okay? Will you hold on for me?"

"Gotta go to the john, huh? Sure. I'll hold on."

Chad brought the chair back around to face the desk as Hart tore the top sheet off the yellow pad, folded that across, and tore again on the fold.

Chad picked up one of the photographs. The man in it stood beside a shiny new car. The left third of the photograph and the front of the car were cut away so carefully that nothing remained of the other person who had posed with the man, except for a woman's hand on his arm.

Into the telephone, Chad said, "I'll be back in a couple of minutes. Maybe more than that. Okay?"

"Sure. But not too long."

Pushing back from the desk, Chad rose, handed the receiver to Reason, and watched her cover the mouthpiece tightly with her palm. To Hart, he said, "Where the hell did you get those things?"

Hart scooped the photographs back into the box. "They were all over his house." Turning to Burke, he thrust the half-sheet of yellow paper at him. "Doberman pinscher puppy. Can't be too many breeders and kennels around. Get people calling them. Find out the women that bought puppies in the last month. Check 'em out."

He headed for the doorway. "Palmer, come out of here so we can talk. You, too, Doctor."

"MYSTERY MEAT and broccoli blastula," Alma said. "And now, desperate dessert."

Beth checked her watch. Dinner had been served even more slowly than usual tonight. "Do we absolutely have to stay for the business meeting?"

"That city franchise tax is on the agenda. You know that."

"I just looked over, and you know what? Hilda Dott even has notes with her tonight. Why do we even come to these things?"

"Because of things like city franchise taxes. And city council members that think there ought to be city real estate licenses. Little things like that."

"Lots of people are leaving. Look, there go Bree and Joe Pickens. And I saw Anne McDonald slip out ten minutes ago."

Alma said, "There's Chuck Saldaña and Angela. And Roseanne Bright. They're not leaving."

Beth shook her head with frustration. "Of course they're not leaving. They work for you, just like I do."

Harmon Brewer, sitting on Alma's other side, leaned over. "We're sure as hell not staying. Joyce and I don't work for you or for Hilda, so we sure don't have to sit around and listen to her. You know they won't get to the tax business, anyway, with her here."

Alma gave up. "All right, Beth. We'll go. We'll just wait until the break, and we'll go. You can hold out for another ten minutes or so, can't you?" She laughed. "I don't know whether I can."

"THESE THINGS are unbelievable," Chad said, taking photographs from the box, spreading them over the kitchen table.

"He had them all over his house," Hart said. "Pinned on the walls, sitting around here and there. And this is

only part of them." He pulled at his tie. "How do you
think we felt when we walked in and saw them?"

"That woman," Chad said. "She could get home at any
minute."

Hart grimaced. Reaching inside his jacket, he brought
out a small spiral notebook, opened it, and handed it to
Chad. "Notes on what we've got on him so far. Ran across
a car repair bill, too. Eighty-three Honda. I put out a bul-
letin on it."

Chad looked over the notes. "His grandmother lives
here in Houston. Maybe she'd know about the hamsters."

"Hamsters?" Pulver said, looking for a place to dump
ashes from his cigarette, giving up, tapping them into the
sink.

"Had them when he was a kid, I guess. And he goes
crazy when you mention them. That was the part of my
note that the captain tore off."

"Hamsters," Hart said, making a mental note. Then he
turned to Pulver. "What do you think? Should Palmer
spring his name on him?"

"Possibly. It could cement rapport. To the point that
Chad could persuade him to leave the house. On the
other hand, it might send him into a frenzy."

"Just give us a recommendation."

"I'd be forced to guess. Possibly, he—"

Chad cut him off. "What if I just leveled with him? Told
him we know all about him. That as soon as he sticks his
nose outside, it's all over."

Pulver was shaking his head. "No, no, no. Now, that's
something I'm sure of. That would be horribly dangerous.
For the woman, if for no one else. As it is, he spends a
half hour or so with the women before he kills them. It's
just too possible that, if you tell him, he'll kill her as soon
as she steps into her house."

Chad looked around angrily, found himself staring at his

reflection in the microwave door, and flinched away. "I wish to hell she wouldn't come home at all tonight. I wish to hell she'd shack up somewhere, and not drag home until morning."

"She's got that dog," Hart said. "She's got to come home to take care of him."

"Christ, yes! I forgot about the puppy."

Hart began returning the photographs to the box. "Whatever she does, she'll be the last one. We know who he is now. He won't get another chance."

"Great!" Chad said. "Terrific! She'll be the last one, and it'll be okay. Fuck you, Captain!"

"You've been gone quite a while," Hart said calmly. "Why don't you cool off and get back to him? If that woman getting killed bothers you so much, well, get off your ass, and get him out of there."

THE FIFTEEN-MINUTE break between dinner and the business meeting came.

Alma stubbed out her cigarette, picked up her purse, and stood up.

But before she and Beth had taken three steps from the table, someone came running up behind them. "Alma! Alma Henderson! Wait!"

"Millie," Alma said, turning around. "Whatever is wrong with you?"

"I have to talk to you, Alma. Hello, Beth."

Beth smiled. Millie Sindler was a predecessor of hers who had left Alma and opened an office on her own.

"Call me in the morning, and we'll have lunch," Alma said. "We were just leaving." Stage-whispering, she added, "On top of that food, we couldn't face Hilda."

Terror came into Millie's face. "I have to talk to you. Tonight. Please, Alma. I just have till one tomorrow."

Alma smiled. "Well, let's go. We'll have a drink or two, and you can tell us what's so important."

Millie neared panic. "But I'm recording secretary. I can't leave before the meeting."

Beth fidgeted.

Alma said, "Oh, for God's sake, Millie. What's so important it can't wait until morning, at least?"

Leaning very close, whispering, Millie said, "The Schimpf home!"

Beth's mouth dropped.

"The Schimpf home. What are you talking about?" Alma said.

Still whispering, looking around with fear of being overheard, Millie said, "I have the Schimpf home. And I can't handle it. I'll split the exclusive with you."

Beth stepped back to the table, set down her purse. "Come and sit down, Millie," she said. "We still have a few minutes before the business meeting starts. You can start telling us all about it."

WHEN CHAD went back into the study, Reason was sitting at the desk, muffling the telephone mouthpiece with her palm while she listened. Burke sat on a corner of the desk.

Softly, Chad asked, "Is he still just waiting?"

"Sitting there playing with the puppy," Reason said.

Burke waited until Chad had taken the handset and blocked the mouthpiece with his hand to say, "We got people calling around about the dog."

Chad nodded, listened for a moment.

A golden strand had escaped from the precise helmet of Reason's hair. He wanted nothing more than to hang up the telephone and touch it. Instead, he handed her the scrap of paper on which was written his note about the hamsters. "Captain Hart wants you in the kitchen."

She rose, and he started to sit down.

"What the hell?" Burke grunted.

They spun around. He was standing between the credenza and the desk, his square face flushed with anger. The pair of Jockey shorts dangled from the tip of his index finger.

Without expression, Reason plucked away the shorts. "Oh, these," she said, holding them by the waistband. "He doesn't wear them with jeans, Ross." Folding them neatly, she opened a desk drawer, tucked them away.

"The kitchen?" she said to Chad, and left the room.

Burke stamped back to the sofa, angrily made a call on the automatic dialer.

Sitting down, Chad took his hand away from the mouthpiece. "Hello. I'm back."

"Yeah. Hi, Chad," the man said. And then, "Hey pup! Hey. What've you got?" There were scuffling sounds and laughter away from the telephone. When the man spoke again, he was out of breath. "He had one of her good shoes, Chad! Jeez. She'd be pissed as hell, if he tore up one of her good shoes."

"What difference would it make? That's funny as hell—you break your ass to save her from a ruined shoe, and at the same time you're waiting for her to get home so you can kill her."

The man chuckled. "Yeah, well . . ."

"Why don't you just give the puppy the shoe and get out of there and leave him alone? And leave the woman alone, too."

The man seemed to be thinking it over. But finally, he said, "I've already started this. You've got to finish what you start."

"Oh, yeah? When did you begin doing that?"

"Doing what?"

"Finishing what you started."

"Well, I try to do that. Listen, I'm not nearly the dumbshit you seem to think I am."

"Sorry. That was a cheap shot. You sure finished those hamsters."

He clenched his jaws at the man's sudden howl of anger. "I didn't finish them! I didn't, damn you! You know that!"

"That's your story."

"You still won't see it right! I'll never forgive you for that!" the man shouted.

"It was for your own good."

"It was so goddamned mean, I still can't even think about it!"

Startled, Chad looked up and saw Pulver standing beside the desk, his eyebrows raised inquringly.

Chad wrote on the pad, "Just following along on whatever he says."

Into the telephone, he said, "You wouldn't listen. You brought it on yourself."

When the man angrily cried, "No, I didn't!" Chad lifted the handset of the extension and handed it to Pulver.

The man didn't notice. Without break, he continued, "You just didn't care! You never did!"

"It was a lesson for you," Chad said, writing on the pad again.

"I don't need any lessons like that," the man said.

Pulver read the scribbled sentence—"Do I use his name?"—and lifted his hands in futility, shrugged helplessly.

Scowling with irritation, Chad looked away from him and, as much for his benefit as the man's, said, "You try to weasel out of everything I say, don't you?"

"You say dumb, ugly things."

Chad looked up at the ceiling, took a deep breath. "Okay, Bart. Let's talk about my going away, then."

"It wouldn't work."

"Why not?"

"I've thought about it, and I wouldn't be able to trust you."

"How could I get your trust?"

"You couldn't. I remember too much."

Pulver was pushing at Chad's shoulder, waving the notepad in front of his face. It said, "Keep using his name!"

"I've changed, Bart," Chad told the man.

"Oh, sure, you have."

"I have. In a lot of important ways."

"I don't think you could."

"I promise you I have, Bart."

There was silence for a moment.

Finally, Chad said, "Bart, I want to make things up to you. I'm sorry about those things."

Now, the man spoke, his voice slow and thoughtful. "I wish I could believe that."

"What can I do to make you believe it? Listen, Bart, I'll do anything to make you believe me and trust me again. I don't want it to be like this between us."

"I think this puppy's getting hungry."

"Bring him with you, Bart. We'll feed him, and you and I can talk this out."

In a voice which seemed much younger, the man said, "She ought to be coming home any minute."

"Bart, just bring him and come out of there."

Sounding like a sad, hurt child, the man said, "You don't care about me. You just want to get me out of here before she finds me."

"I do care, Bart. I don't want you in any more trouble than you already are. We need each other, you and I."

"Why didn't you ever say that before?"

"I don't know. Things like that aren't easy to say. You know that, Bart."

"Yeah. I know it. I know that." After a pause, his voice lost the child's sadness. "Hey, listen, it's getting late. We've been on this phone a long time. I don't think they can trace this at all, but I'm not taking any chances. I'm going to cut this off, and call you back. Okay? Is that okay with you?"

"Don't hang up, Bart. Just when we're getting somewhere."

"I'd better. I'm going to."

"Listen to me, Bart. Leave and go someplace where somebody's not going to come in and interrupt us."

The man seemed to think it over. In a moment, he said, "I'll call you back." Then he hung up.

REASON WAS forced to use the pay telephone in the shopping center parking lot across the side street from Chad's.

She wished to hell Burke had been tending to business

and getting his calling done, instead of standing around with Chad's underwear. She wished they still made real phone booths because it was humid and sweaty out here, and the traffic along Bissonnet made it almost impossible to hear Kate Braden who had evidently used up most of her voice yelling at Santa Ana to get the hell away from the Alamo.

"What?" she said. "Couldn't you speak up, ma'am? Oh. Yes. I'll talk louder, too! This is Officer Reason! Police Officer Reason!"

She swatted at something that buzzed around her neck. "Yes! I am a policeman—a policewoman! I know that some other policeman talked to you earlier! But I need to talk to you now!"

She listened, her eyes closed, her right ear smashed against the receiver, her left hand crammed against her left ear to try to shut out the traffic noises.

"Yes! About your grandson! About Bart! Yes! What?"

Mrs. Braden whispered; she strained to hear.

"What? Please speak up!"

She swore at the bus that chugged slowly past, tried desperately to hear, gave up, and said, "Mrs. Braden, I'm sending a car for you! Yes! A car! Right now! So we can talk! What? No! NO! YOU ARE NOT UNDER ARREST!"

She hung up, fumbled in her purse for another quarter, jammed it into the slot, and dialed.

"Andrews, this is Reason. Send a car to sixteen-sixteen Wroxton Court and . . . What? I AM NOT YELLING! I am not. Okay. All right. All right, I'm sorry, Andrews! Have them pick up Mrs. Kate Braden. Bring her to thirty-one-ninety Bissonnet. Yes. Right. And for God's sake, Andrews, have them tell her they're not arresting her."

THE WAITRESS leaned on the counter. "Telling you you look like Pernell Roberts worked for one drink. What'll get me another one?"

Bill chuckled, checked his watch. Sometimes those real estate meetings of Beth's dragged on half the night. "Tell you what. Tell me I play football just like Joe Montana, and we'll both have another one."

The waitress started rattling ice into glasses. "Why the hell not? Coming right up, Joe."

BURKE WATCHED Chad and Pulver leave the study, and stood up and stretched. "Okay, Andrews," he said into the receiver of the automatic dialer. "The crazy fucker took a break; I can talk like a human being again. So, out of six women those dog-people told you bought Dobermans, you got two that you haven't got ahold of yet. How come you haven't?"

"Well, this Beth Rhodes, there's no answer. But I don't know about her. I think she used a business address and phone number. I asked the old girl at the kennels about it, but she didn't know."

"How come you think it's a business?"

"Well, twenty-nine-fifty-one Kirby? You know of any houses or apartments or anything on Kirby there, but businesses?"

"What about the other one?"

"That's Anne Richards, on West Thirty-third. Her phone's busy."

Hair prickled at the back of Burke's neck. "Busy! Goddamn it, Andrews, that could be it! Try it again right now—no! Don't want to alert him. Get Dispatch to get a car over there—no siren—and tell 'em to take it easy, checkin' the house. Shit! This is it! I can feel it! Tell 'em, if that woman's getting home, not to let her go in till they check it out."

"Sure, Ross."

Burke sat down heavily, grinning. "Damn! I think this is it!" But he frowned. "Hey. Just in case, get 'em to take a look at that Kirby address, too. And move it, Andrews!"

BETH GROANED. Hilda Dott was at it again.

Four tables over, she was standing up, fiddling with the chunk of amber that hung from a chain around her neck, eloquently explaining the wonders of compound interest.

Grudgingly, Beth—and Alma, even—had to admit that the woman was stunningly successful, virtually controlling the real estate market in the substantial suburb of Pasadena. But why couldn't she ever keep her mouth shut?

Leaning toward Alma, Beth whispered, "I have to keep saying, 'Schimpf house,' over and over to myself, just to keep awake."

"'Schimpf *home*,'" Alma corrected, and chuckled. "Home, hell! Palace."

"Look what time it is, and we still have to go by Millie's afterward. Ajax will never forgive me."

Alma laughed. "Listen, dear, we sell this place, you can have Humana Hospital do his ears."

CHAD PULLED a Coke from the refrigerator, snapped away the tab, and drank half of it at once.

"Making any progress?" Hart asked.

Sitting down at the table, leaning forward and pressing the cold can to his forehead, Chad said, "I used his name. I don't think he even heard it."

"I didn't hear him react at all," Pulver added.

Hart rubbed at his face, ran a hand over his pewter hair. "You going to get him out of there?"

Pulver said, "No."

Chad slammed the Coke can down on the tabletop. "Why the hell do you just know about the negative stuff? How come you can't ever make up your mind about anything else? Why don't you make yourself useful, and make some coffee, or something?"

Pulver was unruffled. "I think you're doing very well on your own, Chad. Just following your instincts."

The telephone rang.

HILDA DOTT paused for breath, smiled around, tapped at her plastic hair with a beringed hand, to show that she had diamonds, as well as amber.

Alma leaped to her feet, waved, shouted, "Madame Chairman!"

"Uh, yes, Mrs. Henderson."

Hilda turned to glare.

"I move we adjourn," Alma said.

"I have the floor!" Hilda tried to say, but she was drowned out by shouted seconds and applause.

"Oh, God!" Alma said. "I'll never work in Pasadena again, but let's get Millie, and get out of here."

"THIS'S GOT to be the last one," Bill said.

"Aw, come on. Tell me some more about the Cotton Bowl," the waitress said.

Bill laughed. "Listen, that's ancient history. I never did even like playing football."

"Why'd you do it?"

"Beth wanted me to."

"Beth? Oh, yeah. You mentioned a Beth. Your wife? That one?"

"Sure."

"But you busted your knee. You couldn't play football any more. How come she married you anyway?"

"I don't know. That's ancient history, too." He checked the time. "Listen, I got to drink up and get out of here. It's coming up Reunion Time."

"WHERE ARE you?" Chad asked. "Still at that woman's?"

"Sure," the man said.

Chad's stomach went hollow. Pulling along the telephone cord, he went to the atrium wall. "When you hung up, I was hoping you'd be leaving there."

"Naw. I was just playing with this puppy."

Chad's reflection stared back at him from the glass. "So, what now, Bart?"

The puppy yipped for attention and the man laughed. "She sure does stay out late. Just leaves this poor puppy, and stays out to all hours."

Suddenly, Chad laughed.

"What's funny? What are you laughing at?"

"I had a thought. Funny as hell." He laughed some more, watched his reflection laugh back at him. "What if she's doing the same thing you are?"

Puzzled, the man said, "The same thing I am?"

Chad couldn't stop laughing, didn't want to. "Think how funny it'd be. If that woman went over and sneaked in your a house a couple of hours ago."

Pulver intruded on Chad's laughing reflection. With the

yellow receiver of the extension glued to his ear, he was frowning, shaking his head.

He looked too serious.

Chad moved, shifted him out of the reflection. "Maybe she's sitting over there right now. In your house."

He laughed at his beardless face in the glass. He'd gotten used to it by now. But at this moment, it looked absurd.

"There she is, right now, in your house, with those pictures all over it, staring at her." He had to stop and laugh.

"You're talking crazy, Chad," the man said.

"She's pissed off as hell, Bart. Listen, maybe she calls up her friend, and says, 'Kate, where is that man? I'm over here, waiting to blow his goddamned head off. And he's staying out to all hours.'" Tears streamed down his face. His jaw hurt. But he couldn't stop laughing.

"Chad! What are—"

"She says, 'I'm mad as hell, Kate! Where is he? I want him to get home so I can blow his head off, and then I can take his hamsters, and get the hell out of this creepy place, with these creepy pictures all around.'"

"I don't know what you're doing!" the man shouted.

Chad was crying now. His chest ached. He looked around the room. Pulver. Burke. Where was Sharon?

He wiped at his eyes with a forearm, moved away from his reflection to the fieldstone wall, and leaned heavily into it. "I don't know, either."

"You're saying real crazy things. I don't even understand what you're saying."

Pulling up the front of his T-shirt, Chad rubbed at his face. "I'm saying, 'Let me come and get you, Bart.' I want to get you out of there. Please, Bart."

With no expression, the man said, "You're saying my name."

Chad moved away from the wall. "Yes."

"How'd you find out my name?"

Looking to Pulver, finding only wide eyes and frowning interest, Chad said, "Find it out? What do you mean? Bartley Eugene Braden. Bart. I've always known it. You know that."

"This puppy's hungry," the man said. "She ought to get home and feed him."

Chad went back to the desk and sat down. "Puppies are always hungry, Bart. Like little kids. Listen to me. I'll come and get you right now. The puppy'll be all right."

The man seemed tired. "I don't know what's going on. You never talked to me like this before."

Very gently, Chad said, "I want to get you out of there. Let me come and get you. Please."

Reason was here now, standing pale and still in the doorway. Hart stood behind her in the hallway, listening so intently that he seemed not to be breathing. Burke stared, one hand holding down the switchhook of the automatic dialer while the other held the receiver forgotten. Pulver's teeth were clamped into the filter of a cigarette he seemed not to know he was smoking.

Chad shut his eyes tightly against them. "Please, Bart. I'll come and get you. Or you leave there, and go someplace where you can call me and not get interrupted."

"I don't know," the man whispered. "I don't know what I ought to do. I don't know."

"Please," Chad said.

He waited. And then opened his eyes, blinked against the light, and slowly brought the handset away from his ear.

"He hung up," he said.

"ANDREWS, THIS is Burke. What'd you find out about West Thirty-third?"

"They just reported in. We were lucky, Ross. Dispatcher caught a car out on North Shepherd, and—"

"Damn it, Andrews!"

"Yeah. Okay. West Thirty-third. Forget it. That woman had a migraine and took her phone off the hook and went to bed. She's not the one."

"Shit! I would of bet anything."

"And the other one."

"Yeah. What about it?"

"On Kirby. Beth Rhodes. That address is a Century 21 office. You know, real estate. Closed up. Nobody there."

"What are you laughing at?"

"Well, it wasn't a total loss. They ticketed this car parked out front. Cadillac. Inspection sticker expired."

"Andrews, you screw-up! I don't want to hear about any goddamned inspection stickers. Was that all?"

"Take it easy, Ross. I don't know if you want this or not, but there was this emergency card on the door—how to get hold of the owner. But she's not Beth Rhodes."

"Well, call her and check it out, Andrews, and—no, wait a minute. I'll do it. What's it say?"

"Uh, yeah. Alma Henderson. Five-five-five—six-four-six-seven."

KATE BRADEN stopped halfway out of the police car and looked suspiciously at Officer Reason. "You don't look like a policeman."

Talking with her, Reason had known that she was old, but had not imagined her as being so tiny and frail. Her white hair was wispy-fine. Her hands looked like naked baby birds. The only strongly alive thing about her was her eyes.

Flashing her most sincere smile, Reason said, "Oh, but I am, Mrs. Braden." Looking at the uniformed policeman who had stepped out of the car to assist the old lady, she said, "Aren't I, Joe?"

"She sure is, ma'am."

Hanging tightly on to his arm, Mrs. Braden said, "How come she's not in uniform, then?"

"She's a detective, ma'am. They don't wear uniforms." Smiling toward Reason, he added, "You know, like Angie Dickinson. You never saw her in a uniform, did you?"

"And the last time I saw her, she was peddling avocados, too, wasn't she?" Mrs. Braden said. But she gave up, dropped Joe's arm, and stepped onto the walk, fussily avoiding Reason's proffered helping hand.

She looked toward the doorway of Chad's town house. "That where we're going?"

"Yes, ma'am," Reason said, trying to urge her forward.

But she balked, turned back toward Joe. "Don't you go off and leave me, young fella. I don't want to come out here and find out I've got to hop one of those jim-crackety buses to get back home."

"We'll see that you get home, Mrs. Braden," Reason said. "But let's hurry, please. We're trying to help your grandson, and time is very important."

Mrs. Braden stopped short. "What about Bart? What are you doing to him?"

Captain Hart opened Chad's front door and came down the walk. He smiled, made a slight bow.

The old lady looked as if the sight of someone else with gray hair had cut twenty years from her age.

"I'm Captain Hart. Police," he said, offering her his arm.

She accepted with a bright, porcelain smile, and with courtly solemnity, he escorted her up the walkway.

But at the entrance he paused, motioned with his head to Reason, who slipped past them and hurried inside. Only when she stood with her back against the closed study door, one hand on the knob, effectively blocking it, did Hart guide Mrs. Braden inside.

After they had passed her, Reason left the study doorway and followed them into the kitchen.

"Just have a seat here," Hart said, pulling a chair back from the table.

Mrs. Braden settled herself, placed her pocketbook in her lap, crossed her hands on it primly, and looked around.

On the table, beside the stationery box, sat a tape recorder, but her attention was drawn to the coffee maker which was grunting and wheezing out dribbles of coffee.

Hart switched on the recorder. "Mrs. Braden, we want to ask a few questions about your grandson, Bart."

"Just what's this all about? Some policeman called me early-on in the evening about Bart, and wouldn't tell me why he was asking about him." She cast a sharp look at

Reason who leaned back against the sink counter and tried to smile reassuringly. "And then she called."

"When did you talk with Bart last?" Reason asked.

"Why, it was yesterday, I think. He calls me every two–three days. Are you trying to say he's done something wrong? Well, I won't believe it. He's a good boy. Has a good job. And his own house."

"You must be very proud of him."

"Proud? Of course I'm proud of him. Left alone when he was small. I raised him. He calls me. Stops by to see I'm all right."

Reason said, "Did he have pets when he was a little boy?"

Mrs. Braden looked around, smiled up at Hart. "Pets? Why in the world would she want to know about pets?" She frowned at the coffee maker, turned back to Reason. "Run a little white vinegar through that thing, it'll work right."

Hart pulled the lid off the stationery box, started setting photographs out on the tabletop. "Who is this man, Mrs. Braden?"

She squinted, fumbled in her purse, brought out a pair of wire-rimmed glasses, fitted them on carefully, and without much interest, looked down at the photographs.

And then one hand flew to her mouth while, with the other, she reached out and tenderly touched this photograph, that one. "How did you get these?"

"Who is he?" Hart asked.

She touched the sepia-tone photograph, caressed the man's cheek with a forefinger. "Don," she said softly. "Donald. My son."

"Bart's father?" Hart asked.

"Yes. Oh, yes." She picked up a color photograph of the man in swimming trunks, clowning on a diving board.

"Where did you get these? They were in my attic. In my old albums."

Hart set out more of the photographs. "Where is Donald now, Mrs. Braden?"

"Why, he's dead." She held up another of the photographs, smiled sadly at it. "He's been dead for so long. The ninth of June, 1964. That's when he died."

"HELLO."

"Is this Miz Henderson?"

"No. Mrs. Henderson isn't here. Who's calling?"

"This is Lieutenant Ross Burke. Houston Police."

"What did you need?"

"Who are you?"

"Linda Janssen."

"All right, Miz Janssen . . ."

"*Miss* Janssen. What is it you need?"

"Okay. Fine. Miss Janssen. We got Mrs. Henderson's phone number off the emergency card on the door of her office."

"Yes. Go ahead."

"Well, who are you, Miss Janssen? Are you familiar with Mrs. Henderson's operation? Do you know her employees?"

"What employees?"

"Is a woman named Beth Rhodes employed there?"

"Beth Rhodes? Why do you want to know about her?"

"It could be very important that we find out where Miz Rhodes is living. She could be in danger."

"Oh, I get it."

"What? You get what?"

"Bill Rhodes put you up to this."

"Huh? Who's Bill Rhodes?"

"So. You're a cop, are you?"

"Yes, I am."

"In a pig's butt! You're just some turkey doing dirty work for Bill Rhodes."

"Miss Janssen, I don't know what you're talking about. This could be very important."

"Yeah. Sure."

"We think somebody might of broke in Miz Rhodes' place. Be there waiting for her right now. We've got to—"

"Look. Just give it up, will you? Tell that damned Bill Rhodes you blew it."

"Listen, lady! You stop smart-mouthing me! I want to know where Beth Rhodes lives, and I want to know it now."

"I'll bet you do! Well, you and Bill Rhodes can take a flying jump at a truck. You know what the penalty is for impersonating a cop?"

"I am a cop! I want to know where this Rhodes-woman lives. She may be in danger, and—"

"Yeah, she is! From you. Now you just crawl back under your rock, and take that crappy Bill Rhodes with you! I'm hanging up, and calling the real cops!"

"THAT WASN'T so bad, was it?" Alma asked, holding her watch up into the light as Beth drove through the Kirby-Richmond intersection. "Millie gets a little overwrought. She'll be at the office first thing in the morning, and we'll be all ready for the Schimpfs by one."

"The Schimpfs! My God, Alma. I've never even been in a place that's been in *Architectural Digest*. And this one's been there twice."

"Three times. They did one article just on Caroline Schimpf's closets. One for Yves St. Laurent. One for Valentino. And Galanos. Oscar de la Renta."

Laughing, Beth braked, turned, eased her car to a stop beside Alma's Seville.

Alma gathered up her purse. "Thanks for the ride." Then she paused, fell back as if she were swooning. "My God! Do you realize? A chance at the biggest residential real estate deal ever, in the whole state of Texas."

She started to get out. "Go apologize to Ajax for staying out so late. But give me a minute to get my car started, so I can see you get home okay."

"Alma, please."

"What?"

"Sit back down for a minute. We have to talk."

Frowning, Alma settled back into the seat.

"I don't exactly know how to tell you this," Beth said. "But I feel smothered. I can't tell you how much I appreciate all you've done for me, but you've got to stop treating me like a child. Bill's forgotten about me. And I don't even want to think about him. All I want is to live a normal life. And that means driving home without an escort.

"I don't want to hurt your feelings. You've been wonderful—you and Linda both. But I have to start living my own life."

"Bill's forgotten about you?"

"Yes. Obviously."

"Obviously, my eye! Linda told me I should tell you, but I didn't want to worry you." She turned, looked squarely at Beth. "Last Wednesday night, I ran the son of a bitch off the road when he was trying to follow you home."

"I thought it might open up his eyes, if I scared him enough. But I've been worrying that it just made him more careful."

"You should have told me."

"Well, too much smothering one way or the other. Anyway, don't give me this 'he's forgotten me' crap. I hope to hell he has. But you gave him an ultimatum. He hasn't called you up from his therapist's office, so you can bet he's up to something else." She glanced around. "Damn it! What the hell is that?"

She jumped out, went to the front of her car, and ripped a slip of paper from under the windshield wiper. Steaming with anger, she dropped back into Beth's car. "Look at this! 'Expired Inspection Sticker.' Damn!" She glared futilely at her car, held the ticket slip close to the map light. "Not fifteen minutes ago! Damn it!"

Beth said, "A ticket. Big deal." She laughed. "What's a little ticket to the biggest residential real estate dealer in Texas?"

Alma laughed, shook her head, stuffed the ticket into her purse. "Fine." She looked at Beth. "Okay. I'm tired. Ajax is probably eating the commode. You can have an escort home, or not. Suit yourself."

CAPTAIN HART leaned back against the counter, motioned with his head to Reason to take over.

She said, "I'm sorry about your son, Mrs. Braden. But

now, we have to talk about your grandson. And we have so little time. Tell me about Bart's pets. Please."

The old lady frowned. "Bart's pets." She slipped off her glasses, folded them. "His mother didn't want him to have pets. She said she was allergic."

"But he had some hamsters. Try to remember about them."

Mrs. Braden tucked the glasses into her purse, looked around confusedly. "Hamsters? Why, I don't know . . ."

Reason pulled a chair close, sat down, put her hand gently on Mrs. Braden's thin shoulder. "Hamsters. Bart had a pair of them. Little brown animals."

Shaking off her hand, Mrs. Braden looked up at Hart. "Bart's a good boy. He's made good for himself."

"The hamsters," Hart said. "Tell us about them."

Mrs. Braden shrank down into her chair.

"Please," Reason said. "It's so important to Bart. Try to remember. Little brown, furry pets. He called them Adam and Eve."

"Oh, the . . ." Mrs. Braden began. But she broke off, lifted her knotted, pink hands and, with them, formed the outline of a small meshed-wire cage above the tabletop. "Adam and Eve," she whispered. "Yes. Little, cute micey things."

"What happened to them?" Hart asked.

"What happened?" Mrs. Braden daubed at her eyes. "Please. I don't want to think about that. No. I haven't thought about that in years. Those little animals. No."

Softly, Reason said, "Bart would want you to tell us."

"No," Mrs. Braden said strongly, as if she had suddenly gathered strength from somewhere. She shook her head. "No. You have no right. Bart wouldn't want anything of the kind."

Hart shook his head at Reason, and she sat back, away

son die?"

"It was an accident. A terrible accident."

BILL STOOD up, dusted his hands together, and backed away from Beth's garage door.

Smiling, he looked from one side to the other, at the two bricks that leaned against the foot of the door. The setup looked perfect to him.

Light flashed along the drive by the side of the town house.

He ran. Across the alley. Into the oleanders. Pushing the long, springy branches aside, he burrowed into hiding. Light flared blindingly, and he froze.

Through the branches, he watched Beth's car stop, watched the garage door begin to lift.

He pictured his bricks lying flat on the concrete now, and laughed.

Another car! Alma Henderson!

He didn't breathe. Disturbed insects buzzed around him.

The Seville made the turn wide, around Beth's car, and stopped, branches of the bushy oleanders brushing its right side, its front tire not a yard from Bill's foot.

He could see Alma inside the car, watching the garage door open all the way, and Beth driving inside.

The door started down.

Alma smiled, took her foot off the brake, and drove on

along the alleyway, past the backs of the rest of the town houses.

When her taillights disappeared as she turned to go back to the street, Bill stepped out of the oleanders, brushing at his face and neck.

He saw that his bricks had worked perfectly, falling down flat when the door lifted, lying in its way when it closed down again, preventing it from closing completely and engaging the lock.

He brushed dry twigs out of his hair and started up the alleyway toward where he had left his car parked out of sight in the drive back of a vacant house, squeezed in beside an '83 Honda.

He'd sit in the car for a little while, in the air conditioning, and relax. And let Beth relax some, too. Maybe she'd take a quick shower, be all nice and warm and sweet-smelling for him.

CHAD SNATCHED up the receiver as soon as the telephone began to ring. "I didn't know if you were going to call me back or not."

"I had to think," the man said.

"You didn't leave. You're still there, at that woman's house."

"Yeah."

Chad clenched his jaw. "So, you were thinking. What about?"

"Everything's just seemed to pile up on me, all of a sudden. I'm not sure about things. You're saying some heavy stuff to me."

"I mean it. Let me come and get you."

"Oh, boy. Jesus, I wish it was that easy."

"We'll make it easy. Just depend on me, Bart."

"You're saying my name. That's one thing I'm not sure of. You're saying a lot of things tonight that I didn't know you knew about. You didn't know about them the other times we talked."

"It just took me a while to remember. That's all. But now I do. Tell me where you are, Bart. And I'll get on the way right now. Then we can work things out."

Over at the sofa, talking on the automatic dialer, Burke was having a tough time with someone. It had gotten harder and harder for him to keep his voice down. And now he picked up the whole big telephone set and stamped across to the atrium, pulled the door open, stepped outside, and slid the door closed as far as it would go against the gray telephone cable.

"Come on, Bart," Chad said.

He looked up, found Pulver standing near, with one hand clutching the handset of the extension to his ear, and the other fisted, slowly lifting, while he mouthed silent cheers.

Softly, slowly, the man said, "Okay. Yeah. All right. Come and get me. Come and get me out of here. We'll—"

He broke off.

"Bart? Where are you? What's going on?"

Silence.

Chad wiped at his face, realized his neck was aching with tension, said, "Bart! What's wrong, Bart?"

Now, the man answered. But his voice had changed, gone harsh and excited. "She's coming! I heard the garage door opening. She's coming." He laughed. "It's too late, buddy. Here she comes."

"No! You can still get out of there! Before she gets inside."

"Get over yourself! She's here. I've got business to finish with her." He paused, breathed roughly. "I've got to put this puppy back in the bathroom before she gets inside. Spoil the surprise, if he was out running around all over the place."

"No, Bart . . ." Helplessly, Chad let his voice trail off because all he could hear now was the handset rocking abandoned on the hard top of a bedside table.

ALMA'S CAR telephone buzzed as she was crossing under West Loop.

It was Linda, sounding both angry and scared. "Somebody keeps calling here, saying he's a cop, saying Beth's in trouble."

"Beth? I left her not ten minutes ago."

"I thought he was some son of a bitch trying to get her address for Bill Rhodes. But now, I'm beginning to believe him. I've got him holding right now."

Glancing into the rearview mirror, wedging the handset between ear and shoulder, Alma brought the car skidding around a traffic island, to head back the way she had come.

"Add him on the line," she barked, and accelerated through the amber light and under the Loop.

"This is Lieutenant Burke. Mrs. Henderson?"

"What the hell's going on?" Alma said, accelerating even more to beat a car that was about to cross Memorial along the Loop access road.

The car braked, honked.

Alma threw up her hand, middle finger extended, and jammed the accelerator the rest of the way to the floor.

CHAD WANTED to run away. But he held on to the telephone and kept listening.

To nothing. Until there was a small scraping sound— the man picking up the receiver from the tabletop?

"Bart?"

No answer.

Muffled yappings of the puppy. Faint sounds of a woman's voice. Growing less faint, as she came to release the puppy from the bathroom.

"Answer me, Bart! Please!"

He didn't.

The woman laughed. The puppy yapped again, the sound no longer muffled by a closed door, only by distance.

Chad jumped as Burke shoved back the atrium door, stepped back into the study, smiling hugely. Dropping the automatic dialer on the coffee table, he turned toward Chad, jabbing a thumb exuberantly upward.

But his smile wiped away when he saw Chad's face.

The woman was near enough to the telephone now that her words were distinct. ". . . get these shoes off," she was saying, "and we'll see what we've got for you to eat."

Chad tried to breathe; he heard the man's sudden intake of breath.

The woman cried out. A short, high-pitched cry of startlement.

Chad closed his eyes, bit down hard on a knuckle, waiting for the next sounds, which would be screams of terror.

But the woman sounded angry, instead. "Damn you!" she shouted. She seemed enraged. "You bastard!"

And then, she was laughing.

Chad pushed back from the desk, listened unbelievingly. She was laughing! Laughing in great, pealing whoops. Laughing!

Finally, catching her breath, she said, "I thought you were my husband!"

And now, she screamed in fear and pain.

HART SAID, "After this accident, when you lost your son, you took Bart, and moved here from Dallas."

Mrs. Braden nodded. "Bart and I were all each other had."

"He was what, Mrs. Braden? How old?"

She smiled. "Eight years old."

"His mother. What about her?"

"She was dead."

"In the accident?" Hart asked.

"Yes."

"What kind of accident was this, Mrs. Braden?"

She seemed not to hear him, squinted at the photographs.

Hart and Reason exchanged looks of frustration.

Reason said, "Did Bart have the hamsters while you were still living in Dallas, or did he get them after you moved to Houston?"

"Why does she keep going on about those things?" Mrs. Braden asked Hart. Leaning forward, she touched some of the photographs. "Bart must have gotten these out of my attic." She frowned at Reason, smiled at Hart. "Why won't you tell me why you're asking all these questions? Where is Bart?"

Burke burst into the kitchen, about to blurt out something. But he bit back the words when he saw Mrs. Braden.

"What is it?" Hart asked.

"He's got the woman! She just came in."

"Damn!"

"But I got the location! From her boss. I'm on the way over there now."

Hart nodded, waved him away, and watched him rush off along the hallway.

Mrs. Braden smiled up at him and started to rise. "Please. Will you have them take me home now? I want to . . ."

Reason shoved her back down into her chair. "Those hamsters. You tell me about those pets of your grandson's, Mrs. Braden, and you tell me now."

CHAD WAS hunched forward in his chair, elbows on the desktop, head down, eyes closed in concentration. Huge, dark splotches of perspiration showed under his arms.

"Bart, she's taken care of now," he said. "She won't

bother you. Why won't you just leave? Go on, and get out of there. Why the hell mess yourself up any more? Come on, Bart. It'll be best. I promise you."

Hart came into the study, his hair awry, face drawn and pale. Chad didn't know he was there.

Pulver handed the captain the yellow pad, on which he had written, "Woman angry! Furious! Then laughed hyst. Said she tho't Bart was her husband at first. Then scared. Bart angry! Hit her! Tied her to chair. Put puppy out in patio. Chad won't give up—keeps trying!"

"What can I promise you?" Chad was saying into the telephone. "I'll do anything, if you'll just come out of there now, and leave that woman alone."

BILL HEAVED up the garage door, slipped beneath it, caught it, eased it back down.

Crossing the garage, he patted the nose of Beth's car. He wished there were more light and a mirror so he could get himself looking really neat. But so what?

He paused at the kitchen door, making a bet with himself that it would be unlocked. He'd never been able to teach her to lock that door every time. She always seemed to think the garage door was security enough.

It wasn't locked. Chuckling, he stepped inside and closed it quietly behind him. Looking around in the dimness of the kitchen to orient himself, he scuffed out of his shoes.

There were sounds somewhere in the place. Whimpering, maybe, and a man's low voice.

He chuckled, picturing Beth, right out of the shower,
lying on the bed, drowsily watching TV.

Pulse pounding in his throat, he started toward the
sounds.

TWO BLOCKS away from Beth's, Alma turned off the
street and took the alley shortcut. It was rough going,
with bumps and overgrown shrubbery that whipped
against the car, but she was in a hurry.

She brought the car to a skidding halt, though, fifty feet
from where the alley widened behind the row of town
houses, and backed to peer at two cars almost hidden by
the untended bushes behind a vacant house.

The little foreign car didn't interest her. But she glared at
the other one. She knew it well! Bill Rhodes' car, damn him!

She gunned her car forward. That cop had told her only
that someone was threatening Beth. Well, hell, yes!

She braked to a stop by Beth's garage door and uttered
a curse as she saw the bricks. Bill's kind of dirty trick.

Grabbing her pistol, she got out of her car, gruntingly
lifted the door enough to slip under it, and hurried toward
the kitchen entrance.

At the side door, however, she paused. The striker
plate of the bolt lock was broken away and lay on the
floor. This door had been forced open and closed again.

Why would Bill rig the big door, and force this one,
also?

Sparing only a moment for perplexity, she rushed on.

CHAD SAID, "Leave her there, Bart. Go someplace else. Stop at the first damned pay phone, and call me, if you don't want to go all the way home."

Hart shook Chad's shoulder.

Startled, he looked up, and then slid his palm over the mouthpiece.

Hart said, "Burke got the location. Police are on the way. But no sirens—hostage situation. You can drop him now—we'll take over."

"No!" Chad said.

Moving his hand, he said into the telephone, "Bart. Please. Won't you listen to me? Leave there. Please."

Hart stood back from the desk, watched for a moment, and then, shaking his head tiredly, left the study.

"I'm mixed-up," the man said. "This woman was mad at me. And then she laughed. I didn't know what to do when she laughed at me."

"She was scared," Chad said. "She just reacted strangely."

He looked up, saw Reason hurrying in, carrying a tape recorder.

He pulled the pad of paper away from Pulver, wrote, "The Hamsters???"

Reason put her hand over the word, mouthed, "Stay away from them until you listen to this," and pointed toward the recorder.

She had been crying, Chad saw. He looked a question at her, and she waved it away.

"Bart, we'll talk about what's confusing you," he said. "I'll

talk with you for as long as you want to talk. But not with you    227
there. Somewhere else, we'll sit down and talk it all out."

There was a long silence. And then the man whispered,
"Yes. All right. All right, I'll leave."

"Now, Bart. Now," Chad pled. "Leave there now."

"Yes. Now. I'm putting down the phone. And walking
out."

SMILING, BILL picked his way across the living room. He
wished he had some flowers. But that couldn't be helped.
Tomorrow, he'd bring her flowers home. He'd come carrying a dozen red roses into their house that would be clean
and nice again, and she'd smile and brush away a tear.

He tiptoed on.

Alma stepped into the kitchen, saw Bill's shoes on the
floor, snarled silently, reached down and pulled off her
own shoes, set them on top of the washer. Then she went
on across the kitchen, turned into the dining room, and
saw Bill ahead of her, tiptoeing along, just about to reach
the bedroom doorway.

She hurried, lifting her pistol, getting it ready to jab
into his back. He would absolutely shit! She wondered if
she'd shoot him. She hoped so. But not really. Just scaring
him out of his mind—and out of Beth's life—would be
enough. Besides, if the cops really were on the way, she
wanted some of him left for them.

The bastard!

Stepping into the bedroom doorway, Bill saw the television set first, on its stand at the end of the room. It wasn't

turned on, but that didn't register, so hotly was his mind set on picturing Beth lying drowsily on the bed.

Beth! There she was. Not lying down. Sitting in a chair, between the TV and the bed. Sitting strangely. He couldn't see her arms or hands, and why did she have a scarf in her mouth?

But nothing mattered except the fact that she was his.

She saw him. Her eyes went shock-wide. She screamed through the scarf.

"Hi, baby," he said.

As he spoke, Alma stopped behind him, got ready to ram the pistol into his back.

Now, Bill saw the man!

CHAD SET the receiver down on the desk and stood up and stretched aching muscles, breathed freely for the first time in days, it seemed.

Pulver was still listening on the extension. To nothing. Bart was leaving!

Reason was talking on the automatic dialer, trying to make sure that the police arriving at the town house would stay out of sight and not scare him back inside.

Pulver cried out, "Chad! She screamed!"

He seized the receiver, brought it back to his ear.

A man's voice—not Bart's—said, "Hi, baby." And then, "Beth! Who's this son of a bitch? You got a man here! You dirty, lying slut! I'll . . . a shotgun! No!"

And now, a woman shouted, "Bill Rhodes, you bastard! Where are you, Beth? I ought to blow your balls off, Bill

Rhodes! Wait a minute! Who're you? What're you doing with that shotgun?"

Hart appeared just outside Chad's study doorway. Someone was with him—a tiny, white-haired old woman.

Leaning into the room, seeming to be trying to block the old woman's view of it, Hart tried to reach the knob to pull the door closed. As he did so, she slipped past him, took a step into the study.

Chad shouted into the telephone, "What's going on?" And was answered only by angry, confused shouting.

The old woman stared at him, her eyes going impossibly wide. Her lips quivered. Her skin seemed to be perceptibly going gray. She cried out in a thin, high wail.

Hart grasped her arm, tried to turn her toward the doorway. But she shook away from him, wouldn't give up staring at Chad.

Bart's voice came from the telephone, rising above the other voices. "Stop it! Everybody SHUT UP!"

The old woman took wavering steps toward Chad, tried to speak to him, but her lips twisted and she made only thin, unintelligible sounds. She lifted out her arms to him, reached for him, reached desperately out to him.

And suddenly, her eyes rolled up white, and she toppled forward onto the floor, one outstretched hand almost touching his foot.

From the telephone came the blast of the shotgun.

CHAD FELT as if he were trapped inside a capsule of sound as Captain Hart drove toward Beth Rhodes' town house, siren shrilling.

Holding the tape recorder pressed to his ear, he could just hear the voices of Reason and Hart and Kate Braden. Now, he pulled it away from his head, rewound a bit, hit "play," and pressed it back to his ear to listen to part of it again.

Abruptly, the siren shut off; they must be getting near.

The recorded voices seemed blaringly loud now—the old woman's, halting, thin, sob-punctuated; Reason's, showing that she was crying also, but with more control; and Hart's, thick and hoarse.

He fumbled at the volume control, lowered it, and kept listening, even though, each time he heard it, his face twisted in pain.

Hart was slowing the car.

Pulver sat beside him, looking concernedly back at Chad from time to time.

He shut them out, concentrated on the aged woman's voice, barely aware that the car was making a turn. Then the recording was finished.

Lights flashed in the street ahead. Hart slowed even more, drove between barricades, and stopped.

A uniformed policewoman leaned in to Hart. "It's the one on the end, Captain. We evacuated the one next to it, and Lieutenant Burke's in there. Drive on around and walk in through the garage."

As Hart started the car moving slowly forward again, Chad set the recorder down on the seat between him and Reason. She touched his hand, smiled sadly at him.

This would be over soon, he thought longingly. He turned his hand, held to hers.

He looked at the recorder. "That poor guy."

Reason moved her hand away. "That 'poor guy' has killed seven—no—nine people."

"That's you I hear crying in this recording, isn't it?"

"That's different," Reason said.

"THIS ISN'T Palmer, but don't hang up," Lieutenant Burke said.

He was standing on a two-by-twelve plank shelf for potted plants built against the wall of the patio next to Beth's. The telephone sat on the top of the brick wall and its cord trailed back and through the sliding glass doorway behind him. He had carried out a chair and set it below the four-foot-high shelf as a step.

"I'm not talking to anybody but him," the man said. "I told you that."

"Just listen a minute. I just called you again to tell you he's on the way."

Below Burke, on Beth's side, Ajax stood up against the wall, leering upward, quivering with curiosity. Across the patio, bright light glowed through the draperies in Beth's bedroom.

Burke bent his head to hold the receiver in place against his shoulder and steadied himself with his forearm against the wall, drew his pistol with his right hand, brought it to his left, which he used to grasp the slide, while he pushed the pistol body forward, eased it back, seating a cartridge ready to fire.

"I want to talk to him, not you," the man said.

"Sure," Burke said, bringing up his right hand, aiming the pistol at the sliding glass door, at a spot about five feet up, two feet back from the closure. "Hey, where's the dog? I don't hear the dog."

"He's outside," the man said.

"Outside? You sure he's okay?"

"You're not who I want to talk to," the man said, but didn't hang up.

"Palmer'll be here any second. Just keep your shirt on."

Burke turned the receiver so that the mouthpiece was against the lapel of his jacket. Keeping the pistol trained on the glass door, he glanced down at Ajax, whispered, "Hey! Speak! C'mon, speak!"

Ajax danced excitedly, but did not bark.

"Damn you!" Burke grunted.

A voice behind him said, "Burke?"

He whirled and almost lost the receiver.

He saw Hart and Chad below him in the patio, and Reason and Pulver stepping through the doorway. Awkwardly, he got the mouthpiece covered.

Chad's face was angry. "What're you doing?"

Burke thrust the telephone receiver at him, jumped down, and turned to Hart. "He keeps yelling about talking to Palmer."

Covering the mouthpiece, Chad said, "What the hell were you doing with the gun?" Not waiting for an answer, he stepped up onto the shelf and looked over into the patio. Turning back to Burke, he said, "You son of a bitch! You were trying to shoot him!"

Into the telephone, he said, "Bart, I'm here."

The man's voice sounded young and scared. "I don't know what to do."

"Let's work that out," Chad said. Below him, Ajax cocked his head, studied him. "Is everybody okay?"

"Sure."

Chad looked around. Hart and Burke, Reason and Pulver, were together near the patio doorway, talking in low, urgent voices. Burke was gesturing with his pistol.

"Bart, what about Beth Rhodes?"

"She's okay."

"And the others?" he asked, looking around again.

Pulver had left the group, stood below Chad, his lips thin, jaw knotted with strain.

A uniformed cop had appeared just inside the doorway and was whispering to Hart.

"They're okay, too," the man said. "That big son of a bitch that came busting in here won't stop bawling, but he's okay. And that other woman is."

"What about you, Bart? Are you all right?"

"Sure. I'm fine. What am I going to do?"

"What do you want to do?"

"I don't know. It was all going to be okay, you know. I was going to get out of here, and go to my house, and open up a beer, and call you up and talk to you. And then that son of a bitch came in. And that other woman."

Chad felt the plank give and turned to find Hart standing beside him. "We'll figure out something, Bart."

Ajax excitedly stood up against the wall to stare at Hart, but Hart paid him no attention. Instead, he looked frowningly around the patio and then seemed to be gauging the distance from the wall to the closing side of Beth's sliding glass door.

"Figure out something," the man said. "What?"

"You could just walk out of there."

Hart motioned for Chad to cover the mouthpiece. "Mrs. Braden died. They just sent in word to me. Her heart went and they couldn't get it going again. She couldn't take seeing you, I guess. But her heart was already bad."

Chad waited for himself to react. But there was only dullness left in him, it seemed.

Hart said, "Is he going to let those people out?"

"I'm working on it."

"Time's running out," Hart said, and stepped down and went back to Burke and Reason.

The man said, "Just walk out of here? But there're people out there all over, aren't there? I don't know if I could go walking out there in the middle of those people. I don't think I could do something like that again."

"Let the people in there go out, then. Let them leave. And you stay until they're gone. Then I'll come in and walk out with you."

"I'm scared."

Chad said, "Hey, guy, I know you are. Listen, I'm scared, too."

Pulver had moved back over to the group. He was angry, but Hart was angry, too, and motioned him away.

Chad said, "Will you let them go, Bart? Then we can stop being scared."

"I don't know."

"I'll do anything you want me to do, if you'll let them go."

"Maybe. It seems like we could talk now. Just you and me."

"You figure out how you want to work it, Bart. You tell me how we can do it. So those people can leave, and you and I can talk."

"I'm afraid. I didn't used to be afraid like this when you and I talked. I'd call you up, and you'd be the one that was afraid."

"We'll talk about that, too."

Reason stepped up onto the plank. She smiled at Chad, looked across at the lighted draperies, down at Ajax, and turned back to Chad with a look of warm understanding.

He put his fingers over the mouthpiece. "I'll get him out of there, Sharon. Or get those people out."

The man said, "Will you come in here alone? If you will, well, then, I'll let them go."

"Yes. I will."

Reason motioned him to cover the mouthpiece again.

"Will you not let them hurt me?" the man asked.

Reason's fingers brushed Chad's lips as she covered the mouthpiece herself.

Gently, Chad moved her fingers away. "I promise, Bart. I swear it."

"Please, Chad," Reason whispered.

Tired of being ignored, Ajax made a high, quick bark.

The man said, "There's that puppy. He scratches on the glass sometimes. Maybe he's . . ."

Chad cut him off. "You leave the puppy alone. He'll be okay. Just leave him where he is." He blocked the mouthpiece.

More of Reason's hair had escaped to feather softly over her forehead. "We'll go, Chad," she said. "We'll leave here."

"What?"

She put her hands on Chad's. "It's over. You've done all you can."

He looked behind them. Pulver was staring at the side wall. Hart and Burke were looking up at him. Burke held his pistol tensely in front of his belly.

Reason said, "Please, Chad. Just hang up. It's no use. I'll take you home, and we'll be through with this."

The man said, "Are you going to come in here? Please. You said you wouldn't leave me. And I'll let them go."

"Not yet, Sharon," Chad said.

She moved closer to him, lifted her face, whispered, "Please. I want you to."

Sounding frightened, the man said, "Where are you? Please don't leave me."

"Please," Reason said, touching Chad's face.

He stared at her.

"Just hang up. We don't have any more time. It's over with." She smiled at him. Her warm fingers urged his to release the receiver.

"I can't stop now, Sharon. He'll let them go."

She shook her head. "We can't let you go in there."

He stared at her. "So you're just going to shoot him!"

"Chad . . ."

"How're you going to do it? Put Burke down there to hurt the puppy, so he'll look out, and you can shoot him? Or does Burke get the shot because it's his idea?"

Into the telephone, he said, "Don't be scared, Bart. I'm coming in there," and shoved the telephone and receiver into Reason's hands.

Backing away from her for room, he saw Burke lunging forward, saw Pulver step in his way to block him jarringly with his thin body and, as he heaved himself up onto the top of the wall, heard Reason cry, "No, Chad!" and heard the telephone clatter against the plank and down to the ground.

He jumped down into Beth's patio, sending Ajax scurrying away, went to one knee, pushed himself up.

Hart and Burke were yelling.

He lunged against the sliding door, shouted, "Bart! It's me!" pushed at it, found it locked.

"Stop it, Chad!"

He jerked at the door. "Unlock it, Bart! Hurry! Please!"

"Get away from that door!" Reason shouted.

He looked up to see her leaning over the top of the wall, leveling her pistol, her left hand professionally cupping her right.

"I warn you, Chad!" she cried.

He heard a metallic clicking at the door behind him. "What the hell are you going to do, *Officer* Reason? Shoot me, too?"

As if struck, she bent her elbows, pointed the pistol upward.

Chad slid the door open, slipped inside.

CHAD'S HEART was pounding out of control. Visual images seemed compressed. Burke's and Hart's angry shouting and the puppy's yapping boomed and racketed at him.

Slamming the door closed, clicking it locked, he fought out of the folds of drapery, blinked at bright room light. An older woman stepped quickly away, her hands open and lifted, her gaze not on Chad, but directed warily to his right—it must have been she who was instructed to unlock the door.

Sitting in a chair with her back to him was Beth Rhodes, gagged with a green silk scarf knotted at the back of her head. In the corner cowered a dark-haired man chewing at his hand, his eyes red and staring. Above him, in the ceiling, was a ragged, fist-sized hole—the result of the shotgun blast Chad had heard over the telephone line—when?—only an hour ago?

Blood was barely visible against the coppery shine of Beth Rhodes' hair, but it darkly stained the shiny fabric of the gag.

Ice in his belly, blood pounding in his throat, Chad turned toward Bart who sat cross-legged near the head of the bed. His black T-shirt was soaked with perspiration and there were bruises of fatigue under his eyes. He wore filmy-white plastic surgical gloves. The shotgun was in his right hand. The left held Alma's .357 Magnum revolver. Both weapons were pointed toward Chad and the others.

"Bart, we made a deal," Chad said, his voice sounding

hollow and thin to himself. Before he could continue, he had to force himself to breathe. "The deal—I'm here; you let them go."

The frightened dark-haired man whimpered.

Bart's eyes flickered toward him, returned to Chad. "He's really something," he said contemptuously. "You could teach him a few things."

Keeping his hands in Bart's view, Chad moved slowly toward the chair to which Beth was tied.

"They can leave," Bart said. "But you have to stay."

Bill made a high-pitched sob and began a shaking, uncoordinated effort to get to his feet.

To Alma, Chad said, "Watch him. Keep him quiet until Bart says it's okay."

He was at Beth's chair now, and he looked at Bart inquiringly. "I'll untie her now."

Bart nodded. "I want them to get out of here."

Chad knelt, worked at the knots in the drapery cord binding Beth's wrists, worried them loose, rubbed her cold hands for a moment, and then stood and untied the knot in the scarf.

The silk caught where blood had soaked through it and Beth winced as Chad tried gently to pull it away. Bringing up her hands to work it free, she looked up at Chad and mouthed, "Thank you."

"Get out of here," Bart told Alma. "You first. And then him."

Bill pushed himself away from the corner and entreatingly held out his hand to Alma as if for help. Distastefully, she reached out to him.

"No," Bart said. "If he can't get out on his own, he stays."

Bill cried out, a harsh, sobbed shriek. His eyes were mostly white now.

Beth went to him, pushed at him, hissed, "Get out of here, Bill!"

He was far into panic. He staggered against her, held to her.

She slapped him, pushed him away. "Move, damn you!" she said, and propelled him through the doorway and out of the room.

Chad held to the back of the chair, watched as Bart sprang up from the bed to go to the door and push it closed.

Then he motioned with the shotgun. "Sit in the chair."

Chad did so, and Bart sat cross-legged on the bed again.

"Now, we can talk," Chad said.

"I didn't really think you'd come in here."

Chad's heartbeat was thunder now. "I had to."

"I guess you did. And now, I have to kill you."

CHAD STARED into the guns. "You don't have to kill me. You don't have to kill any more, at all."

Bart made a sad chuckle, shook his head, lifted the hand that held the pistol and rubbed at his forehead with the back of it.

On the underside of his arm, so close to his armpit that the T-shirt sleeve almost covered it, was a small round scar, visible only because its texture differed from the pale skin around it.

In the harsh artificial light, with his face flushed and damp, a tiny line no bigger than a pencil mark showed on his forehead, running from his left eyebrow up into the hairline. Under his left eye was a small crescent-shaped indentation scar.

"We could go out of here now," Chad said. "I could take you out, and keep those people away from you."

"They're going to grab me and put me away. They're really going to handle me, man."

"You've done some bad things. Someone's going to have to take care of you for a while."

Bart looked pleadingly at him. "Will you take care of me? Would you—" He broke off, lifted the shotgun slightly. "No. That's silly. You'll be dead."

"I thought we were going to talk."

"We're talking."

"I mean, for a while, Bart. Talk things out. That's what we said we'd do."

Bart chuckled. "That was just to get you in here. You knew that."

"A half hour. We can talk for a half hour."

Bart looked at the clock on the table beside the bed and nodded. "Okay. Until twelve-ten. Does that make you happy?"

"Is it a promise? You promise me a half hour?"

"Promise? Sure." He laughed. "Cross my heart, hope to die."

Chad said, "I'm going to grow back my beard."

Bart looked away toward the draperies.

"You haven't called me Chad for hours, Bart. You'll call me Chad when I get the beard going again, won't you?"

"That puppy hasn't barked, or anything, in a long time. Maybe something happened to him. Maybe we should—"

Chad interrupted. "The puppy's all right. There are people out there with guns."

Bart looked at him with surprise. And then he seemed to understand, and shivered slightly.

"Why are you going to kill me, Bart?"

"You let me down when I thought you were the last person in the world that'd let me down."

"I know how your father let you down."

"We're not going to talk about that."

"We've got to talk. And say true things. That's why I'm here. To say true things to you."

"You'll make me kill you sooner."

"You were eight years old. Your father let you buy the hamsters, even though your mother didn't want you to have them."

"I'm going to kill you, if you say another word!"

Chad stared into the muzzle of the shotgun. "You're as yellow as that man that was in here."

"I am not!" Bart shouted. But he didn't shoot.

"I'm going to talk true to you."

"Stop it."

"This has to be truth. No matter how much it hurts."

"I don't want to do this."

"Your mother hurt you," Chad said. "We have to talk about it. Will you let me talk about it? Please. I'm hurting, too. It'll be easier because you're not hurting alone. It's why I came back."

Bart set down the pistol and rubbed at his face, the plastic of the glove squeaking against his skin. He looked everywhere but at Chad, his expression that of a small boy showing exaggerated resignation. "Okay. I'll talk to you. About it."

"She hurt you sometimes, didn't she?"

Bart looked down at the bedspread, extended his finger, drew a line, studied the indentation it left.

"Didn't she hurt you, Bart?"

He shook his head, studied the line.

"She hurt you with lighted cigarettes."

Bart pushed down into the fabric with his finger, studied the indentation, seemed aware of nothing else.

"She'd get angry, and hurt you in other ways."

"YES!" Bart shouted, and lifted the shotgun, used both hands to level it at Chad's face. "Nobody was supposed to know! You didn't even care."

Chad forced himself to say, "I know. I care." And waited for the explosion of the gun.

But Bart didn't fire. He looked directly at Chad, sobbed out a breath, and lowered the shotgun to his knee, let its aim waver.

"She didn't like your pets," Chad said.

"You're scaring me."

"I don't want to scare you. You know that. She didn't like your pets, did she?"

Bart made a child's grimace of helpless grief, and shook his head.

"She didn't like them at all. And you had to be careful of them because of that."

Bart frowned at him, adjusted the shotgun so that it pointed at him more definitely, and then looked past him. "I hid the cage most of the time. Or kept it at Grandma's."

"Why?"

Exasperation. "So she wouldn't hurt them."

"Adam and Eve. They had babies, didn't they?"

Bart grinned shyly and his voice turned very childlike. "Yeah. Boy, were they funny!"

"You lived in Dallas then. Down the block from your Grandma Braden. And you stayed all night at her house a lot. To keep away from your mother."

"Grandma and Momma had fights. Grandma'd get mad when she hurt me. And when she did other things."

Chad grimaced, hearing in his head the thin wail of the old woman's recorded voice. "His mother'd say, 'Go ahead and tell your precious son! I wish you would! I'm sick to death of him, anyway. But just you remember that I'll get Bart. And I'll move so far away from here that you won't ever get to see him!' And she would of got him—she was the mother. She'd of taken Bart off somewhere."

Shaking off the memory of Kate Braden's sobbing pain, Chad said, "One night, when you were staying at your grandma's, you forgot your hamsters. And you went home to get them."

Bart's face showed fear. "Oh, boy. I don't think we ought to talk about that."

Chad hurried on. "You tried to get them without bothering your mother. You went in the back door. To your room. And you got the cage, and the can of food."

"I dropped that can. Right in the hall. And it rattled around all over the floor." He looked fearfully around, seeming not to be aware of Chad or of this room.

"Your mother came out of the bedroom," Chad said softly.

Bart nodded jerkily.

"She caught you in the hall. And what else?"

"Somebody was with her. In the bed. It was a man and they didn't have any clothes on and she was mad at me. She was so mad at me!"

"Then what?"

Bart stared coldly at him. "What do you care?"

"She hit you. And you ran. You dropped the hamster cage, and you ran away from her."

The coldness faded, went to hopelessness. "I ran away from her."

Chad waited.

In a moment, Bart said, "I ran out in the backyard. And I hid under the bushes. She was awful mad. That man was mad, too, and he left, and that made her madder at me. She came out on the back porch, and she yelled at me, 'You little sneak! You get up here, and get what's coming to you! You get up here!'

"But I didn't. I wished my daddy'd come home. Then she ran in the house, and came back out with my hamster cage. She waved it around and yelled. But I stayed hid.

"Then she yelled, 'You better get up here, or I'll fix you!' And I was scared! She said, 'You better get up here, or I'm gonna feed these nasty things to the cats!

"'Kitty-kitty-kitty-kitty!' she went, and the cats came running up on the porch."

He was crying now. Huge tears rolled down his face.

"No, Momma! Please don't!" he shouted, and followed with an eerie small boy's imitation of a grown-up voice. "'I'll teach you to sneak around on me!'"

He sobbed, choked for a moment, and continued. "She opened up the cage. And I yelled, 'Please don't, Momma! Here I come! I'll let you hurt me!'"

Pausing, he wiped his face with a forearm, but the shotgun continued to point at Chad. "I went running up on the porch, but she was shaking the cage, and my pets came out, even the baby ones, and the cats were grabbing them! And fighting over them! And they grabbed the babies! She shook them all out to the cats, and they grabbed them all up!

"I tried to get the cage, and she hit me with it! She hurt me. She hit me some more. And the cats were grabbing up my pets, and she still hurt me.

"I ran! She got me in a corner, but I ran in the house. I had blood all over my head because she hit me and she was always hitting me and she gave my pets to the cats."

He went silent, seemed to be using all his strength to stop crying. Reaching down, he pulled up the front of his T-shirt and used it to wipe roughly at his face.

In a moment, he looked at Chad, as if he were just remembering that he was there. In a nearly normal voice, he said, "I talked about it. Are you happy now?"

"You didn't talk about all of it."

"Enough of it."

Chad shook his head. "No. You didn't tell about running into your mother and father's bedroom."

Bart took careful aim with the shotgun. "I think I'd better kill you now."

Chad tried to smile. "Not without finishing." Promptingly, he said, "You ran into their bedroom. . . ."

Shaking his head in frustration, Bart said, "I ran into their bedroom. To the phone. I was going to try to call my daddy . . . why are you nodding like that?"

"Just understanding something—why you used the phone."

"You never understand anything."

"My name is Chad Palmer. Tomorrow, I start growing my beard back again."

Bart giggled. "You can't. I'm going to kill you."

"There was blood all over your head, and you were trying to call your daddy."

"Why are you doing this to me?" Bart shouted.

Chad shouted back, "Trying to save my life! And yours!" He lowered his voice. "Your mother found you there, hiding in the corner. By your daddy's shotgun."

Bart sucked in breath. "She yelled at me, and she started hitting me again!" Lifting the shotgun with both hands, he made jerky, fending-off motions with it. "My head hurt! There was blood in my mouth! And it shot her!"

He went silent, his body frozen, with the shotgun aiming over Chad's head. Then slowly, he lowered it.

"I want to show you something," Chad said.

"What?"

"I have to get it out of my pocket." Keeping watch on the shotgun, he twisted in the chair, reached slowly into a back pocket. "One of your photographs." He brought it out and unfolded it, smoothed the creases, and leaned forward to toss it onto the bed.

Keeping the shotgun trained on Chad, Bart tilted his body forward until he could reach it. "Where did you get this?"

"It was in your house."

Setting the photograph face-up on the bedspread near his knee, Bart frowned down at it.

"I know what happened next, in that bedroom," Chad

said. "And I know what happened to you when I came back."

Bart looked up at him, his face twisted with anger, and grappled the shotgun up to his shoulder.

Chad sucked in breath and spoke in a rush. "My name is Chad Palmer. You saw me a thousand times, Bart. We said, 'Hi, how're you doing?' to each other a thousand times." He paused and continued more slowly. "But we didn't pay any attention to each other. I was just the guy with a beard at thirty-one-ninety Bissonnet that got *Architectural Digest* and *Omni* and bills, and bitched at you about the junk mail, or if I thought something was late."

"I'm tired of this," Bart said, his voice distorted because his cheek was pressed against the shotgun in firing position.

"I was just somebody on your mail route. And then, one morning, I shaved off my beard. First time in years. I just shaved it off without even thinking about it. And went out front, and you were coming up the walk with my mail."

"Shut up!"

"I said, 'Hi, how're you doing?' and you handed me my mail."

"I told you to shut up!"

"Your mother was beating hell out of you with your hamster cage. And you accidentally shot her."

Bart's grip tightened on the shotgun. His finger tightened against the trigger. "I'm killing you now!"

"No!" Chad shouted. "I still have some time!"

"Time?"

"You promised. It hasn't been thirty minutes yet."

Reluctantly allowing his grip on the shotgun to relax, Bart turned to look at the clock.

"Thirty minutes," Chad said. "You crossed your heart. I kept my promises to you."

Bart grimaced, but took the shotgun from his shoulder,
lowered it to his knee.

Chad said, "Look at that picture. That's a Fifty-seven
Chevy. I never had a Fifty-seven Chevy."

Bart looked down at the photograph.

"They must have bought that car when you were still
just a baby. Did they still have it? Is that what he came
driving home from work in that night?"

"Don't do this."

Pleadingly, Chad lifted up his hands. "I have to."

Slowly, Bart nodded. "Yeah. My daddy was parking it,
and he heard the gun go off. And he came running in."

"Into the bedroom. You were hurt and scared, and your
mother was dead."

"You came running in. You saw Momma! She was all
bloody! Her face was all bloody"

Chad said, "I saw you a million times bringing my mail.
I raised hell when a magazine was torn, or something."

"You picked Momma up and her face was all bloody and
you looked awful! You cared about her!"

"I shaved off the beard and laughed at myself in the
mirror. I didn't know it was going to turn me into somebody else."

"You cared about her! And you yelled at me!"

"Everybody was saying, 'Hey, who're you?' and laughing because they'd never seen me without a beard before.
But not you, Bart. You looked at me, and you saw your
father."

"You yelled at me! You were going to hurt me, too!"

"You saw me, and it all started over again for you."

His face white with anger, Bart stared at him. "You
were mad at me! You wanted to hurt me. Just like she did!
You didn't care how much she hurt me."

"He was shocked," Chad said. "He was horrified. He
didn't know what had happened."

"You came at me, just like she did! And I had my

daddy's shotgun! You were going to hurt me, too! You didn't care! And I pulled the trigger at you!"

"I do care!" Chad shouted into the muzzle of the shotgun. "I care about you, Bart! I do care!"

Bart's body shook. He stared.

"I wouldn't hurt you. I wouldn't have let her hurt you."

"You never even knew she hurt me. You just thought I hurt her with the shotgun. And you ran at me. You wanted to hurt me, too!"

"I wouldn't hurt you. I wouldn't."

"I killed you!"

"It's all right. I care about you."

Bart's body shook with sobbing. He dropped the shotgun, put both hands to his face, cried into them.

Slowly, Chad stood up, walked along the side of the bed, and sat down. "I care," he said softly.

He touched Bart's arm, pulled him to him, held him while he cried it out.

In a while, with his arm around Bart's shoulders, he brought him to the door.

"I'm scared," Bart said.

"You don't need to be. I'm here."

Opening the door, Chad looked out toward the living room, called out, "It's all right. We're coming out now. I don't want you to frighten him."